Hart's Grove

Christmas, 2015

Hart's Grove

■ ■ ■

STORIES

Dennis McFadden

To Emily — I hope you enjoy these — Keep writing!

Colgate University Press
Hamilton, New York

The paper used in this publication meets the minimum requirements of
American National Standard for Information Sciences—Permanence of Paper
for Printed Library Materials, ANSI Z39.48-1992. ∞

ISBN: 978-0-912568-20-1

The author gratefully acknowledges the journals that first published these
stories, in slightly different form: "A Penny a Paper," *The Green Hills Literary Lantern* 15 (June 2004); "Radaker's Angel," *The Saint Ann's Review* 7, no.
1 (Summer 2007); "Glitter and Grace," *Washington Square* 15 (Winter 2005);
"Muddy Bottom," *The Seattle Review* 28, no. 2 (2006); "Strauss the Butcher," *The
Massachusetts Review* 50, no. 3 (Fall 2009); "Bye Baby Bunting," *CutBank Literary Magazine*, no. 68 (Winter 2008). Excerpt from "Peckin'" by Shel Silverstein
from *A Light in the Attic* (New York: HarperCollins Publishers, 1981). Epigraph
from "When Place Becomes Character: A Critical Framing of Place for Mobile
and Situated Narratives" by Glorianna Davenport, in *The Mobile Audience: Art
and New Technologies of the Screen* (BFI, 2005).

All the characters in these stories are fictional.
Any resemblance to any real person, living or dead, is purely coincidental.

Library of Congress Cataloging-in-Publication Data

McFadden, Dennis, 1943–
    Hart's grove : stories / Dennis McFadden. — 1st ed.
    p. cm.
    ISBN 978-0-912568-20-1 (alk. paper)
    1. City and town life—Pennsylvania—Fiction.   I. Title.

PS3613.C436H37 2010
813'.6—dc22

                               2010008896

Text and cover design by Mary Peterson Moore

Colgate University Press, Hamilton, New York 13346

1 2 3 4 5 6 7 8 9 0

for Brookville, Pennsylvania,
aka "Hartsgrove"

and

for Vera Catherine Hall McFadden,
aka "Mom"

■　　■　　■

Before there was story there was place:
landscapes are the archetypal containers for the lives of people.

—Glorianna Davenport

Contents

Hartsgrove was founded in 1797 by Eli Hart, the pioneer settler. Intending to erect a saw mill, he selected as his site a tract of timber in the center of which was a particularly splendid hemlock grove; as other settlers arrived, the location quite naturally became known as Hart's Grove. Over the decades, the name eventually contracted to Hartsgrove, but I have chosen to remember Eli Hart and the history of the town by using the title "Hart's Grove."

PART ONE

■   ■   ■

A Penny a Paper

They say Hartsgrove was built on seven hills just like Bethlehem but I can only count six and I've lived here for over a year. My paper route is on Longview which is probably the steepest hill in town. Weasel Fleager's who showed me the ropes on my paper route. He always says how's your heart when he first sees you the way other people say hello. He didn't say it to me at first but he does now. I guess I must have grown on him. Weasel Fleager doesn't care much for the hills at least not for hauling papers up them. He's got a wagon with a rope tied to the handle he hauls them up in. I like the hills the way you can look down on the town like you're sitting up there on a cloud.

I get up when it's still dark out to deliver my papers. The tree leaves in the streetlight look silvery green on top and black on the bottom. Most mornings they just droop there fat and lazy but when it's windy like this morning they flip and twist like they're trying to escape. My grandmother always got up early before the chickens she called it. She told me a story one time about a little boy who was lost in the woods. Then one afternoon his family looked down the road and there he came and he was all alone. But he was swinging his arm like he was holding hands with someone and when he got closer they could see he was looking up and talking and smiling. And when he got home they asked him who he was walking with and he told them Jesus. He told them Jesus had found him when he was lost in the woods and had taken him by the hand and led him home.

My mother and I moved into Hartsgrove last year after my father

3

took off. He's looking for work down south. We used to live out near Coolbrook which is about seven miles north of town. My best friend Buster Clover still lives out there. I don't see him so much anymore because he still goes to school out there and will until the ninth grade and we're both out of Little League now. He swears Roy Campanella winked at him one time when we went down to Pittsburgh with Little League to see the Pirates play the Dodgers. I always say yeah and Ralph Kiner blew me a kiss. My father played ball. He was pretty good I guess. He was in the minors for the Washington Senators and I've seen some old newspaper clippings calling him a hot prospect. Fireball Johnny they called him. He used to make me play catch with him. Then he played for the Hartsgrove Grays and I used to go to their games all the time but I don't so much anymore because everybody's always asking me about him. Heard anything from the old man they say. Man we sure could use old Jacey's fastball now.

Mom's a nurse up at the hospital and they're talking about going out on strike. They make way less than the nurses over in Harmony Mills Hospital so I don't really blame them I guess. She works eleven to seven so she doesn't get home until I'm already out on my paper route. Dad always used to say put your dukes up when he was fooling around like we were going to start fighting. I remember one time him and mom with their dukes up. They were standing beside the big stone fireplace in the house out near Coolbrook with their dukes up like they were going to start fighting. At least I think I remember it. I was just a kid then. It was dark so maybe I just dreamed it.

I made friends with this kid Bub Allgier when we first moved here. He lives in the apartment above ours. We live down in the basement. It's on the side of a hill though so our porch is still on ground level down a set of steps from the sidewalk where Bub's porch is. Next door to us Twila Ruffner lives with her two little kids. Half the time she's not even home. She drinks. She leaves Mikey who's only about seven watching Millie who's four. So half the time they end up pestering me. Mom's thinking about calling the cops on her but she hates to cause trouble. What are the cops going to do anyhow?

Weasel Fleager wears suspenders that pull his pants halfway up his legs. He's an old guy. In the afternoons he sweeps out stores on Main Street and sweeps the sidewalks in front of them and sometimes washes the windows too. The worst part about it is Randy he says which he calls a dang occupational hazard. Randy's a dog who lives on Main Street but doesn't belong to anybody in particular and he tries to diddle everybody's leg all the time. Weasel says at least once a day he looks down and there's Randy humping away on his ankle.

Sterck's down on Main Street is one of the stores Weasel Fleager sweeps out. I stop there about every day to buy a Baby Ruth and a Pepsi-Cola. Bub Allgier and I read the comic books till they tell us to leave. We were leaving a couple of days ago and Randy comes trotting over panting and jumps on Bub's leg. Bub kicked him. Randy never bothers my leg. Maybe he thinks it's too little. Too little to diddle.

Too little to diddle. The cat and the fiddle.

Weasel Fleager told me about this woman called Wahoo who's part Indian. She lives down towards the bottom of Longview where the houses are kind of shabby and close together like ours. Up on top some of them are like mansions with lawns like the golf course out at the country club. Wahoo doesn't get a paper but you go right by her house. Weasel told me he looked in her window once and saw two guys diddling her at the same time.

So yesterday we were sitting up on Bub Allgier's porch and I told him about what Weasel Fleager told me. I try to stay outside as much as I can so mom can sleep. Bub was swinging on the porch swing and eating a baked bean sandwich he had his mother fix him. I was peeling loose paint off the rail. All of a sudden he stops swinging and says to me you know I bet we can diddle Nora Jean Vandevoort if we play our cards right.

I said oh yeah? I didn't know what else to say.

Bub nods his head up and down like Father Thomas does when he's giving out communion and he finishes his sandwich in about two bites. I'm sure of it he says.

I said what makes you think so?

He says I know women.

I was going to say Nora Jean Vandevoort's only about eleven but I didn't. Bub Allgier was in seventh grade with me but he is a year older and he's lived in town all his life and all. So I was thinking he might know what he was taking about. Just then Millie Ruffner pops up the steps next door. She's wearing torn green shorts and she's dirty from head to toe. She starts hopping down the sidewalk waving this thing that looked like a man's belt. From her porch downstairs Mrs. Ruffner's yelling Millie Millie stay out of the street. Jimmy are you up there? Like it's my job to watch her. Then Millie spots me on the broken chair on Bub's porch and comes running over and jumps up on my lap.

My grandmother's favorite hymn was The Old Rugged Cross which starts out on a hill far away stood an old rugged cross but Buster Clover and I always sing it on a hill far away stood an old Chevrolet. Sometimes it starts running through my head when I'm delivering my papers. I guess because of the hills. Grandma's on a hill in the cemetery behind the Methodist Church out past Coolbrook. From her hill you can look around in every direction and see nothing but woods except for the church and a couple of farms along the road. You can see two barns in opposite directions and they both have Chew Mail Pouch Tobacco Treat Yourself To The Best painted in big red letters on their sides. Woods is about all you can see from the hills in Hartsgrove too with a few houses showing through here and there where the streets are. Hartsgrove is mostly in the woods except for Main Street and the Sylvania plant next to the ball fields down by the where the creeks meet up.

Six years ago two little sisters named Mary Lou and Katie Mc-Cracken went into the woods and were never seen again. They were visiting their grandparents up on Jimtown Road out past Coolbrook and they took their pails out berrying. Two years later a hunter found a pail deep in the woods. Their bodies were never found but another hunter claimed a couple of years ago he saw their ghosts. He claimed he was coming out of the woods at sunset when he saw them holding hands and running away carrying one pail between them.

I think about them sometimes when I'm on my paper route. When I left the house this morning Mikey Ruffner was sleeping outside on his porch just across from ours. Their porch roof's a slab of tin with rusty nail holes in it and there's a dim little porch light which is why I could see him. He was sound asleep in a rocking chair he had pulled up in front of the door so the door couldn't open. I don't know if he was locking Millie in or she was locking him out but he looked okay so I just tiptoed on up the steps. Probably their mother wasn't home yet. They don't have a father living with them either.

Jum's Bar is down on Main Street. We used to go in there after baseball games when I was a kid. A lot of the players stopped in still wearing their uniforms. I was allowed to drink all the Cokes I wanted but I found out six or seven is plenty. There's only so many Cokes you can drink. My father let me taste his beer. He drank Iron City. I used to like it but then it got so it tasted bitter. My father laughed a lot then. Weasel Fleager hangs out in Jum's usually with his pal Doodle O'Hanlon. They like to sit near the front windows and watch Randy try to diddle the legs of the lawyers going in and out of the Court House across the street. He says it's better than the circus. One block down from Main Street on Pershing is the Grace Episcopal Church where we go now since we moved into town. For a long time we didn't go to church at all but when we moved my mother said it was about time we started again. She said we did a lot better when we were going to church. My father always chewed gum before we visited my grandmother and grandfather. They didn't believe in smoking or drinking and he didn't want them to know he smoked and drank.

Halfway down Coal Alley the trees open up and you can see across to the side of Rose Hill rising up above the creek. I like to listen to the birds waking up. The sky's turning from black to blue and there's fog hanging over the creek. You can't see the houses on the other hill because they're all in the shadows or hidden by the trees and there's no cars out yet so all you can hear is the birds. I put down my bag of papers. President Eisenhower's playing golf on the front page. I look in Wahoo's window every morning but I've never seen any diddling going on. One time she was asleep on the couch with all her clothes on snoring so loud you could hear her through the window which was closed. The windows in the church are stained glass and they remind me of the colors in the sky early in the morning the pinks and reds and blues. I wonder how two guys could diddle one girl at the same time. Up on Pine Street I saw a lady in her bra and underpants drinking coffee but I don't know who she is. She doesn't get a paper. Weasel Fleager told me that some mornings he used to diddle some lady over on his paper route when her husband wasn't home but he wouldn't tell me who she is. He said she's a high church lady who doesn't smoke or drink or swear but she sure likes to diddle a lot. She used to make him take his shoes off.

Three creeks run through town. Potters Creek comes in from the north and meets up with the Sandy Lick to form the Red Bank Creek down by the ball fields across from the Golden Days Supermarket. Way up Potters Creek in Coolbrook there's a swimming hole with slippery rocks where Buster Clover and I used to swim. Just north of Hartsgrove they built a dam across Potters Creek a long time ago for the waterworks. They made it a place for picnicking and swimming with a diving board just below the dam. Kids hang out there swimming in the afternoon because there's nothing else to do. Judy Lockett was sitting on her towel with her knees spread apart one day and I saw her thing. It had a little bit of hair around it but not much. The youngest of the McCracken girls Katie was my age. In seventh grade last year I'd look at an empty desk every now and then and wonder if Katie McCracken would be sitting there if she hadn't disappeared up in the woods with her sister six years ago.

The preacher at Grace Episcopal Church is Father Thomas. He asked me if I'd be an altar boy and I said yes. I didn't really have a choice. Mom was standing right there. Sometimes I serve at the early service which means I have to get up before the chickens on Sunday too. Father Thomas showed me the ropes at the church just like Weasel Fleager did on my paper route. You wear a cotta and cassock over your clothes so that nobody looks any richer or poorer than anybody else in the house of God. The ceiling inside is made out of polished wood the color of chocolate candy and goes way up to a peak. When Father Thomas told me the candles were made out of beeswax I said holy smoke and I didn't realize until later what a dumb thing that was to say. Every Sunday during the sermon in church I'm thankful I'm wearing a cotta and cassock because I keep thinking about Judy Lockett's thing and it always gets hard. When it gets hard in the bathtub it reminds me of a periscope. It gets hard almost every time I take a bath when I'm looking to see if I can see any hair yet or not. Sometimes I pretend it's Katie McCracken's thing I see not Judy Lockett's.

Bub Allgier and I were up in his living room last night watching Milton Berle with all the lights out. We were trying to think of where we could diddle Nora Jean Vandevoort. We came up with this place down between Main Street and Jefferson Street where there's a patch of thick brush and trees where there used to be a tennis court. We figure we could clear the brush out to make an opening in the middle that we can crawl into and get some cardboard boxes and tear them open and put them on the ground for her to lay down on.

We were talking about it and Bub says man I got a hard-on so big I could use it to clear the brush with. We were on our stomachs on the living room floor and for some reason that struck me funny and I started laughing so hard I had to roll over. And there's his mom standing in the doorway to the kitchen with her arms folded. She heard every word we were saying.

Well Bub looks up and he doesn't bat an eye. He says mom fix me a sandwich will you. You want anything Jimmy? I said no.

And so what's his mom do? She goes out in the kitchen and starts fixing him a sandwich. She yells in are you sure you don't want anything Jimmy? Bub told me not to worry she'll never tell my mom.

Sure enough the nurses are going out on strike. Saturday they were over making signs to picket with. Mom asked me to help them and I did and mom kept saying I make really neat letters. They all did. I think they were buttering me up just so I'd keep helping them. It's not real hard to make neat letters. Mom read this letter to the editor in the newspaper out loud from the man who runs McCrory's five and ten cent store down on Main Street. He said he didn't know why the nurses think they should make more money because they already make more than his cashiers do. Well you should have heard them. Mrs. Morley had a fit.

When he was laid off my father went for hours on end without saying a word sometimes. I'd have to tiptoe around the house. Now I still have to tiptoe around the house because my mother's sleeping. I bring in the mail while she's sleeping and yesterday there was this plain white envelope addressed to her with no return address on it. She opened it up and pulled out a newspaper clipping and read it and turned as white as the envelope but she didn't tell me what it said. She still tickles my back sometimes. I took off my shirt last night and laid across her lap while we were watching The Perry Como Show and she tickled my back. I guess I'm getting too big but it feels too good to quit. She's been tickling my back like that ever since I can remember. After mom went to work I found the envelope under some stuff in the little nightstand beside her bed and read the clipping. It was from a South Carolina newspaper and said that John C. Plotner who is my father was in jail on a charge of moral turpitude. There was no letter or anything just the clipping.

I couldn't fall asleep. Then I hear Millie Ruffner screaming like somebody was trying to murder her and I run out and she and Mikey are up on the sidewalk in front of Bub Allgier's. This is around midnight. All she did was fall down and cut her knee a little bit but you would have thought it was the end of the world. Mikey's trying to pull her up. I didn't even push her down he says. I didn't even push her down. I took her downstairs and washed her knee and put some mercurochrome on it and stayed with them until they fell asleep. So I'm bushed this morning. Mrs. Ruffner wasn't around.

I had to go with my mother to the YMCA down on Main Street to pick up surplus food. They hand it out every Tuesday. She talked about it and talked about it before we finally got around to going. We got a box of cheese and some canned meat and dried milk. I was afraid Randy would turn up and try to diddle somebody's leg when I was there with my mother but he didn't. The man who was handing out the food asked if we heard anything from Jacey yet and carried the box out to the car for us. I could have carried it out myself.

At the dam there's a footbridge across Potters Creek with a trail on the other side heading up through the woods. People go up in there camping. Bub Allgier and I went with Snuffy Guth and Walter Mertz a couple of weeks ago. We camped near one of the Scripture Rocks. That's another story my grandmother liked to tell me about the Scripture Rocks. Old Dan Slagle was a painter who was living in Hartsgrove when the Lord told him in a dream that he should give up all his worldly possessions and dedicate himself to making the Scripture Rocks. He borrowed a hammer and chisel and started carving Biblical verses on big rocks and boulders in a circle around Hartsgrove. There were almost five hundred of them in all. He worked all by himself and became the subject of ridicule. It took him 30 years. Eventually they decided he was crazy and put him in a mental hospital. I never said it to Grandma but it does sound like he was about three bricks shy of a load. Most of the rocks are lost now.

The verse on the one up in the clearing by Potters Creek says the water that I will give will become in them a spring of water gushing up to eternal life. I have no idea what that means. Neither does anybody else if you ask me. We built a campfire and ate sandwiches and started telling ghost stories after it got dark. Snuffy kept wandering off beyond the light and he'd come back and try to tell us he'd seen the McCracken girls. When we got tired of ghost stories Bub said we ought to have a circle jerk but I didn't feel like jacking off in front of anybody. They did though and Snuffy showed us some jizz on the tip of his cock. I never saw any before.

Sandt's Drugs on Main Street is owned by Eugene Sandt. The old timers talk about when his grandfather and some of his friends who were doctors robbed a grave and stole the corpse of a Negro fellow who had just died. This was about a hundred years ago. There aren't any

Negroes in Hartsgrove now. There used to be one family the Van Pat-
tens but Mr. Van Patten quit his job and moved to Pittsburgh. He was
real well liked and the editor of the Hartsgrove Herald wrote a piece
and said he was the whitest black man he ever knew. When that Negro
fellow's body was robbed from his grave a hundred years ago there
was quite an uproar in town and when they found out who did it Eugene Sandt's grandfather just said they took it to dissect and study because good corpses were hard to come by. Weasel Fleager told me that
Negro fellow had a twelve inch cock and that it's still in a jar in the back
of Sandt's Drugs. He said he saw it with his own eyes one time when he
was sweeping out.

We got the middle of the brush cleared out where the tennis court
used to be. Then we got the cardboard boxes from the Golden Days
Supermarket and flattened them out and put them in the clearing for
Nora Jean Vandevoort to lay down on. It looks pretty cozy actually. It
might just work. We laid down on them and talked about how we're
going to talk her into it. That's the part that's got me worried. Bub says
don't worry about it. Leave it up to me he says. I'll handle it. I know
women. But Nora Jean Vandevoort's only about eleven I told him.

And he says if they're old enough to pee they're old enough
for me.

It's bad enough delivering newspapers in the rain anyhow but all I can
think about is how it's messing up our cardboard. Bub Allgier wasn't
around yesterday. His mother said he had to go visit his father who's
working someplace down in West Virginia. She talked to me just like
nothing had happened so I'm hoping she won't say anything to my
mother about Nora Jean Vandevoort.

Weasel Fleager always says think the rain'll hurt the rhubarb? And
Doodle O'Hanlon always says not if it's in cans it won't. Man I sure
hope I never get to that stage. Last night I just got to sleep when I heard
this squeaking noise. I looked outside. Mikey was swinging on the
swing set down in the yard. It's all rusty. The moon was out and I could
see him plain as day. I went down and said Mikey what are you doing?

He kept swinging and looking away. Swinging he says. I said do you know what time it is? He said no. I said how come you're swinging in the middle of the night? He says Millie was keeping him awake. I said where's Millie?

We found her up sitting in the middle of the street playing with dirt. She was under the streetlight and kept throwing the dirt up in the air and it kind of glittered spraying out. She said it was magic dust. I said Mikey you should be watching her. He said I am Jimmy.

I got them into bed and waited for Mrs. Ruffner who got in about two hours later. She was drunk. I told her what had happened and she just kept shaking her head and saying they know better than that they know better than that. She kept thanking me. She said it would not happen again. But I left mom a note anyhow.

Sure enough Mom had me go picket with them. My sign said Equal Pay. Hers said Full Staffing. I don't mind helping my mom and the nurses but I was a little bit embarrassed. I kept hiding my face behind my sign whenever a car went by. You can look down on the whole town from up there on the hill by the entrance to the hospital. The steeple of the Catholic Church is below you and so is the Court House down on Main Street even lower. I could see the side of Longview where my paper route is but I couldn't make any sense of the streets or houses through the trees. It was hot and the whole town looked kind of wilted down below. Out the Harmony Mills road there's another Chew Mail Pouch Tobacco Treat Yourself To The Best barn. There were a bunch of nurses and relatives and everybody was excited and laughing like they were nervous. A cop was sitting in a Hartsgrove Police car just across the street. He just sat there watching us for a long time.

Mom didn't look embarrassed picketing at all. She had her shoulders back the same way my father always did when he was on the pitcher's mound.

Buster Clover was supposed to show up too but he never did. I guess he's not quite as dumb as he looks. Mom told me she talked to Mrs. Ruffner. Mrs. Ruffner's been home the last couple of nights which is good. I wonder if she tucks Mikey and Millie in. I can still remember when mom used to tuck me in and dad too. Of course that's a while ago. I was thinking about mom and dad standing by the fireplace in the house out near Coolbrook with their dukes up like they were going to start fighting. I think I must have just dreamed it.

I hitchhiked out to Coolbrook the day before yesterday to see if I could talk Buster into picketing with me. We decided to walk out to the Strawcutter grave. Another one of my grandmother's favorite stories was about this man called Richard Strawcutter. She said he was an evil man who lived during the Civil War. When he was dying he decided he could outsmart the Lord so he got himself buried underneath the over-hanging edge of a big boulder that looked like the slightest tremble of the earth would send it tumbling down. He figured that on Judgment Day when the graves are all opening up the rock would fall over and hide him. He figured the Devil might be able to snatch and torture everybody else but not him. The wages of sin is death my grandmother used to say. I never said anything to her but it sounded to me like Richard Strawcutter didn't quite have all his oars in the water. She never told me how he was evil. I don't know if he killed somebody or stole money or if he just smoked and drank like dad and didn't go to church. I wonder if Grandma would have thought her own son was an evil man.

It's a long hike out through the woods but Buster and I used to take long hikes through the woods all the time playing army. We haven't done that in quite a while now. Buster's dog Pupady came with us. He's about Randy's size but he doesn't try to diddle your leg. I was standing outside Sterck's when a bunch of guys came out of Jum's Bar to watch Randy sniffing this lawyer's leg and just then Wahoo got out of some-body's car to go into Jum's. They all started hollering and pointing at Randy who was humping away on the lawyer's leg and Wahoo told them a joke. What do a rooster and a woman have in common she said. Everybody said what? And Wahoo said the rooster says cock-a-doodle-do and the woman says any-cock'll-do. Weasel Fleager walked out of Jum's Bar and saw me and hollered how's your heart?

After we got home from picketing mom went in to lay down. There's this little shelf in the hallway with dad's trophies on it which are little golden pitchers on top of golden baseballs. They're all dusty. I peeked in and mom was laying on her back on top of the sheet with her arm over her eyes. I don't think she was sleeping. Then I noticed the picture was gone. It usually sits on the nightstand next to the bed a picture of dad standing there with a big smile on his face and his hands on his hips. His uniform says Oxen Hill across the front of it. Then I saw it beside mom's hand. It was laying face down on the bed beside her. The triangular thing that holds it up was pointing up in the air like the sail of a little boat.

Bub Allgier's still down in West Virginia. His mother told me she's not sure when he's coming home. I spotted Nora Jean Vandevoort on the sidewalk across the street from Sterck's with two other girls. She looked over at me and waved. I could feel my face getting red.

Pupady kept chasing things on the way out to the Strawcutter grave. I couldn't tell what he was on the trail of but I kept looking around in the woods and wondering if that hunter really did see the ghosts of the McCracken girls. My grandfather was a blacksmith before he worked on the roads for the county and he used to shoe horses in all the lumber towns in the woods up north. Places that aren't even there anymore. Places like Willow Well and Blue Run. They're not even on any map anymore. That night around the campfire up by Potters Creek I kept hearing noises in the woods and I know they were only animals. But it seems different remembering it. It seems like there could have been something creeping around us just outside the light getting closer and closer as the fire died down like two little ghost girls wanting to come into the light but afraid to. But I guess I'll keep that to myself.

Buster doesn't know what moral turpitude means either. I can't ask my mother because then she'd know I read the clipping.

Richard Strawcutter was 43 when he died. The wages of sin is death Grandma used to say. She was right about the boulder. It's tipping clean back the other way now. She said the Lord reached down and picked it up and tilted it back the other way. I guess. Either that or Richard Strawcutter was a moron to begin with.

■ ■ ■

Bub Allgier's back. He said he wasn't supposed to go visit his father. He was just there last month. So he thinks they sent him down there because of what we were planning with Nora Jean Vandevoort. We got some fresh cardboard boxes from the Golden Days Supermarket and tore them open and put them down on the ground for her to lay down on and got rid of all the soggy stuff. Then we hung around her house on Jefferson Street but she never came out. We waited and waited. I asked Bub what he was going to say to her and he told me don't worry I'll think of something.

I bumped into Weasel Fleager coming out of Deitz's Funeral Home on Main Street last night and I told him my heart was just fine before he could ask. I think that hurt his feelings a little bit. I asked him who was dead and he said it was some old guy from out by Bootjack he wasn't sure who. Weasel likes to go to all the funerals he can so that when he dies somebody might show up at his. Then he told me the news. Wahoo got beat up and raped by a bunch of college guys. Weasel says they'll never even go to jail for it because their families are all rich. Everybody says Wahoo was asking for it. Everybody says if Wahoo had as many sticking out of her as she's had sticking in her she'd look like a porcupine. The nurses are still out on strike and they moved most of the patients out of the hospital. Weasel said they took Wahoo over to Harmony Mills Hospital.

Nora Jean Vandevoort finally showed up. We were standing on the sidewalk up on Jefferson Street. I was pretty nervous wondering what Bub was going to say to talk her into it. But all he did was jerk his thumb towards me and tells her me and Jimmy wants to f—— you. She ran away or so Bub told me later. I didn't see her because I was running the other way.

My mother made me egg on toast for breakfast. Then she came over and stood behind me and tickled my back through my shirt while I was eating my egg on toast. It doesn't feel as good that way but I still got goose pimples on my neck. I figured something must be up. She doesn't usually make me egg on toast for breakfast and she hardly ever tickles my back like that. Sure enough she told me she heard from my father.

I said oh yeah? I didn't know what else to say.

She said he probably won't be home for a while yet. He's still looking for work she said.

I said I hope he finds some.

Me too mom said. I do too. The faucet in the kitchen sink was dripping. Mom went over and tried to turn it all the way off but she couldn't. My father could because he has a real strong grip. He used to shake me and Buster's hands and just about crush them. He used to punch us on the shoulder all the time to see how tough we were. He was kidding around but it hurt. Sometimes he drank shots of whiskey and chased them with cold water from the faucet in the kitchen leaning over the sink. Dad always said his three favorite vegetables were lettuce turnip and pea and every time he said it mom always said that's so corny. I went over and tried but I couldn't turn the faucet all the way off either. Mom said don't worry about it. Let it drip she said.

This place on Coal Alley where the trees open up is the best view on my paper route. I decided there's only six hills in Hartsgrove I don't care what anybody else says. I also decided Bub Allgier is a moron. The sky's dark blue halfway between night and day and the fog coming up out of the creek makes me think of ghost fingers reaching up out of a grave. Fifty people drowned when this boat called the Andrea Doria sank. I hold my breath and try to imagine what it's like to drown. And I wonder who'd come to my funeral. Besides Weasel Fleager I mean. Main Street runs right over Potters Creek and sometimes I stand in the middle of the bridge and look straight down at the water. The way it rushes around the stone support that holds the bridge up makes it feel like you're on a boat sailing away to someplace where you've never been before. Maybe the McCracken girls are in one of the places my grandfather used to go to like Willow Well that isn't there anymore. I dreamed about Katie McCracken again. I've invented a face for her in my dreams because I never saw her in real life but her face in my dreams isn't one that belongs to anybody else. I wonder if it's what she would really look like. I dreamed we went berrying in the woods and we sat down to eat some berries and I looked over and I could see her thing because she was sitting with her knees apart like Judy Lockett. And she was smiling at me like she didn't mind me looking at all.

There's a siren way across town which sounds like a big mosquito. I can see smoke coming from over on School House Hill which is where I live. The Boy Scouts are working on a project to restore the Scripture Rocks. It was in this week's Hartsgrove Herald. They want to find them all and open them up with trails for people to visit. Old Dan Slagle died in the mental hospital my grandmother said. My grandmother told me the Scripture Rocks would withstand the test of time and they would be as enduring as the Bible itself which outlived centuries of ridicule. She never thought Old Dan Slagle was crazy. I wonder what she'd think of this guy in the paper who killed his milkman in Indiana and cut off his ears because he said the Lord told him to.

More sirens. A swarm of them. People are coming out of their houses to watch the smoke. They point and shout and yell where is it where is it and yell for everybody else to come outside and see. Where is it? Can you tell where it is? People stop their cars and get out and look at the smoke going up. You can hear people calling on the other hills.

The trucks and the hoses had my street all blocked off so I had to go around and up through the backyard from Valley Street. They were down by the rusty swing set. Mrs. Ruffner was gray not red like she normally is. She was holding Mikey who had his face buried in her like he was never coming out again. My mother had her arm around her. Millie was nowhere to be seen. The firemen were still pumping water into Ruffner's house. Most of the roof was burned away and the smoke was going up and every now and then a tongue of flame would leap up out of it. The big window in the back had black all around it. It looked like Millie's mouth after she's been eating dirt.

I got on the swing. Everybody else was standing back. It seemed like the whole town was standing there watching the fire and watching my mother and Mrs. Ruffner and Mikey. I started swinging. The swing started squeaking. Nobody was making any noise like they were in church except for the sound of the water shooting and the fire hissing and the swing squeaking. I started swinging higher and the wind filled up my ears and my stomach started flying away and the higher I went the more I could see. It was like I could see down on everything. I went higher and higher and I saw Millie throwing magic dust in the air that glittered under the streetlight and the leaves flipping and twisting and trying to escape from the tree and my grandmother whispering the wages of sin is death and I went higher and there was Katie McCracken and Millie Ruffner holding hands in the woods and running away. And I watched the smoke how it curled up into the sky into God's eye the way smoke from my father's cigarette used to curl up his cheek and into his eye.

The Other Sister

She was not the prettiest girl in Cookie Zufall's fifth period social studies class, an honor clearly belonging to Margie Allshouse, nor was she his smartest student, a dubious distinction in Cookie's mind anyway, usually associated with spectacles and pudginess, which fitted Denny Lindemuth to a T. Short, well-proportioned, with a sweet, round face and moon-pie eyes, she might have been just a normal girl, an average student, a member of Sub-Deb and Tri-Hi-Y, a girl who dated now and then and went to the Hartsgrove High School football games along with everyone else. But to anyone who lived in Hartsgrove, she was not just your typical high school senior; Becky McCracken had a history.

Seven years earlier, when she was ten, her two little sisters, Mary Lou and Katie, had gone to pick blackberries in the woods near their grandfather's farm, and were never seen again. Becky should have been with them, had she not been grounded by her father following a squabble over which pail should be carried by whom. Whether she would have vanished too, or whether all three would have safely returned, no one of course could know, but ever since that day, no one could look at her without seeing that history, without thinking, in so many words, "That's the *other* McCracken girl."

On the Monday following the historic launch, Cookie wrote *SPUTNIK* on the blackboard; then he memorialized it, adding the year, *1957*. Sunbeams slanted through the high windows above the cast-iron radiators mounted on the wall of his basement classroom. "Who can tell me what this means?" he said.

Bobby Fetzer, the class clown, said, "Isn't that the telephone number for the Kremlin?" which rang a distant bell in Alvin Brocious's mind: "Ain't that that satellite thing the Russians put up?"

"That's what it *is*," Cookie said. "I asked what does it *mean*."

"It means the Russians were first," Barb Bennett said. "It means they got more know-how than us now."

"It means they can launch nuclear missiles at us from Russia," Denny Lindemuth said.

In the pregnant pause that followed, Becky McCracken said, "It means we better make hay while the sun shines." She sat in the front row wearing a smile and a snug pink sweater, the top three buttons of which were fetchingly unbuttoned. Intrigued by the implications of her remark, Cookie was also annoyed; this was a serious matter. To him, a war was a war, cold or hot. A decade and a half earlier, as a twenty-year-old MP, he'd been wounded by a German POW booby trap, a severe, war-ending injury.

"Certainly," he said, waving his chalk. "But keep in mind the real meaning of Miss McCracken's wisecrack. 'Making hay' is not the same as 'making whoopee'"—here a chuckle or two escaped the classroom—"making hay means hard, hard work."

After class, he turned from erasing the blackboard, nearly bumping into her. "Sorry," Becky said. A head shorter than him, she was standing close, books clasped to her chest. "I just wanted to tell you I like your jacket."

"My jacket. Really."

"Blue looks good on you."

"Thank you."

"But you keep getting chalk on it. Here." She brushed at the chalk dust in the area of his right hip. "It's on your pants too."

He took over the brushing before she got to his pants. "Yes. It drives my wife nuts."

"It drives me nuts too. What's your wife's name?"

"Mabel." He frowned.

"You should put the chalk back before you put your hands on your hips."

"Excellent advice."

"It doesn't really come off," she said, spanking at his jacket again, "this just smears it around. How does Mabel get it off?"

Cookie eased his jacket from her grip. "I don't know. I'll have to ask her."

Truth was he didn't have to ask. Truth was his marriage was currently under siege, Mabel boycotting the chalk on his clothes, as well as other of what Cookie considered to be her wifely duties. It went back three years, to summer vacation. He'd just finished mowing the lawn, a tough, two-hour job with his big yard and little mower, and, washing up in the bathroom before supper, he was examining himself in the mirror. A man in his prime, he wanted to stay that way, looking for early warning signs—fat, wrinkles, moles, a sneaky gray hair in his neat black brush-cut. Peeling off his tee shirt, he admired how the sweat made his pumped-up muscles glisten. He threw the sweaty shirt on the floor by the hamper—thoughtfully, he thought, so as not to taint the other laundry.

Next day, the shirt was still there.

Mabel was at the kitchen counter slicing fresh tomatoes from the plants Cookie grew along the fence in the backyard. "How come my shirt's still on the floor in there?"

"You threw it there, you pick it up." She didn't turn around.

Cookie explained that he hadn't wanted to get the rest of the laundry sweaty.

Still she didn't turn, looking over her shoulder, a coquettish tilt to her head. "You've been in the bathroom seven times since it dried."

"Fine. Next time I'll throw it in there all sweaty."

"Fine," Mabel said.

"Fine," said Cookie.

It was quiet at supper that night. The kids—Eddy and Linda, six and four at the time—sensed something wrong. Linda made a mashed potato pyramid with her fork. There'd been quarrels and arguments before—bedtimes for the kids, the need for a new rug, where to go on a Saturday night—but this was new ground. This seemed to be a wobble in the very foundation of his marriage, a wobble he'd been fearing since the day he married Mabel.

Mabel was gorgeous; Cookie could never quite trust his good fortune in having won her. With a warmth of black hair, a dark, glowing complexion and a sparkling smile, she'd been the most beautiful girl in their class, a cheerleader, the one everyone watched, the rest of the squad in her shadow. It wasn't that Cookie lacked confidence. He considered himself handsome, a good pitcher on the baseball team, an adequate guard in basketball—but while he was good, he wasn't the best at anything, not quite the smartest, not quite the best-looking, and he hadn't played football, like Bill MacBeth, the star quarterback; football was where the real glamour was. Cookie'd come home from the war with a wound not quite from the battlefield, a wound not quite visible, not quite heroic, while Bill MacBeth and the others were still overseas, and so he'd made hay while the sun shone. Mabel was not a patient girl, not the type to wait for a better offer to come along. Cookie had been looking over his shoulder ever since.

His shirt stayed on the bathroom floor for two weeks. He found it difficult to relax on the toilet with his *Reader's Digest* while it was there. It didn't seem to bother Mabel. She was an adequate housekeeper at best, and he began to notice the cobwebs in the corners, the dust bunnies under the chairs. One day the shirt was gone. He figured Linda, not Mabel, had picked it up. Cookie was watching television that evening when Mabel said, "When are you going to burn the trash? There's no more room to put it." They collected the trash in the pantry for Cookie to burn in their burn barrel at the far end of the yard.

Cookie said, "You threw it there, you burn it."

■   ■   ■

A week after *Sputnik*, Cookie's lesson was on how World War II still af-
fected the world in which they lived today, twelve years later. This was
one of his favorite subjects, one he felt especially qualified to teach.
Discussing the reasons for Hitler's rise to power, Denny Lindemuth
cited Hitler's powers of oratory.

Alvin Brocious's mouth fell open. "You mean he could tell the future?"

Becky McCracken raised her hand as the laughter died away. "Mr.
Zufall? Where were you wounded in the war?"

A hush. No one had ever thought, or dared, to ask such an excellent
question before. "In France," Cookie said, "just outside a little village
near—"

"No, no," Becky said, "I mean what part of your *body*."

Cookie grinned, shaking his head, the titters running their course.
Becky's face was proud and red. Every year there was a girl—at least
one—who flirted with him, sometimes in hopes of a better grade, sometimes just showing off. It was obvious who this year's flirter was.

Two days later he asked the class to imagine nuclear war had destroyed the earth's population, except for ten people who'd survived in
a bomb shelter. They must wait at least three months for the atmo-
sphere to clear, yet there are supplies enough for only six of them to
last that long. The future of humanity depends upon them. Which six
should stay, and which four should be made to leave the shelter and
die? On the blackboard he wrote the names, ages, and other characteristics of the ten hypothetical survivors.

"You can't send the little girl and the little boy out to die," Barb
Bennett said.

"Why not?" said Becky McCracken.

"Well," Denny Lindemuth said, "the little boy has the highest IQ
up there."

"So what?" said Joe Spare, a letterman. "He can't hunt or build
things or do any work."

"Just throw out the four oldest ones," Bobby Fetzer said.

"That's stupid," said Rhonda Stewart. "Have them draw straws."

"And what if the four best ones lose?" Denny said.

"Who's to say who the best ones are?" said Rhonda.

"You are," said Cookie. "That's your assignment. We'll break up into four groups, and I want each group to pick the six survivors, write down your reasons, select a spokesman, and be prepared to defend your choices. Be objective. You can't be ruled by emotions. You have to decide which characteristics are most important for the survival of the human race."

After class, when he turned around from erasing the blackboard, Becky was there again. "Mr. Zufall? I have a question. How can they have babies?"

"How can they what?"

"Aren't they going to have to start having babies to repopulate the planet?"

"I would certainly think so."

"None of them were married."

Although her big round eyes seemed sincere, her hint of a smile was unmistakably flirtatious. "They'll have to manage somehow, I guess," Cookie said.

"I guess," she echoed, with a sudden swipe at the chalk dust on his jacket. Then the smile was gone. "We might be leaving soon," she said. "My dad wants to move away from here in the worst way."

That was common knowledge, had been for seven years. He watched her walk away, the sexy strut for his eyes. Becky's flirting was different. The others had usually confined it to the classroom, in front of their classmates; not so Becky. He'd always reciprocated good-naturedly, for he'd always been able to see through to the essential innocence of it. Becky's was much more opaque. Now she was practically giving him a deadline. If there was any essential innocence there, he couldn't see it. If any was there, it was hidden by the mystery of her past.

After school Cookie often worked out in the high school gym. Although he belonged to the YMCA down on Main Street, he preferred the gym because there he could work out alone, as aggressively as he pleased, dribbling the basketball up and down the court as fast as he could, slamming the ball as hard as he could, then shooting, chasing, dribbling again.

He was running down the court when a flash of color caught his eye. Pink. He pulled up, still pounding the ball. Becky was there, sitting in the stands, her books stacked neatly beside her. He hadn't seen her come in. The gym was a big, empty cavern, pads like mattresses hanging behind the backboards, windows bright on the south wall above the stands. "Becky?"

"I wanted to see if I could see where you were wounded in the war." The words echoed. He dribbled the ball over, his eyes even with her knees which were slightly apart, a white glimpse of panties. "Can you show me?"

His right buttock was throbbing from the old wound. "Exactly what's on your mind, young lady?"

"My sisters," she said, "Katie and Mary Lou." Cookie felt the cool chill of the sweat on his neck. "They'll never know what it's like."

He'd been away at college when they'd vanished. He remembered seeing them only once, three little girls, at the Fourth of July parade when he was home from school one summer—'48, it would have been. They were marching, carrying batons they tried to twirl, dressed in red, white, and blue spangles, and the littlest one—Katie?—kept running off giggling, while the oldest, Becky, kept chasing her down. He wouldn't have known who they were, but Mabel had pointed, laughing, "Aren't those McCracken girls cute as buttons?" He hadn't thought of that in years, but now he did as he stared at Becky. "What *what* is like?"

"*Any*thing. *Every*thing." Then she smiled, crossing her knees, smoothing her skirt down her thigh. "I just don't want the same thing to happen to me."

"Then you'd better stay out of the woods," Cookie said.

"Oh no," said Becky. "The woods is where I want to be."

He enjoyed the flirting. He couldn't help it. He was addicted to adoration. The less he received at home, the more he craved at school. Adoration was easily recognizable in the eyes of the adorer, say in Becky's eyes, a certain sparkling expectation, the anticipation of delight. As opposed to the dull, indifferent glaze in the eyes of the unadoring—in Mabel's eyes, for example.

It hadn't always been that way. At one time that sparkle had inhabited her eyes. The honeymoon at Niagara Falls, eating hot dogs at the card table in their first apartment, the day he'd earned his degree, the morning they'd learned she was pregnant with Eddy, the candle-lit dinner at Frankie's Band Box in Pittsburgh, fixing up their new house, painting the walls yellow, singing along with Rosemary Clooney, "Come on-a My House."

He couldn't remember when the adoration had left her eyes, but it was certainly gone by the time his dirty shirt lingered on the bathroom floor for two weeks. What he could remember, if he tried, was the general course of the escalation that followed, which action on her part led to which reaction on his, which reaction to which revenge, which tit to which tat. When Cookie wouldn't replace the broken clothesline, she did it herself, then quit folding his laundry. When she quit helping him wash the car (he loved soaking the front of her shirt, the way her nipples rose to the occasion), he quit clearing the table after supper. When she began drinking more, he began drinking less, having never much cared for it in the first place. When she quit going to his softball games, cheering from the bleachers with the other wives and girlfriends, he quit going to her parents' house, Dick's and Verna's, on Friday nights to play Hearts, something he didn't miss at all; Dick, a plant manager down at Sylvania who made twice as much as Cookie (the better to spoil his only little girl) tended to make up the rules as he went along. She quit fixing him snacks, so he quit sharing his bacon—he loved bacon, frying big, sizzling heaps of it—actually slapping her hand once when she reached for a piece. She quit making him lunches, so he started buying them at the cafeteria, deducting the cost from their food budget, giving her less every week for groceries. So she prepared fewer meals. Their marriage had taken on the aspect of a badminton match, the gentle lobs of the birdie picking up steam as the game went along, picking up heat and passion.

In the end, the rules were these: Civility was maintained, even friendliness and a modicum of affection (the occasional spat notwithstanding), not only for the sake of the kids, but for the pride of the combatants; neither would admit that anything the other could do could possibly ruin their day. Neither ceded an inch; whatever territory might be lost here, an equal or greater amount was reclaimed there. In the end, the battle hinged on the thing each possessed that the other couldn't live without: Cookie the money, Mabel the sex.

Early that summer, Cookie had finally given in and bought Mabel a dryer, a shiny new $189 GE model from Matson's down on Main Street, an event that marked the end of a two-month period of Mabel-imposed celibacy. That night, after she'd put the kids into bed and a load of laundry into her new dryer, she'd tickled his ear, passing behind his chair. "Why don't you go put on your headdress, lover?" she'd whispered, the flicker back in her eyes.

For his Eagle Scout pioneering merit badge in high school, he'd made an Indian headdress, a finely crafted article of colorful beads and rawhide and real eagle feathers; just after they were married, they'd occasionally used it in their sex games. It tickled her fancy, she liked to joke. She liked the feel of the feathers on her skin, though they hadn't used it in years.

That night they didn't either. Cookie had refused, fucking her instead without affection, like a customer in a whorehouse, annoyed by the high cost of her favors.

Cookie spent his free period in the teachers' lounge smoking with Bill MacBeth, a man with a clenched jaw and perpetual Chesterfield. He liked Bill. He remembered with awe how Bill had been able to throw a football sixty yards in the air, and how, on defense, the whole pile had moved three yards whenever he'd slammed into it. When Mrs. Ishman left the room, Cookie mentioned Becky.

"You nuts?" said Bill. "She's jailbait."

"You don't believe in messing around with a girl under eighteen?"

"Hell, I didn't say that. Sex after puberty is the way God intended it—eighteen's just a number picked by a bunch of fat lawyers. All I'm saying is because they did pick that number, you could go to jail."

Cookie nodded. "She's started dotting all the *i*'s on her homework with little hearts."

"Don't make me puke," Bill said. "She did that on my homework, I'd flunk her."

"C'mon. She's cute as a button."

"Don't make me puke. Besides, she's gotta be pretty screwed up in the head, after what happened to her sisters."

Cookie doubted it. Having a crush on him was de facto evidence of clear thinking. "But what a body," he said. "What a set."

"Jailbait," Bill said.

Cookie nodded again. He knew. Left unspoken was what they both knew: they were all jailbait, all the high school girls, always had been, and yet in the illustrious history of the school, woven into the musty fabric of the place, like the undefeated football team of '38, or the famous alum who'd produced a Broadway play in the twenties, more than one teacher was known to have yielded to temptation.

He didn't feel like company, but Ron and Betty Stahlman were coming for supper. Betty was a wide woman—not fat, not unattractive, but possessed of a wide freckled forehead and wide shoulders, and, to Cookie, she was devoid of sex appeal. Ron was a nice enough guy, quick with a quip, lean and good looking despite his thinning hair; he helped his father run their boiler manufacturing business. He and Mabel had grown up in the same north-side neighborhood, near the school, and Cookie, from the south side of town, hadn't known either of them then. Mabel had told him a story once, a story she thought was funny, how she and Ron had set out one summer morning when they were six to catch a bird by sprinkling salt on its tail, an easy enough feat, they'd figured. When that hadn't panned out, they'd ended up in the middle of the laurel thicket behind Ron's house taking down their shorts to examine each other's parts. They'd each peed to see where it came out; Ron, unfortunately, had peed on the salt shaker, so they'd buried it in the thicket, hoping his mother would never miss it. This was a story that had stuck with Cookie ever since.

It was warm enough to cook out, and they ate at the picnic table in the backyard, twilight creeping across a scattering of crisp brown leaves. Mabel complained that Cookie had burned the burgers, so Cookie pointed out with glee the spots on the silverware, the crusty scab on the end of the ketchup bottle. "Mabel! Black Label!" was Ron's joke of the evening. He'd brought two six-packs of the stuff, though Cookie knew for a fact he preferred Schlitz. "Mabel! Black Label!" he would call, holding up his empty. "Get your own damn beer," Mabel would snarl, then bring him another, along with another highball for herself. Cookie didn't particularly like beer. He had two—it was, after all, free—while Betty drank orange pop with the kids.

When it was nearly dark, the kids went inside to watch *Your Hit Parade*. Mabel and Ron started swinging on the swing set. "You break it, you're gonna buy a new one," called Cookie from the picnic table. He tried to sound as though he were joking. The thing had cost him thirty-nine dollars last summer.

"Let's try," Mabel said to Ron, just loud enough for Cookie to hear.

"What a couple of kids," Cookie said to Betty.

Betty shooed a fly away from an uncleared plate. "I think I better drive home."

From the swing set came a snatch of conversation, the only words of which he could make out were "salt shaker," and Ron and Mabel laughed so hard they had to stop swinging and cling to the chains. Cookie smiled, fuming. Betty shook her head. It was a pattern: the less sex they had, the more Mabel flirted with other men, and the more she flirted with other men, the angrier Cookie became. He knew it was all a part of her strategy to get him to buy her that damn sewing machine. But he wasn't buying.

Stars had emerged overhead. From the swing set, tips of cigarettes flared and glowed. Cookie lit a Lucky of his own. From inside, Snooky Lansen warbled an unlikely version of "Wake Up Little Susie." A faint motion in the sky caught his eye.

From out of the west, a tiny point of light came at him, a fast-moving, faint-twinkling star. Cookie started to call to the others, but caught himself.

Across heaven it raced, ominous and beautiful, sinister and miraculous. Catching his breath, swaying, he thought he felt the picnic table shiver. No one else noticed, Ron and Mabel giggling on the swing set, Betty clearing a plate.

On sped *Sputnik*, marking the end of the world as they knew it.

Cookie kept it all to himself.

When Cookie left the cafeteria, he strolled over to the trees beyond the playground for his after-lunch Lucky, guessing Becky, whom he'd spotted on her way over, would follow. She did. She asked what he was doing all alone in the trees.

"I was just thinking about Skippy and MacArthur," he said, leaning against the old maple carved with a hundred broken hearts. "Skippy was our dog, MacArthur was our cat. One day—I couldn't have been more than ten—MacArthur got run over and killed. We were devastated. I don't know who cried more, my sister or my mom. So Dad buried him. Next morning we got up, and there's Skippy on the front porch with MacArthur—he'd dug him up. He was lying there on the porch with him between his front paws, licking him. So Dad buried him deeper. Next morning, there's Skippy again, holding MacArthur in his mouth—three times. Three times that happened. Finally we took him out in the country, and buried him there."

"That's so sad," Becky said.

"Really? You don't think it's funny?"

"What's so funny about a love that'll never die?" she said.

"I didn't finish. About a week later, Skippy disappeared for a couple days. Next morning, there he is on the porch again, with MacArthur in his front paws. Of course by now MacArthur's getting a little worse for the wear."

Becky's moon-pie eyes narrowed considerably. "Are you pulling my leg?"

"So Dad happened to be going down to Pittsburgh on business, and he took MacArthur with him—stuffed him in an old shoe box— and buried him down there, out towards the airport. Well, about three weeks later—"

"You are such a *liar*."

"Scout's honor," he said with a scout salute, a gesture he often used to drive home a point. He looked at his watch, dropped his cigarette, grinding it out with his foot. The kiss was spontaneous, nearly inadvertent, intended as only a peck on the cheek, and exactly how it hit her lips he wasn't sure, nor, certainly, how their tongues came together, how they licked and lingered.

Pulling away he said, "The fish sticks are delicious." She nearly missed his parting smile, her eyes opening slowly to twice their normal size. He walked away. Halfway to the school, he heard her rushing up behind him. "My God," she said, "I can't believe how soft your lips are!"

"Becky—"

She clung to his elbow as he kept walking, her head cocked, burrowing closer. "God—they're so *soft*!"

"Becky—go to lunch. I'm late for class."

"I've never been kissed like that. I didn't know there *were* kisses like that."

He stopped. People were looking. He saw Mrs. Ishman in her haughty amble, staring straight at them. He turned, making space between them. "Becky—people are watching us. Do you want me to get fired?"

The hypnotist had snapped his fingers. She backed away. "No."

"Good," he said and walked away, feeling her eyes upon him. He hopped onto the curb. He *was* a good kisser—even Mabel used to say so. Into the building, down the steps to his classroom, like skipping down a cloud. He was a great kisser; he was a good athlete, a man who'd shed his blood for his country, a father, a teacher, a molder of young minds. He was good looking, well conditioned, clean-living;

how could all those attributes be so completely voided by Mabel? What had happened? When had his outlook turned so sour? He could hear Johnny Mercer singing the words—*ac-cent-u-ate the positive*—singing along in his mind. Midway through his fourth period class, he was cruising, rocking up on his toes as he did when a lesson was going well, hitting home, the kids all attentive, not a napper in the back. He glanced to his left and saw Becky, outside in the hallway, peering through the small window in the door, her breath hot on the pane.

Good days. Days when living was a breeze. Everything on good days was easy, the pieces falling together, fitting perfectly, the test a snap, the fastball moving, the set-shot dead on, Mabel eager and early for their date. There were plenty of good days before the war; during the war they were fewer. After the war and the healing, during his college years, there was a time when nearly every day was a good day. Where had they gone? What had happened to them? Was it Mabel alone? Was it aging alone? Was it inevitable? Now a good day almost never was—the best he could hope for was a few good hours, and even those had become distant and random. And when he had a few good hours, he always thought about the good days.

Today had the makings of a very good day. Cookie was riding the high. In fifth period Becky was attentive and devoted—but cautiously so. He had a good workout after school, no papers to grade, a game of catch with Eddy, a delicious meal—chicken and dumplings—which Mabel prepared ungrudgingly. They watched *Gunsmoke* together without bickering, a new episode, the kids went to bed willingly, Mabel's latest sewing machine argument was feeble and easily deflected, almost as though she were giving up. His bath felt luxurious as he thought about the kiss. About Becky. Thoughts of her caused a happy apprehension, as though he were on an adventure, one slightly risky, but under control. He looked at his body in the water, at the prime muscles, and he felt the faint stitch in his buttock where he'd been wounded in the service of his country. Sex was not far from his mind, part of the happy apprehension, the imagined body of Becky, the real one of Mabel, and when Mabel came into the bathroom, he suspected this good day might go on and on.

She hadn't interrupted his bath in years. But when she used to, it had often ended well. "Do you mind?" She nodded toward the toilet. "I really have to go." Cookie smiled. As she sat and peed, she looked at him—a good sign—though her expression was neutral. He put his hands behind his head, the better to display his body, and mouthed a kiss in her direction. Though she neither smiled nor frowned—nor returned the kiss—her eyebrow arched minutely, and he thought he saw there an inkling of a flicker. He tried to read her expression even as she was leaving, closing the door behind her, even as his penis began to plump up.

He rose from the tub, quickly dried, shaved, splashed on after-shave, inspected himself in the mirror, every tooth, under his chin, each profile, brushed his hair and his eyebrows, put on a fresh white pair of shorts. In the bedroom she lay waiting, propped against pillows, reading a magazine, smoking. A glimpse of color in the closet—*inspiration*! He retrieved the Indian headdress, putting it on. If that didn't tickle her fancy, nothing would. Headdress on his head, hands on his hips, throb in his shorts, he posed at the foot of the bed.

She looked up with a crooked smile and, surely, a sparkle. "Come here, lover."

Leaning to kiss, he heard the click. Then he felt the heat and saw the flash and noticed the Zippo in her hand. With a yelp and a leap, he knocked the flaming headdress to the floor and started to stomp it out. Smiling distantly, Mabel watched the war dance with pure appreciation. "I'd sew you a new one," she said. "If I only had a machine."

Hartsgrove High School, stately and aging at seventy-five, was an imposing Victorian building of brownstone and brick, its crowning mansards towering five stories high, all but invisible on this October Saturday night—all shadows, glints and mystery. The scent of burning leaves in the air was pungent, thrilling. "Scared?" Cookie said.

"A little bit," said Becky, gripping his arm. She'd never been inside the place dark and empty. Cookie had keys. Inside, the ceilings were high, hallways wide and barren, dreary and dim. The silence made their footfalls echo. The light of a single bulb illuminated the stairwell as they descended toward his classroom. The windows high on the wall were barely brighter than the room, light skimming the tops of the cast-iron radiators suspended there, the rows of desks only vague suggestions of themselves. By his desk, he kissed her. Her mouth was dry at first, moistening quickly as her hand without hesitation found the front of his pants.

He unbuttoned his shirt, started on her blouse. "You okay?"

"I think so," she said, and he kissed her again. They stood in front of his desk, her bra against his firm abs, her hand exploring with a hint of urgency. In all his fantasies she'd mounted his desk, but now that seemed too awkward. "I love you, Mr. Zufall, I really do."

"Call me Cookie."

"Cookie—there's no place to lie down."

"We can go up to the teachers' lounge."

"There's a sofa in the janitors' room. I saw Blinky Mumford one time taking a nap on it." Blinky Mumford was a janitor, an odd duck with a facial tic that left him perpetually cross. "He has dirty pictures tacked up behind the door."

"How do you know?" Cookie said. Taking his hand she led him down the dark corridor where the light didn't reach. "How can you see?" He lit his Zippo, holding it high like a torch to get his bearings. The scent of burning leaves infiltrated the stale schoolhouse air, a disorienting incense.

"Come on," she said, tugging at his hand. A few yards farther she whispered, "Here." He felt the doorjamb. He couldn't see a thing. Because of the darkness, they whispered. "Did you hear something?" he said.

"No. Come on."

Inside the door, he heard the noise again, a soft growl. He lit his Zippo and they gasped; there on the sofa lay Blinky Mumford, dead to the world, mouth open, snoring. Cookie snapped the lighter shut, as Becky's eyes, never bigger, were coming at him.

Down the corridor they hurried, in a blind rush of faith. A soft squeal, a stifled giggle, and they lost control, falling to the floor together near his classroom, laughing, shushing, rolling, giggling. She wiggled to the top, pinning him, her hand groping, and he was astounded at finding himself here in this place at this time of his life, nearly blind, flat on his back on the floor outside his classroom, one of his students, a girl half his age, unzipping his pants, fumbling inside, covering his face with wet kisses. "Slow down," he said. "We should go somewhere else—it's not safe here."

She didn't answer, having found what she was looking for in his pants. With the touch came a new sense of urgency, one without caution, and he said, "In here—in the classroom," and they made their way to the darkness of the far wall beneath the sheltering radiators. He dropped his pants and shorts, sloughing off his shirt, and he was naked. She looked at him, her moon-pie eyes growing bigger in the dimness of the room. They kissed, her tongue suddenly shy, her hand no longer touching, and he unsnapped her bra with one-handed proficiency and began pulling at her panties. "Wait a sec," she said, holding a hand to his chest. "Hold on a minute."

He kept pulling, but she squirmed away. "*Wait.*"

"*What?*"

She was still for a moment, as though listening, then she murmured something, then she listened again. "Okay. Okay." Cookie reached for her. She pushed him away. "I'm sorry."

"Sorry?"

"I'm sorry, but we can't do it." She sounded as though she wanted to cry.

"What do you mean?"

"I'm sorry." A quiet sob. "I really love you and I really want to, but we can't. Katie's too scared."

The words scarcely penetrated, a weak joke at best, and he reached for her again, finding her breast beneath the dangling bra. Pushing his hand, she slid away. "You can't stop," he said. "You can't stop now." He reached again, grabbing, holding, squeezing her breast, pushing her down, climbing on top, and she struggled, resisting.

"*Stop!*" she cried in an altered voice, the voice of a little girl. "*Mommy! Daddy!*"

Cookie pulled back, chilled. Becky scrambled away, standing, feverishly fastening her bra, buttoning her blouse, gasping little sobs. He watched in horror from the floor. In the faint light he saw the flurry. When the final button was buttoned she stood for a moment before him, a dark form, a glint from her hair, another from her cheek, and she said, "I'm sorry—but it's Katie's fault, not mine." Then she turned with an odd, garbled sob and hurried away, a vanishing shadow.

For the next two months, Cookie's was an anxious existence. The night after the aborted seduction, he awoke at two a.m. on the edge of a razor, soaked with sweat, adrenaline pulsing through his head. The specter of shame and ruin loomed over him like a gleaming ax; if Becky talked, it was over.

The clarity was terrifying. Mabel would leave him, take the kids. He would be fired. Possibly jailed. His life as he knew it would end. How had it come to this? How could he have let it? Becky's instability was an ambush waiting to happen. He felt helpless, more helpless than he'd felt in the war, when every waking moment had been pregnant with fears of being shipped to the front. God only knew what she might say or do, when, or in front of whom.

After a week or two, she began to apologize for Katie. Began flirting anew. She began hanging on his every word again, leaning toward him in the front row, tongue on the tip of her pencil, moon-pie eyes worshipful. She cornered him whenever she could, after class, in the hallway, on the way to the cafeteria. She hinted that Katie was growing up, getting bolder. Cookie remained charming, keeping it light, counseling that it had been wise not to rush into anything, avoiding any hint of another rendezvous. Never mentioning her sisters. Gazing into her eyes, he never asked who was in there; he didn't want to know. He didn't want to disturb a pebble that might cause an avalanche.

Just before Christmas they moved away. There was little notice. Becky's father had been laid off from his job with the county, he had relatives in North Carolina, and he'd been wanting to leave for years. Most were surprised they'd stuck it out this long. They left behind unpaid bills and an unsold house; the house, as it turned out, unsellable, the inside a trash-ridden shambles that hadn't been cleaned in years— probably seven years. Becky's room was an oasis, clean and tidy, the room of a normal teenage girl; or the room of teenage girl feigning normalcy, was Cookie's guess. He withstood her final onslaught of anguish and regret, spouting platitudes about fresh starts, new beginnings, adroitly dodging her groping hand at the final farewell, when he couldn't avoid a consolatory hug.

When she left, he was born again. It was springtime in December. The awful specter of shame and ruin dissipated into the blue skies and warm breezes, and he began to feel that he'd overreacted, began to feel, in fact, ashamed of his weak and sheepish overreaction.

It was the best Christmas the Zufalls ever had, Eddy and Linda reveling in Cookie's overindulgence, their new Schwinn bicycles and Radio Flyer sleds. Mabel was caught up in the surfeit of joy as well, although, as it turned out, there was nothing permanent about the period of grace Cookie purchased with the new Singer.

When he returned to school in January, the place brought back Becky. There was the empty desk in the front row fifth period. There was the floor just outside his classroom doorway, the spot on the far wall beneath the radiators. Darkness came early. Smoking in the teachers' lounge one day, Bill MacBeth asked him what he ever did to that McCracken girl. "Man, that kid sure vamoosed in a hurry."

Cookie threw his hands up, innocent. "I had nothing to do with it." He took a drag of his Lucky. "You were right about one thing though. She sure was screwed up in the head."

"I don't think so," Bill said.

"What do you mean?"

"She got you going with the whole kid sister thing, did she?"

"She told you about her kid sister?"

"Hell, she told everybody about her kid sister. Katie made her do this, Katie made her do that. It got to be a running joke. She told me she didn't have her homework done one time because Katie had scribbled all over it with crayons. I mean, she could barely keep a straight face."

Cookie pondered the revelation. He pondered too the garbled sob he'd heard as she'd rushed away from him that evening in October. The sob that, it occurred to him now, might just as well have been a stifled laugh. "So you don't think there was anything wrong with her?"

"Oh, I think she was crazy all right," Bill said. "Crazy like a fox."

Bill stubbed out his Chesterfield and left. The bell rang, and Cookie heard the corridors fill, teeming with Hartsgrove's youth, heard the calls and shouts and laughter of the flirters and adorers of the future. He heard the laugh of the next one, a laugh that wanted him to believe in its pure adulation, and the hairs on the back of his neck stood up, his breath coming shallow. In the ashtray, the smoke rose up from Bill's imperfectly snuffed cigarette, and Cookie could only watch it, smoldering.

Diamond Alley

The year we were seniors in high school, a girl in our class was murdered and the Pittsburgh Pirates won the World Series. Which was
the more momentous event? No contest of course; how could a game, a
boys' game at that, compete with the death of a classmate, a girl who
was our friend? Yet somehow, despite our lip service to the contrary,
these two happenings seemed to attain a shameful equality in our
minds. And if anything, now that so many years have passed, Mazeroski rounding the bases in jubilation after his homer had vanquished
the big, bad Yankees is more vivid in our memories than the image of
Carol Siebenrock, young, beautiful and naked, as seen from the darkness beyond her window.

The Pirates were with us everywhere that autumn. They filled the
air. Every evening when we went out, we didn't need our transistors—
we could hear Bob Prince calling the game all over town, his friendly
baritone drifting from radios on porches, in kitchens and living rooms,
pervasive as the scent of burning leaves. We would often pause, inter-
rupting whatever nonsense we were up to, holding a hand in the air to
signify an at-bat worthy of our attention: Maybe Smoky Burgess coming up to pinch hit with the tying run in scoring position, or Clemente
connecting, sending a screamer through the gap, or big, dumb Dick
Stuart approaching the plate with enough runners on to win the game
with one mighty swing of his lumber. And every time they played the
Pirates' jingle, we would sing along:

Oh, the Bucs are going all the way,
All the way, all the way,
Oh, the Bucs are going all the way,
All the way this year!

We might have been anywhere in Hartsgrove, the hilly, leafy town of our youth that most of us have long since abandoned. We came out after dark, after our homework was done, savoring our first heady taste of freedom—seniors now! When we weren't at Les's Pizza Palace down by the bridge over Potters Creek, we were at the elementary school playground on the north side, back in by the swings and seesaws near the trees, watching the stars, smoking the Winstons and Luckies we'd pilfered from our old man's pack on the kitchen counter. Or walking down East Main Street, by all the crowded houses sorely in need of paint and repair, or trudging up Pine, where the leaves on the trees were burnt orange in the scattered streetlights. We might have been crossing the swinging bridge over the Sandy Lick Creek by Memorial Park, seeing how perilously we could get it to sway in the dark, or taking the shortcut down Rose Hill, shrieking like ghosts in the woods on the rutted, littered path that had been a turnpike a hundred years before. Everywhere we went, we smelled the burning leaves and listened to the Voice of the Pittsburgh Pirates. The darker it got, the better we liked it.

Many nights found us in the pine shadows of Carol Siebenrock's backyard on Diamond Alley, waiting for the light in her window.

Her house was on a hill—Hartsgrove was built on seven hills—the backyard at eye level with her second-floor bedroom. We didn't venture there till late summer, when the days were getting shorter, the concealing nighttime longer. We'd heard the rumors a year or two before, from older guys, guys since graduated and gone, but we were younger then, our curfews earlier, it was the fifties, and we were timid; peeping was a serious offense in Hartsgrove, Pennsylvania—that and running stop signs were about all the cops had to live for. But now we were seniors, bulletproof, brave, bold and fast, our ears attuned to the slightest hint of a cruiser on Diamond Alley, a dozen escape routes mapped out in our minds.

On the good nights, her light would come on. And there she was. "Ladies and Gentlemen, it is now showtime," Wonderling would whisper. At the foot of her bed she unbuttoned her blouse, looking out at the darkness hiding any number of eager eyes, then she turned, blouse open. Steadying herself, hand on the dresser, she stepped from her shoes, loosened her belt. Then the snaps and crackles would begin, as we positioned ourselves in the pine needles for a better view, louder than dancing elephants. She stepped from her pants, shrugged from her blouse. White bra and panties. Heavenly curves and crevices. Her bra fell away, nipples staring us down like little red eyes. Her thumbs went to the sides of her panties.

The nights were rare and precious when the planets aligned to allow us the perfect sighting. She might have gone to bed too early, or too late, or it was raining, or we were spotted on Diamond Alley, or we heard a car, or we had too much homework, or we were simply giving it a rest. But when the planets finally did align, it was ecstasy, nearly unbearable.

"You're blocking my view!" Wonderling whispered hoarsely, shoving Nosker. But his inflated state amplified the whisper, and the ensuing chorus of shushes must have sounded to Carol as though her backyard had sprung a leak.

She came to the window holding a pillow over her tits, and yelled through the screen, "Why don't you guys grow up! Go get a girlfriend!"

We were gone. Down Diamond Alley in the dark, wind whistling past our ears, coming out on Pine beneath the streetlight, where we slowed, ambling down toward Valley Street. Suddenly we stopped. In the air we heard Rocky Nelson line a shot up the right field alley, scoring Groat all the way from first with the winning run—*How sweet it is!* cried Bob Prince, *How sweet it is!*—and we pumped our fists and yelled, falling to our knees on the sidewalk, nearly weeping.

■　■　■

Next time the curtains would be closed. They would inch open again over the next few nights, first a visible sliver, followed by a gradual widening. We wondered if Carol could guess we were there, and we tried to believe she was willing to play the game, willing to be seen as long as we didn't let her know we were seeing. That was what we wanted to believe. It never occurred to us that she might simply have felt she had the right to fresh air, that she might have believed that we had given up, or, better, that we had grown up now and respected her privacy, and were above crawling on our bellies in the dirt and darkness for a cheap glimpse of flesh.

She stood out from the other girls in our class. Other girls were pretty, sexy, smart and popular, but none of them packaged it quite the way she did. None of us had been her boyfriend, but we'd all been her confidante at one time or another, the one chosen to rub her back between classes, to sit with her at lunch, to dance with her at Les's, to have those privileged, personal conversations when her clear blue eyes would mesmerize you.

When we rubbed her back, she would put her arms on her desk, her head down as if she were going to sleep. "Higher," she would say. "Right there—between the shoulder blades." And she would moan. That moan. That skin. We would have to pretend our heavy breathing was caused by the physical exertion of rubbing. And we would have to cross our legs.

"Do you have a date for the record hop?" she would ask.

"I hadn't really thought about it," we said, panting.

She was concerned about our social life. She didn't want any of us left out, left behind. It was as though she wanted us all to experience life in the same, expansive, wonderful way that she was. She was always offering helpful advice: *Bobby, you should be more serious—everything's not always a joke, you know.* Or, *Jimmy, how come you never smile? You look so serious all the time.* Or, *Doug, why don't you comb your hair in a DA? You'd look really sharp with a DA.* Or, *Don't squeeze that, John. If you squeeze it, it'll leave a scar.*

"Why don't you ask Brenda?" Carol said. "She likes you."

"I don't know. I'll think about it." We wanted to play it cool. "You going with Bucky?" Bucky was her boyfriend. Her boyfriends were always three or four years older than us, always with cars and the coolest of reputations.

"Yeah. Wait'll you see his car." Bucky had a new, midnight blue GTO, leather seats, four on the floor, competition clutch. She told us all about it. Then she put her hand on ours, leaning close, adding conspiratorially, "But I don't like it—the backseat's too small."

A comment such as that could fuel our masturbatory fantasies for a month. She was mature, sexy without being slutty, no easy feat in 1960. Her silky blond hair and clear blue eyes seem almost suspect now, as if our memories have polished them to perfection, but her picture in our yearbook—which we dedicated to her—bears out the truth of it. She always seemed to wear the skimpiest briefs beneath her cheerleader's outfit, and Nosker in fact claimed that once she wore none at all, swears to this day he saw her beaver that fateful Friday night. We insisted he was full of shit, secretly allowing ourselves to entertain the possibility, masturbatory fuel for another month.

The teachers seemed to hold her apart as well. She challenged Mrs. Ishman, an elegant and earthy lady, over the amount of trigonometry she assigned. Mrs. Ishman, grim and determined, defended herself as she would to an adult—the rest of us would have ended up in detention. Carol debated Mr. Zufall, our social studies teacher: Why should we bother watching the presidential debate? Everyone knew Kennedy didn't have a snowball's chance in heck anyway, because then the Pope would be running the country, so it was all just a waste of time. Mr. Zufall laughed, shook his head. He let her get away with it. Mr. Zufall, in fact, almost seemed to encourage her.

He almost seemed to be in Carol's confidante rotation along with the rest of us. He was one of those teachers who try to be one of the guys, and he came close. We liked him. He had a habit of rocking up on his toes while he was teaching, which we often mimicked but secretly admired. He was graceful, athletic; he'd been a pretty good basketball player for Hartsgrove High, then got a medal in the war. He used to make fun of the non-athletic types behind their backs—the same as we did—mimicking their pigeon-toed strut across the front of his class-room. He told us dirty jokes and gossip, the only teacher who did. And every day he could talk to us about how the Pirates had fared the night before.

He pulled us aside before class. "I came in the back way this morn-ing," he said. "No sooner do I open the door than who do I see standing there, behind the back stairwell, but a good friend of ours, with her boyfriend—I won't mention any names, but you know her well. And her boyfriend is holding her breasts! One in each hand! Buoying them up!" Mr. Zufall was positively gleeful. He repeated the phrase—*Buoy-ing them up!*—holding out his hands, buoying a pair of imaginary tits. We shared his zeal, wondering exactly who he was talking about, when we noticed Carol Siebenrock across the room, watching us.

The last place we saw her was Les's, the evening she disappeared. Les's was overflowing with the usual after-school crew. Carol was sitting with some of the other cheerleaders, planning a bonfire and pep rally for Friday night. We had a big game Saturday against Cranberry.

"Hey," Carol yelled over to us. The music was too loud for talking. Everybody yelled. "Do you guys know where we can get any wood?"

"I know where you can get some," Wonderling said, snickering.

"I don't know," Nosker said, "I haven't been getting any either."

"Get your minds out of the gutter," Carol said.

"I'd like to lay the wood to her," Knapp whispered, and we grinned.

Plotner dropped a nickel, reaching down to get it so he could look up their skirts, smacking his head against the table on the way back up, good for another laugh. He swore Brenda Richards had jerked her legs apart while he was down there, displaying her crotch for his viewing pleasure. "Sure, sure," we said, refusing to allow the remotest possibil-ity it was true, believing it all the while, because it's what we wanted to believe. We were hooked on the implications of a free peek willingly given. The cheerleaders kept talking wood and fire, while we lapsed into our typical topics: Who was getting bare tit off whom, who was getting bare ass, who was finger-fucking whom, and who was actually getting laid. And, most importantly, with whom. The jukebox stopped playing, but no one stopped yelling. Allshouse chased Judy Lockett around the pinball machine, and Les Chitester, his long, white apron bloody with sauce, yelled from beside his pizza oven, "Hey! Take a cold shower!" Linda Pence was dancing, shaking her perfect ass in our general direction, and Nosker said, "Say this five times real fast: Tiny Tim tickled Tillie's tit till Tillie's twat twitched," and we were up to the challenge. Many times. And every time we looked at Carol Siebenrock, all we could see were her nipples.

Les brought out the cheerleaders' pizza, and Carol, taking her first bite, dropped sauce on her white blouse, close enough to her boob to prompt another outbreak of hilarity on our part. She tried to wipe it off with her napkin, but only smeared it around. She stood to leave, shoulders back, making no effort to conceal her sullied boob. "Grow up, you guys," she said.

We wanted to run after her. We wanted to leapfrog over the parking meters down Main Street, fly up the hill, get to her backyard before she got home, but we didn't. It was still light out, and we wondered why she was leaving so early, assuming it was the stain on her blouse, never guessing she might have had a date. It was a school night. So we stayed, laughing, leering, the occasional erection springing to life on our young, healthy bodies, and later we walked home listening to the Pirates' magic number dwindling down toward zero. The last thing Carol ever said to us was *grow up*. We remembered that later, smitten by the twist, sure that we were the only ones on the face of the earth ever to witness an irony so deep and true as that.

Carol's two older sisters, Dottie and Mary, were married and gone. She was the baby. Some years before, her mother had tried to commit suicide with her father's rifle—trying to pierce her ears, went the old, black joke. She'd managed to only graze her brain, leaving her more or less lobotomized. Mr. Siebenrock was a chubby, earnest fellow who owned a shoe store down on Main Street, and we all knew him pretty well—he'd been one of our Little League coaches, even though he'd apparently never held a bat in his own two hands before taking over the reins of Sterck's Terriers. He cheered enthusiastically—maybe the source of Carol's talent. As a coach, he made a pretty good shoe salesman.

He'd left Little League about the same time we had, when his wife had shot herself with his .22, which he'd kept in a closet and seldom touched. He was not a hunter, but for some reason thought he should own a gun. Everyone else did. Now, when he wasn't selling shoes he spent most of his time taking care of his wife, bringing her to church and school events, trying to maintain some semblance of a social life.

The night Carol disappeared he'd taken his wife to the Hartsgrove Businessmen's Association Banquet out at the Country Club. Home late, he'd assumed Carol was upstairs asleep. Next morning he discovered his mistake, along with her blood-stained blouse.

By the time we learned the blood was pizza sauce, a hundred different rumors had swept through town: Her bracelet had been found here, her shoe there, a stranger spotted here, Carol herself there. She'd run away with her boyfriend; she'd run away by herself. She'd been abducted from her bedroom; she'd been abducted walking up the hill from Les's. She'd gone kicking and scratching; she'd gone willingly with someone she knew. She'd been raped; she'd eloped; she was being held for ransom. The rumors were flimsy, yet they lived and died and were born again, endlessly, it seemed. In the end, she was simply missing.

Her empty desk filled every classroom. Every blond head we saw in the hallway brought an instant of expectation, which dissolved again just as quickly. Mr. Zufall seemed as stricken as any of us. *She'll be fine*, he told the class. *Leave her alone and she'll come home, wagging her tail behind her*. And he grinned a rueful grin.

Shuffling down Main Street one afternoon on our way to Les's, we saw Mr. Zufall coming out of Siebenrock's Shoes with his arms full. It looked as though he'd bought half a dozen pairs of shoes. Seeing us across the street, he only nodded a greeting, his arms too full to wave.

It struck us at the time as some sort of magnanimous, mature gesture, a show of support, the sort of thing we'd have been incapable of. We wouldn't have had the slightest idea of what to say to Mr. Siebenrock in a circumstance such as that.

Evenings at Les's were quiet, filled with the whisper of rumors. The pep rally and bonfire at Memorial Park were cancelled; we lost to the Cranberry Rovers the next afternoon, 45–6. The cheerleaders' efforts were half-hearted, as were the team's, although the outcome of the game wasn't all that far from the norm. No one was in the mood for a pep rally the next week either, but there was a large pile of lumber that had to be disposed of somehow, so the pep rally was rescheduled for the next Friday night, before the Harmony Mills game.

Like the crowd, the fire was large and nervous, shooting jittery red trails of sparks and shape-shifting plumes of smoke into the night over the black running waters of Potters Creek. The speakers—the captain of the cheerleaders, the football team captain, the school principal—all spoke about our team, our school, our town, our pride, about giving our best and winning. No one mentioned the big white elephant sitting just beyond the bonfire. It was a decidedly pepless rally.

All the while Carol stayed missing.

The rumors grew silly and cruel. She was living with beatniks in New York City. She was living with cousins in Oil City, having been knocked up. She'd run away to join the circus girlie show. She'd run off to become a Playboy Bunny. She'd had to leave town because someone had spotted her in a skin flick. All the silly, cruel rumors tried to imagine where she was. None of them imagined her dead.

All the while the Pirates kept winning.

Carol's disappearance, magnificent mystery that it was, never distracted us from the heat of the pennant race. There was plenty of room in our hearts and minds for both. When the Pirates finally clinched on a Sunday afternoon in late September, joy erupted and settled back over the town like a golden mist. It was the only topic of conversation at school Monday morning—*How sweet it is! How sweet it is!* We sang, *Oh, the Bucs are going all the way!* The first fifteen minutes of Mr. Zufall's class were devoted to nothing but Hoak, Groat, Mazeroski and Stuart, Clemente, Virdon, Skinner and the boys. By the end of class, however, it was business as usual; Mr. Zufall reminded us—warned us, really— that the Kennedy-Nixon debate was taking place that evening.

"Who watched the debate?" he asked next morning. "Raise your hands."

No one was foolish enough not to. Mr. Zufall rocked up on his toes, his approving smile turning wistful as he glanced at the empty desk. "I'm only sorry Carol wasn't here to see it," he said. "History in the making. I think even Carol would have appreciated that."

The collective sigh was audible, the moment of silence spontaneous. It was the first time anyone had spoken of her as though she weren't coming back.

They found her two weeks later. Evan Shields and his grandson, hunting squirrel in the woods along Potters Creek just north of town, spotted her body snagged on a log in the water. Her skull was fractured, and she'd probably been dead since the day she disappeared. That was about all the coroner could determine, given the state of her body.

It was assumed she'd been raped. She was naked from the waist down.

Every generation or so there's a murder in Hartsgrove above and beyond the usual run-of-the-mill, heat-of-the-moment killing, a murder with a certain cachet. About twenty-five years earlier, before we were born, a lady had been raped and stabbed to death in the railroad yard signal tower on the south side of town where she worked. Les Chitester, manning his pizza oven with his long-handled paddle, remembered it well, though he'd been only ten at the time; the town had been in a frenzy of fear till the killer had finally been caught. Years later, after we'd scattered and were slogging toward the end of our own middle ages, a pack of drunken, drugged-up kids stripped and hanged a girl in a clearing in the woods by Potters Creek. The young always think these flashy crimes are unique, that life has devised this outstanding drama just for them, and them alone. That's what we thought. Now we know better. Now we know it's just part of the cycle, just another run-of-the-mill murder that happens to have a certain cachet.

Girls cried in the classrooms. Boys shook their heads. There were hollow-eyed stares down the hallways of the school. *Gone but not forgotten*; Mr. Zufall must have uttered that hackneyed phrase a hundred times. Les's was even quieter. We hugged self-consciously, in solemn unawareness of what else we could possibly do. We talked about it, tried to exorcize it. We talked about Carol, every last little thing we'd ever done with her, every last little minute we'd ever spent with her, competing to have known her best, as if whoever had been closest to her would be closest to this new mortality, and therefore the most worthy among us.

Who had done it? Who could have done such a thing? Bucky Morrison, her boyfriend, naturally came to mind, but Bucky was away at college, and though his alibi wasn't airtight, he was reputed to be a gentle creature, who, Brenda Richards let it be known, kept a kitten in his dorm room against all regulations. Mark Schoffner, the boy Carol had dumped for Bucky? In the army now, at Fort Drum. There were the usual local toughs in Hartsgrove, the high school dropouts and misfits, but we inventoried and dismissed them one by one, group by group. The crime was a quantum leap from picking a fight on a street corner with a bellyful of beer, from stealing hubcaps or keying the car of an antagonist. It was beyond them, just as it was beyond any of us, beyond anyone, really, that we knew. It would have to be a stranger. No one we'd ever laid our eyes upon could possibly commit such an evil.

She was buried on a Wednesday, the same day as the sixth game of the World Series. We were conflicted to say the least, though we never dared suggest we'd have preferred spending the afternoon in front of a television, rooting for the Pirates to wrap it up; they led the Series three games to two. But the Buccos made it easy on us that day. Their resounding 12–0 loss dovetailed perfectly with the tragedy, reflecting ominously on the future. We were sure they'd lose tomorrow too. It was how the planets were aligned.

Mr. Siebenrock looked softer than we remembered, like a marshmallow that had been stepped on. He followed Carol's casket down the wide aisle of the Presbyterian Church, his jowls inflated, his comb-over glistening with sweat, his hand fidgeting in his pocket like a squirming mouse; we could hear the coins jingle in the sniffle-filled silence. His wife, her hand clutching his coat sleeve, her hair too black, her gaze unanchored, looked as though she were wandering through a fog. Carol's two older sisters, Dottie and Mary, not nearly as pretty as Carol, followed with their husbands. Our hearts ached at how sad they looked, and at the fact that we were missing the game, and as soon as the service was over we rushed out to Nosker's car and turned on the radio—the Pirates were trailing 6–0 after two and a half! Crushed, we joined the funeral procession to Chapel Cemetery a couple miles south of town, Bob Prince filling us in: Bob Friend, in whose right arm we'd trusted, had lasted only two innings. Clouds swelled with gloom over the cemetery at the top of the hill.

We did our best to say goodbye to Carol there. The view from the cemetery was wide, but the sweep of bright trees was dulled by the gray of the day. We were too far away to hear the words of the preacher, a skinny man with white hair and big ears. When it was over we drifted away. We weren't in a hurry to get back to the game; we knew a lost cause when we saw one. Over our shoulders we watched Carol's mother, her hand fluttering at the pile of dirt like a toddler just learning to wave bye-bye.

Next morning during homeroom, they interrupted the announcements over the PA system to call for a moment of silence for Carol. We felt it applied just as much to the Pirates. That afternoon they suspended classes, and we gathered in the auditorium to watch the seventh game of the Series on the televisions they'd set up on the stage. We were absorbed from the first flickering image of Forbes Field, immersed for the next four hours, emotions soaring and plummeting, as the lead went back and forth, ecstasy and anguish in the balance. The Pirates blew a four-run lead and trailed, 5–4, after seven. When the Yankees tacked on two more in the top of the eighth, Allshouse actually snuffled and blew his nose, and we were actually too upset to ridicule him for being such a baby. We were on the verge ourselves.

In the bottom of the eighth, a routine ground ball took a bad hop and hit the Yankee shortstop in the neck. We rejoiced, Tony Kubek's evident agony notwithstanding. This could be the break—pun intended—we needed; this might be the omen, the sign we'd been waiting for, and sure enough, when Hal Smith capped the five-run rally with a three-run homer, joy once again erupted, echoing through the cavernous old auditorium. With a two-run lead in the top of the ninth, and Bob Friend coming in to nail it down, it was all but over.

Incredibly, impossibly, the Yankees tied it up.

Blackness settled over the congregation. The wooden seats never felt harder. "I can't watch," Plotner said, and he was the stoic one among us. The big, bad Yankees were bearing down on us like an oncoming freight train. Nosker buried his head in his hands. And Carol Siebenrock revisited us, tragedy in all its guises, as we went to the bottom of the ninth.

Then, when Mazeroski homered, we were born again. We leapt in the aisles, teachers and students alike, hugging, cheering, delirious with bliss. Clover and Mrs. Ishman were dancing. Plotner and Nosker were dancing. Wonderling hugged Brenda Richards and Judy Lockett, every girl he could find, copping as many feels as he possibly could. Mr. Zufall, at the peak of his powers, lifted Allshouse over his head. And Carol was gone again.

Gone but not forgotten. Less than a week later we paid our final respects. It was a spontaneous tribute, unpremeditated. Leaving Les's, we crossed the crumbling bridge over Potters Creek, heading up toward Main Street in the dwindling twilight. At the Court House, we turned up Pershing, still paved with bricks as all of Hartsgrove's streets had been at one time, onto Coal Alley, and up the concrete steps that

climbed the hill through the trees. The steps were tilted, old and uneven. By the time we reached the top, we were winded, our thighs aching.

The mansards and gables high on the school were nearly invisible
in the dark. The streetlights couldn't throw much light up through the
trees, only a glint off a window here and there. We cut through the
school yard. Mary Lou Allgier lived on Maple, just beyond the baseball
field. We checked out her windows: The lights were on, but the shades
were down, and we couldn't see a thing. Halfway up Pine, we cut across
to Diamond Alley. The best place to pay our last respects was not in the
graveyard, but in the backyard.

Solemnly we filed in, taking our places among the pines. From the
shadows we stared at her darkened window, remembering. Everything
was black. We spoke in whispers. "Remember how she used to piss off
Mrs. Ishman?" we said. We thought, *Bobby, don't try so hard—if you pretend you're not interested, you'll have her eating out of the palm of your hand.*
"How about the way she argued with Zufall?" *Jimmy, your teeth aren't
that bad—is that why you never smile? You have a nice smile.* "Remember
the time she called Mrs. Stockdale a bitch? Man, she had balls." We
stared at her window as though the light might come on at any moment, as though she might appear. *Doug, you have to work harder on your
grades. You have to get into college. Do you need any help studying?* "Remember the time she was cheering without any tights on?" *You should
learn how to dance, John. It's easy. Want me to teach you?* "What a body."
The shadows sighed. "What a shame."

*You have such beautiful hair, Jimmy. You're going to get taller. By next
year at this time, the girls are going to be chasing you like a hawk.* Her clear
blue eyes were still gazing into ours, holding us hostage, verifying the
truth of every word she said. Her beautiful face was still resting on her
hands as we rubbed her back, the warm, soft, living heat of her.

The whispering desisted. The moment of silence was long and true.
The air was empty, except for the scent of burning leaves, the sound of
crickets. No Bob Prince. It was over. We began to stir, our tribute paid,
our obligation fulfilled, feeling a little ennobled, a little restless.

The light came on. Carol's mother appeared in her window, looking around the room as if she'd never seen it before. "Ladies and Gentlemen, it is now showtime," Wonderling whispered, and at that moment we hated him. Carol's mother came toward the window and we crabbed back farther into the shadows. Absently she raised a hand to her ear, looking around again with a frown, then to her other ear, taking off her earrings. She placed them on the dresser, straightened the tilted mirror, then began to unbutton her blouse. The look on her face was as though she were trying to recognize a song, a song that no one else could hear. We watched, uncomfortable with the hollow thumping in our chests. A pinecone dropped with a soft plump that jolted through us like a shot. We watched Carol's mother step out of her slacks.

We watched. Not watching was no more of an option than speaking. We watched until she was naked, until every inch of her aging flesh had been revealed in all its faded splendor, and she stood bewildered looking around the room again, perhaps for her nightgown, perhaps for nothing at all. Carol's father came in, a look of relief on his face, and we watched him gather up his wife's clothes, put his arm around her shoulder, and guide her toward the doorway. There he paused, looking around the room again. Spotting something, he came back, crossing our field of vision; when he returned he was carrying a doll that appeared to be quite old, a well-worn, well-loved doll with yellow hair. Putting his arm around his wife again, he led her out of the room. We watched him reach back and flick off the light with a nervous glance toward the window.

We watched the dark of the house again, in silence, until our erections and galloping blood, our shame, had finally subsided enough to allow us the freedom to leave.

They arrested Blinky Mumford a month later, but it wasn't the closure we needed. It was anticlimactic. We never suspected him; furthermore, we never really believed he did it. One of the school janitors, Blinky Mumford was sullen and ill-tempered, with a facial tic that animated his scowl. He had no family and was often seen walking up and down

Main Street muttering to himself. The story was that he'd been left in Hartsgrove when he was six by one of the orphan trains that used to stop on the south side in the early years of the century, but no one had taken him in. Like the other candidates we'd inventoried and dismissed, a crime like this was beyond him—too important, too notable. Despite his conviction, we were never convinced. They found what they said were strands of her hair in his battered old wreck of a Ford, and the key piece of evidence was a pair of panties found hidden in the janitors' closet near Blinky's buckets, brooms, and mops. Her father identified them as Carol's.

We wondered how he could possibly have been so sure, so Bruner came up with a theory: Skid marks are like fingerprints, he hypothesized, no two exactly alike.

Not much is left now. The old high school on the hill came tumbling down, and a whole generation of kids has graduated from the new school out by the new interstate, neither of which is new anymore. Les Chitester built a new place too, the Colonial Eagle Interchange Hotel Restaurant, not far from the new school, and our old hangout by Potters Creek was razed, a hardware store built in its place. For over thirty-five years, its motto has been *Buy By The Bridge*. Even Memorial Park was buried, all the towering elms and oaks along the banks of the creeks cut down and burned, victims of Hartsgrove's flood control project.

We scattered. The teachers are gone too, retired and died, most of them. A few years after we left, Zufall quit teaching to become a carpenter. That didn't surprise us; we figured he must have wanted a manlier profession, something more in line with his athletic sensibilities.

And Blinky Mumford? He faded away in his cell, a self-proclaimed innocent man.

We still gather in Hartsgrove now and then for reunions and funerals. Tomorrow we're burying Nosker's mother. We'll be next in line. Unlike Carol, we're waiting our turn. Thanks to Carol, we know how to die.

We talk about the Pirates. They won two more titles in the seventies but haven't come close since; it's beginning to look as though they never will. We complain about the state of baseball, the small-market quandary, convinced the sport will never be the same. We don't complain about our own aging bodies, however, which will never be the same again either. We don't ogle and leer at the pretty girls like we used to, because we're mature now—unlike Carol, we got to grow up. At least that's what we tell ourselves. The truth is, ogling and leering would only be mocking our own aging bodies. The truth is, we miss it, everything about it; we miss our young, healthy selves, the dependable, eveready erections of our youths.

Sooner or later, as if to atone, we set aside the Pirates, put to rest the small talk, and Carol Siebenrock arises from the grave. We speak of her reverently, honoring her. We never speak of our adolescent indiscretions, the nights we spent on our bellies in the black shadows of her yard, the primordial thrill we felt at the sight of her lush, naked flesh.

But in our minds she is naked. In our minds she will always be naked.

She is naked even as she sits in a classroom a lifetime ago, raising her hand, sunlight streaming through the window, touching her with grace and radiance. Where is our place in this picture? Where is our place in this world? We maintain our innocence. We blow away any trace of guilt, like blowing dust off the top of a locked box, but the dust swirls and swirls in the sunlight, swirls and swirls, refusing to disperse and disappear. And so we talk about the Pirates. We talk about Carol as if we never loved her. And always it ends up the same. "Who do you suppose really killed her?" we always say, never looking ourselves in the eye.

PART TWO

Radaker's Angel

When he swung the hammer too hard and missed, nearly falling from the tree, Radaker's first reaction was to look around. Had anybody seen him? He was, after all, a professional; hammering was what he did. Now here he was, hammering like a damned accountant. Of course there was nobody there, not in his own backyard—certainly not his own family. Climbing down from the remains of the tree house, he trudged back up to the house to call Gwenda again. In the ten years she'd worked for him, he'd never called her twice after work, but things were different now. The miss had filled him with doubt.

"Gwenda?"

"Earl?"

"You think fifteen's too old for a tree house?"

"Hell, I don't think fifty's too old for a tree house."

"Watch your mouth, Little Folks."

"Heck, I don't think fifty's too old for a tree house."

"Me neither," Radaker said. "She never once set foot in the thing after Christmas morning." Tammy, his stepdaughter, had seemed unimpressed when he'd given her the tour, leaving him baffled. Why? Real glass windows, mitered molding, shingled roof, working trapdoor, all the trimmings . . . Rita, his wife, had said from the beginning Tammy was too old.

"Different strokes," Gwenda said.

"I'm tearing it down."

"Don't do that, I'll move in." His response stalled as the joke registered. "Did you call up Rita yet?" she said.

"I ain't calling her up. She can call me up."

"That oughta work," said Gwenda.

Radaker had to hammer. Too long without hammering and his mind compensated, flashing images of his hammer smashing a long nail into a plump plank, the muscles in his forearm twitching along. It could happen anytime, watching television, reading the sports page, at dinner. It happened especially when bad weather marooned him in his office, a converted fast food joint a mile outside of town.

Today he hadn't hammered. Steady rain had washed him and his crew off the roof they were putting on Mrs. Stockdale's place, and he'd spent an entirely unsatisfactory day at his desk shuffling papers, figuring bids, trying to comprehend the vagaries of profit and loss. But all he could think of was hot fudge sundaes. He'd stood at the wide front window much of the afternoon, chewing on his pencil, staring across Route 302 at the rain pelting the parking lot of the Tastee Freeze. He hadn't had a hot fudge sundae in years. The phantom hammer struck again and again, he was restless and depressed, and the last thing he needed to come home to was another vanishing.

His life was filled with vanishings: a key here, a boot there, a family now and again. When he was two, nearly half a century before, his parents had disappeared. Then, today when he'd come home from work, his wife and stepdaughter were gone too. That was when he'd phoned Gwenda the first time.

"Did Rita call today? Nobody's at home."

"No, Earl, I never heard anything. No note?"

"Nope. Nothing. I searched the whole place high and dry."

"Did you look on the refrigerator door?"

"First place I looked." He paused, staring at the proof, the cold bottle of Rolling Rock beer in his hand. "Hold on a minute." Returning to the phone, he said, "Says they're gone. Up to her mother's."

"Gone? For supper? For good? What? What do you mean *gone*?"

In the hallway mirror his face stared dumbly back, the weathered features suddenly cracking at the edges, a troubled knot just below the varnished wave of hair that had crowned his forehead since first grade. Taking his beer, he stepped over Luther, his old sleeping dog, out to the back porch swing, watching the storm clouds slip away, counting the creaks of the rusty chains. The phantom hammer commenced in earnest. The sun peeped low through the clouds, glittering off his little round pond. He counted a hundred squeaks.

Trying to think was like trying to swim through Jell-O. He felt an odd sense of mortality, as though his life were unjustly bleeding out of him. There had to be a connection between this abandonment and the one that happened when he was two, but for the life of him, he couldn't figure it out. Two was before living memory; he'd been innocent then, by definition. Now, guilt was implied; it was an accusation. *Bored?* Who did she think she was marrying—Errol Fairbanks?

With sudden purpose he tromped back inside. She'd better not have taken his good meat thermometer! He rattled through the drawer till he found it. His favorite twelve-inch iron skillet? Still hanging on the beam by the cupboard. Taking another beer, he stared at the gray, symmetrical pattern of the linoleum. Upstairs, he went into Tammy's room, like entering the Forbidden City. Not knowing what he was looking for, he didn't find it. Then, through the window, he spied the tree house he'd built her for Christmas.

Radaker hammered into the dark, alternating blows for Rita, for Tammy, for his mother, for his father. The hammering never ended till Mrs. Shingledecker next door called out, *Earl! Could you please leave a body rest in peace?*

It was a mystery to him, why Rita would leave. Of course, much of life was a mystery to Radaker, which was why he lived it as gingerly as possible, like a man walking in the dark, hands out before him, fearful of stubbing his toe. The phantom hammering persisted even after a fitful sleep had finally overtaken him.

■　■　■

Next morning turned up brilliant and blue, a good omen he never noticed. Up early as usual, he was out of the bathroom by six thirty, unnecessarily, since no one was waiting for it this morning. He whistled "I've Been Working on the Railroad" making his toast and coffee in the quiet of the kitchen. He'd never whistled.

Hammering away on Mrs. Stockdale's roof, he was surprised when she came out and yelled up that Gwenda had called wanting to meet him for lunch. They often met to discuss business over a burger when he hadn't been in the office for a while, but he'd spent the whole day there yesterday.

The Golden Steer was one of Hartsgrove's finer restaurants, built of stones and old barn beams, smelling of leather from the antique horse and buggy trappings that provided the decor. It took him a moment to spot Gwenda sitting alone where the sun between the heavy red curtains threw a slice of light across the table. It took him even longer to realize that his ex-partner Fuzzy Huffman was there too, at the bar with three of his friends. Huffman nodded, unenthusiastically. Radaker returned the nod in kind.

Sitting beside Gwenda, he heard Huffman and company laugh. "You hear that?"

Gwenda said, "What?"

"Them laughing."

"Yeah?"

"You didn't let the cat out of the beans, did you?"

"About what?"

"About Rita leaving."

"You didn't see that ad I put in the paper?"

He thought about it for a moment. "Paper don't come out till Thursday."

Osborn waddled from behind the bar, his meaty hands dwarfing pencil and pad. Ordering the half-pound Steerburger, fries and Coke, Gwenda pulled the clear frames of her glasses back tightly to each ear, her fingers brushing the short hair away. Then she pressed the glasses firmly onto the bridge of her nose with her middle finger, no rude gesture intended, or so he'd always assumed. Her cheeks were round and full—like a chipmunk's, he'd noted, but politely never mentioned. He ordered iced tea.

"That's all?" Gwenda said.

"Brought my lunch." He lifted a brown paper bag. "Didn't know we were meeting."

"What is it?"

"Peanut butter and mayonnaise."

"Let me see it." She took the bag, rifling a perfect spiral to Osborn. "Dump that, John. Make it two burgers and fries."

"Shit," Radaker said.

"How come it's okay for you to swear, but not me?"

"Well, I didn't mean to swear."

"That's what I love about you, Boss. You never mean to do half the things you do."

He shook his head, the varnished wave of hair unruffled. "I swear, Little Folks."

"But you don't mean to."

Radaker sighed and blinked. "What'd you want to talk about? That tax audit?"

"Hell, we talked about that yesterday. Heck, we talked about that yesterday. I just wanted a date, now you're single again."

He allowed a little smile. "Guess I am, sorta."

"I just can't believe it was right out of the clear blue sky like that. No clue, no warning?"

"No, nothing." He drummed his fingers on the checkered table-cloth. "She did say something about the magic being gone, something like that."

"When?"

"Oh, I don't know. Any number of times."

"You could call that a clue."

"I didn't know there was any magic to start with."

"I think I sense the problem here. So what are you going do? Call her up?"

"I ain't calling her up."

"Sunday's Father's Day. You're not going to do anything?"

"Probably drive out to see Shorty." His Uncle Shorty and Aunt Carrie had raised him.

"What about Tammy?"

"She knows where I'm at. Course, I ain't her real father."

Gwenda studied his face, his lips holding back a smile. "You *don't* want to talk to her."

"Well," Radaker said, "maybe I will just live and let sleeping dogs live a while."

What had Rita left him? His house and the old sleeping dog. All this glorious silence. No racket of TV, stereo, chatter. He could hear the house groan in the stillness, settling its old bones as if recuperating after a workout. He could sit on the porch and hear birds, children playing in the yards, the growl of a big truck climbing West Main, the bell tolling the hour from the Court House down below. If he sat still and didn't squeak the swing, he could hear the voice of the announcer drifting up from the ball fields at the bottom of the town where the creeks converged. Bits and snatches only in the fickle air, like a voice from another time or place. *Now batting for Hartsgrove* . . .

He should miss Rita—shouldn't he? But he found he liked the bed sheet tucked in tightly instead of rumpled out in a tangle by the time he got there, and he liked going to bed as late as he pleased, without having to tiptoe in. He liked not having pizza twice a week. He liked looking over the *Pittsburgh Press* without the noise of the *Wheel of Fortune*. He didn't mind cooking; he'd always done most of it anyhow. Now he could enjoy his liver and onions with impunity.

He tried to rehearse exactly what he would say when he bumped into her at the supermarket, or the post office, or pumping gas at Carberry's. Over and over he tried to write the script in his head, but he never got past *How's everything up at your Mum's?* There were too many possible replies. He couldn't keep track of all the possible responses he might make to all the possible replies, let alone to the next generation of possibilities. But he never bumped into her. Driving by Bartley's Furniture on Main Street where she worked, he never caught a glimpse of her, though he always looked. She never called. He never answered.

He hammered July away. Once a week or so he lunched with Gwenda, as the weather seldom forced him into the office. One day they met at the dam. Next to the waterworks on Potters Creek, the CCC in the thirties had built a recreation facility for the town, a large swimming area, bathhouses and picnic tables near the tall, cool pines.

"You want the roast beef or the tuna?" Gwenda said. She wore a blue dress, the uncharted skin of her bare, sun-soaked shoulders foreign to him, as were her sunglasses. He relied on the bill of his R&H Builders cap to shade his eyes. The sun released in her dark hair a red highlight he'd never noticed before.

"Whichever one you don't want," he said.

"I wear dresses all the time."

"I didn't say nothing."

"You're looking at me like I'm all dressed up for Halloween."

"No I ain't. You look just fine."

"Thanks. Jeees."

"*Little* Folks."

"I said *cheese*. Not Jesus." She handed him the tuna. "How's Uncle Shorty?"

"About the same." Shorty was up at the Memorial Home, failing. As often as he could, Radaker found excuses not to visit; the old man seldom said two words. Radaker often wondered if Shorty had been as taciturn the first half of his life, or if resentment at the unwanted burden of Earl had shut him up. Radaker's daddy, a gangly young man from the hills beyond Dagus Mines, had headed south seeking work when Radaker was not quite two. Then his mother, Uncle Shorty's little sister, had run off to find him. Neither was ever heard from again. That was Shorty's story, and he was sticking to it.

Gwenda poked straws in their Cokes, hitching up her glasses, ready to go. She was worried about meeting payroll. They'd lost the bid for the Borough Garage addition to Fuzzy Huffman, which irked the hell out of Radaker. He listened, giving his best attention, distracted by the sheen of the sun on the water, by the sunbathing mothers and sitters watching over the splashing toddlers. The talk twisted back to Rita. She'd been to the house a few times to pick things up, he told Gwenda, but never when he was around.

"Have you thought about what you're going to do?" she said.

"About what?"

"About your marital situation. You got a company, remember?"

"I don't know who owns what anymore."

"Well, if you're not careful, she's gonna wind up owning it."

Radaker hoisted a thoughtful brow. "I doubt it."

"Did you have some kind of arrangement?"

"We didn't have one of them prenatal agreements, if that's what you mean."

Gwenda stared. "Have you thought about a formal separation? Or divorce? Or getting back together?"

Her sunglasses were impregnable, hurling back only his own twin images; her face was blank, full cheeks red in the sun.

"I ain't thinking about nothing," he said.

"I think I sense the problem here." A small bee darted toward the tuna, and Gwenda shrieked. Radaker struck it dead with a resounding slap. How a woman who was fearless in the face of a tax auditor could be afraid of bees was beyond him. He shook his head.

"I can't help it," she said. "My cousin Alice was stung by a bee one time."

"Is she allergic to 'em or something?"

"Not that I know of," Rita said. "Why?"

Radaker shook his head again, examining his hand.

"Splinter?" she said.

"Yeah."

"Lemme see." He held out his hand, which she studied like a far horizon. "Want me to go get some tweezers?"

"I'll dig it out with a needle after work."

"Tough guy," she said, crumpling up the papers. "I gotta get back." A few steps away, she stopped and turned, blue dress swirling reluctantly. "Earl? When are you stopping up? I smelled that skunk again." She'd bought a house in the spring and feared a skunk was living under the porch.

"I'll bring you up a trap."

He watched her dingy Chrysler pull away, still wondering at the image she left behind: the graceful pirouette, the glistening of her skin, the lilt of the blue dress in the blaze of the day. Who was this pretty girl? It couldn't be Gwenda Sowers, plain and steady, his girl Friday all these years.

He watched a young mother drying a toddler, squatting at the edge of the water in a bikini. Hiding beneath the bill of his R&H Builders cap, he soaked it up. The bikini wasn't much more than a pair of panties, a scant pair at that. The heat was getting to him. He hadn't thought about sex; he wasn't used to having to think about it. Rita had always done it for him.

With a blink he realized that right over there, in the backseat of his old green Mercury, parked among the pines, was the first place they'd ever made love. That was the night, with the moon dodging the clouds over the creek, that he'd fallen for her. Fourteen years ago. It was the first time he'd had sex with anyone livelier than a ladder, with someone who talked and loved and laughed, all at the same time.

They'd come here often those first summers. Sometimes in winter. Sometimes they couldn't make it the whole two miles out the dirt road to the dam. God, they were young. It suddenly dawned on him: This must have been the magic that Rita meant. What had happened? A trickle of sweat inched down his spine. The novelty had worn off. It had gotten old; *they* had gotten old. He considered the evolution from sexy and reckless to steady and stable a normal part of maturing, a ripening consistent with Tammy becoming a teenager, with a job more demanding, with *aging*. Magic wasn't built to last forever.

But Rita was ten years younger than him. The trickle of sweat began to flow freely. She was still attractive, breasts still big and comfortable, though the rest of her had begun to join them a bit. Still sexy. God how she loved it. It had been, what, over six weeks now.

Over six weeks? Rita had *never* gone more than two. Never.

What had Rita taken? What he missed was watching her eat a meal he'd made, the way she sighed and savored, her eyes wide and rolling. She would moan sexually, floating away; and Radaker would enjoy his helping all the more, flavored by the pride he took in casting his spell.

He smelled the bacon even before he reached Gwenda's door. "Don't cook it."

Gwenda turned from the stove. "You said bacon."

"Raw. Gotta be raw. Skunks can't resist raw bacon."

"Now you tell me. Want a BLT?"

"Already ate." Gwenda in shorts and Gwenda at the stove were both sights new to him. "You look real domesticated."

"Thank you," she said. "So are my skunks."

There was a crawl space under the porch. Her house was an old fixer-upper on Longview Hill, where Maxwell Alley dropped precipitously down the wooded hillside behind her house to East Main. The old detached garage, weathered boards warping, had a basketball hoop above the door. Radaker figured that was the only reason she'd bought the place.

After he'd set the Havahart Trap, she made him shoot baskets with her. He lost a game of HORSE in seven turns. "You could shoot better with sneakers on," she said.

"My boots are fine. You don't shoot baskets with your feet."

Afterwards, they sat on the porch, Radaker sweaty. She brought him a beer, a Rolling Rock, sweaty too. "Anything new on the home front?"

"Nope. Well, I did call her up."

"Oh yeah? Been what, two months?"

"Near three." The day before, he'd braced himself, held his breath and touched the first six digits of Rita's mother's number nine times before finally completing it—with an assist from the phantom hammer.

She'd sounded surprised to hear from him. Said she still needed time. Still adjusting, still needed room to breathe, still thinking things over, still going through changes. "Blah, blah, blah," said Radaker. "Said she's still trying to find herself."

"All she's gotta do is look down," Gwenda said. "I don't see how she could miss something that size."

He stared at the sweaty bottle in his hands. "Couple nights ago I dreamt I was talking to her on the phone, and I looked down and I wasn't wearing nothing but an apron."

"Cool." Gwenda smiled. "So what were you wearing when you called her up?"

He furrowed his brow. "What I got on now. That was just a dream, Little Folks."

"I keep having this dream where I'm going in for a layup but I can't get off the ground. It's like my legs weigh a ton."

"I keep dreaming about this angel."

"Oh yeah? What kind? Like a guardian angel?"

"Beats me. Her face looks familiar, but all glowing like. Lit up."

"Does she have wings?"

He stopped to think. "I don't know. I don't think so."

"Maybe it's not a dream. Maybe you're just remembering something from when you were little."

"Like one of them repossessed memories?"

"Yeah. Something like that."

He took in her brown eyes, the gravity, the earnestness of her theory. A sudden gratitude filled him, for her competence, her loyalty. Where would he be without her? Where would his business be? Though her habit of showing up pretty much whenever she pleased still irked the hell out of him.

"So how come you ain't got a boyfriend?" he said.

"What makes you think I don't have a boyfriend?"

"Do you have a boyfriend?"

Gwenda shrugged. "I guess I'm just not too good at it. I liked Bobby Dickey so much I just about peed my pants every time I saw him."

"I can see where that could wind up being a problem."

They heard a rattle and shuffle from under the porch. "Oh shit," Gwenda said.

"Watch your mouth." He tiptoed down the steps in his work boots. "Okay, Little Folks, this is it."

They squatted by the edge of the porch, where the battered lattice had gone from white to gray years ago. Gwenda knelt behind him in the weeds, peering over his shoulder, the August sun drenching their backs. Just beyond the glare, in the darkness under the porch, two eyes shone out from the cage.

"Easy does it," he said. "Easy does it."

"What are you doing? What if he sprays?"

He turned to her, his hands holding an imaginary beach ball before him. "The trick is not to startle 'em, no fast moves. Slow and easy—why don't you wait back up there on the porch?"

Slow and easy, he retrieved the cage. The skunk glared with frightened, angry eyes, tail twitching threateningly. "There," he cooed, "there, there."

"What are you going to do with him?"

"I'm going to take him over—real slow like—and plunk him in my little pond. Then I'll come back up and set the trap again. There's probably a whole family of 'em up in under there."

"You're going to what?"

"Plunk him in my pond."

"You catch him in a *have-a-heart* trap and drown him? You don't see the irony in that?"

"I ain't really looking for any."

"You can't drown him. Take him out somewhere and turn him loose."

"You can't turn him loose. He'll spray you the second he's clear of the trap."

"Not if you do it *slow and easy*."

Radaker crept slow and easy to his pickup. Placing the cage in the back, he covered it with the tarp and eased into the front seat, ignoring

Gwenda glaring from the porch. He drove home, slow and easy. Half-way across his backyard he heard her pull in behind his truck. He heard her yell, "I want my goddam skunk back!" and turned to see her running toward him, neither slow nor easy.

Gwenda supplied the tomato juice. Radaker felt foolish. He imagined what Rita would say, seeing him sitting in a tubful of tomato juice, scrubbing it into every square inch of himself. He imagined how she'd throw back her head and laugh, how her wild blue eyes would flash. Then he imagined how she'd insist on climbing in, the unholy mess, tomato juice all over everything, floor, towels, bedclothes, and he was almost glad she wasn't there to see it.

Almost.

Hartsgrove's hills burned with color on the sunny September afternoon of the Autumn Leaf Parade. Radaker spotted the big nose of his buddy Buster Clover in the crowd in front of Lindemuth's Olde Coin and Gun Shoppe. They jeered another old pal, Jim Wilson, President of the Borough Council, who was riding by in a classic car. The Hartsgrove Area High School Band was next, followed by VFW Post 511 shambling by in vague formation, a squad of beer bellies. The Harmony Mills Volunteer Fire Department Pumper Engine Number Four had just passed by when Radaker saw them: Across the street, near the reviewing stand, stood Fuzzy Huffman; beside him was Rita.

Clover laughed, pointing at Harry Nosker, the VFW Post Commander, nearly stepping in a pile of manure deposited minutes earlier by a prancing member of the Elk Forest Dude Ranch contingent.

They were just talking, Radaker told himself, though he could feel the veins in his forehead ballooning. Didn't mean a thing. Couldn't read anything into that. Just small talk. Then Rita's blue eyes flashed, filling her face as her head went back in a laugh. There was nothing small about that talk. It was how she used to talk with him.

Fuzzy and Rita began to walk, vanishing behind the reviewing stand, reappearing. From beneath the bill of his R&H Builders cap,

Radaker watched intently for signs of contact between them, any touch. He began strolling parallel.

Clover said, "Where we headed?"

Through the crowd at the corner of Pershing, dodging spectators, Radaker saw them wave goodbye, Rita getting into her mother's car as Fuzzy kept walking. He felt relieved, then sheepish in rapid succession, glancing at Clover's poker face.

"You look like a man who could use a beer," Radaker said.

"So do I," said Clover. They stood before Jum's Bar and Grill, an old hangout from a decade ago. When he went out—not as often as when he was younger—Radaker tended now toward the Golden Steer or the Green Lantern, places a little less . . . casual. He wouldn't call Jum's a dive, exactly. Nor would he call himself a snob, exactly; it was just that he wasn't likely to see any potential customers in Jum's. At least that's what he told himself.

But today a cold beer in a friendly haunt with an old drinking buddy was just the tonic. He was still abashed at overreacting to his wife and his ex-partner in casual conversation. After all they'd known each other for years. They'd socialized together, the four of them (with Fuzzy's then-wife), then the three of them.

Jum's was a cloud of smoke, jammed with Autumn Leaf revelers. From the middle of the din came the drunken bellow of Smokey Bowersox: "Hey Radaker! I hear Fuzzy Huffman's porking your old lady!"

Luther slept through it all. In his younger days Radaker had always been the last to quit a night on the town. *I gotta get some sleep*, Clover would complain. Radaker would chalk up his cue. *You'll get all the sleep you need when you're dead.*

Radaker with his Rolling Rock sat on the porch swing, watching the paws of the old dog twitch, watching dead leaves bury his yard in the twilight. It was quiet; the birds were sleeping, the kids indoors, the Autumn Leaf revelers sealed away in soundless taverns. The phantom hammer flexed his forearm. Autumn had left the skeleton of the tree house nearly naked, a stark monument to his folly.

What had Rita taken?

The rumor wasn't necessarily true; Smokey Bowersox was an ignorant drunk. Clover had assured him he'd heard nothing, and Clover, who worked for the paper, was accustomed to harvesting rumors. But Radaker's where-there's-smoke anxieties couldn't be doused by Clover's haven't-heard-a-thing assurances.

He decided the truth of it didn't much matter. What mattered was this silence that was eating him up. Back inside, he called Rita.

"Earl?"

"I was just thinking. Why don't you come on up tomorrow for one of my famous seafood suppers? I got the urge to cook."

"Well. Let me see—"

"And we can talk."

He waited. And waited. Did he hear whispering? "Well tomorrow's no good, Earl. How about October the tenth?"

Two weeks? "Sure."

"Okay," Rita said. "What time?"

"About sex?"

"Sure. See you then."

He spent all afternoon in the kitchen, glancing into the living room at the TV only when a roar from the Steelers game occasioned it. He hadn't made his famous seafood supper in over a year. He didn't worry about making too much; Rita loved good food, and lots of it: shrimp cocktail, oyster stew, baked lobster stuffed with crabmeat, baked potatoes, coleslaw, and garlic bread.

He sipped Rolling Rocks as he cooked, whistling "She'll Be Coming 'Round the Mountain." He'd become a whistler. Normally he didn't drink before quitting time, but he was nervous. In his cooking he was confident, in his conversation, less so. What do you say to a woman who's left you? To a woman to whom you don't want to say the wrong thing? When you don't know what the right thing is?

The shrimp were chilling, the ice had been cracked, and the dishes were lined with lettuce. The stew was simmering, aromas tantalizing, the crabmeat stuffing concocted, the lobsters dazed and ready to go. The bread was slathered with butter and garlic, the coleslaw marinating, the potatoes scrubbed and baking. The phone was ringing.

Rita couldn't make it. She'd have to take a raincheck. She didn't say why. Dazed, he didn't ask. He knew she knew he'd slaved over a hot stove all day. He wouldn't give her the satisfaction of asking. He was angry.

The anger was deflated as quickly as the click of the phone by the feast of the silence that followed. The Steelers had lost, the house lay hushed in mourning, the only sounds the abject bubbling of the stew and the pitying tick of the oven. He pondered rash action, destroying the dinner in a fit of rage, before dismissing it as too extravagant.

He pondered eating alone. Too extravagant too. A truck roaring down West Main sliced through the silence, which swallowed it up again.

He called Gwenda. "Listen, I was just cooking up one of my famous seafood suppers and I got all this food up here—got way too much. Why don't you come on up?"

"Tonight? Now?"

"Well, I know it's short notice."

"I don't know, Earl. I was over at my sister's this afternoon playing football, and those kids about wore me out . . . "

"I got shrimp cocktail, oyster stew, lobster . . . "

"The horse can't make it?" Gwenda said.

"What?"

"I said of course I can make it."

"Well, great."

"Got any wine?"

"Nope. I ain't much of a consommé."

"I'll bring some up," Gwenda said. "You gotta have wine with a meal like that."

Next morning Radaker arrived at the office two hours late, wearing the shirt Rita had given him for Christmas last year; on the back was a portrait of a twelve-point buck in the woods, looking timidly over his shoulder. He knew Gwenda disliked the shirt.

Nevertheless, she gave him a smile. "How come you're not up at the site?"

"My head's hammering," he said.

"Guess you never had champagne before."

"That stuff sure packs a wallop."

"You probably shouldn't have switched to gin."

"I switched to gin? Holy moly. I don't even remember that."

"You don't?"

"Nope. Matter of fact, I don't remember much of anything. You make it home okay?" This wasn't exactly true. There were gaps and lapses, but he remembered what had happened; of course he might have dreamed it. He hoped he had. But he thought if he pretended he didn't remember it, they could pretend together it had never happened.

Looking down miserably at the floor, he noticed the toilet paper stuck to his heel. Gwenda hitched up her glasses. "You don't remember anything?"

"Nope," he said. "I have complete anesthesia."

He got through November like a dull saw through an oak plank. Gwenda grew grouchier every day. Uncle Shorty, failing fast, was uttering fewer and fewer syllables. And Rita kept her distance except in his tortured imagination. She never called to cash in her raincheck; he responded in kind. He had his pride. He spent long evenings with his pride, missing pizza, *Wheel of Fortune*, rumpled bedclothes; missing the abundance of Rita, her wild blue eyes and quick laugh. He avoided the bars in town, the gossip. His own imaginings were cruel enough.

Gwenda quit inquiring, becoming as distant as Rita. Her hours became more erratic. Gone were the bright dresses of summer, so strange and new, replaced by her familiar floppy shirts and baggy pants. In the office one bleak morning it took him several minutes to identify what else was missing: the smell of coffee. None in his mug that she used to fetch steaming, none on the hot plate at all. Gwenda was having tea, he was gruffly told. He discovered an hour later, in a manner most inconvenient, that she'd also quit stocking the restroom with toilet paper. He avoided the office even more than before, clinging to the sites like a shipwrecked man.

The day before Thanksgiving he brought in his customary batch of turkeys for the crew, sneaking out quickly without risking Gwenda. Bob, his foreman, called him at the site before noon; Gwenda was gone. Radaker hurried back to the office.

"Where'd she go?"

"How the hell should I know?" said Bob, his three hundred pounds dwarfing her desk, exasperation red on his face. "Some female thing I expect, the way she stomped outta here."

"What female thing?"

"How the hell should I know? Look, Earl, I got the union on one line, some guy about health insurance on the other—"

"When's she coming back?"

"How the hell should I know?"

"Ain't that her turkey?"

"Oh yeah. She told me to tell you to stuff it."

The Sunday before Christmas, Radaker decided to go to church. He didn't know where else to turn. He wasn't necessarily turning to God, but if he happened to bump into Him, that was fine too. It was not to soothe his soul that he dressed up in his itchy blue suit, but to satisfy his curiosity, though maybe the two were akin.

He'd occasionally attended the Lutheran Church, down by the Red Bank Creek, but that wasn't where he pointed his pickup. The United Presbyterian Church, a gothic castle of brown stones and steeples, anchored the west end of Main Street. He parked well beyond it and walked back, wind blowing through his parka, which failed to reach the bottom of his suit jacket. It was the church of his ex-partner, Fuzzy Huffman.

Arriving late, during the first hymn, he sat in a rear pew beneath the balcony, smelling the polish and pine. Evergreen boughs with red bows decorated the altar and aisles, the great chamber filled with the thunder of the organ and the voices of the engorged congregation. He opened a hymnal to a random page, moving his lips silently as he searched from pew to pew, head to head, up one row, down the next. He spotted his friend Buster Clover and his wife, Peggy, Clover staring at him, eyebrows in a quizzical knot. Across the main aisle, midway up, he finally found what he was looking for: the graying hair of Fuzzy Huffman, swept over the familiar bald spot, next to the freshly coifed hair of Rita, raven black. Tammy stood beside her. Radaker looked away, to the nearest window.

Stained glass brilliantly illuminated by the morning sun, a magnificent angel watched over him, arms and wings extended.

The next hymn was "Adeste Fideles." He sang along in a shaky voice, seeing his wife and his ex-partner sharing a single hymnal. Then Fuzzy's arm floated up, touching Rita's back, where it rested. Radaker looked up to the angel again, to the rich, glistening hues of heaven more brilliant than ever, and his forearm flexed a mighty ripple.

Two days later, the hospital called: Uncle Shorty was failing. He'd called for his nephew Earl.

The hospital was on the highest hill in Hartsgrove, higher than the Catholic Church on Irishtown Hill. On the third floor, Radaker stopped for coffee at the vending machine, unaware of the sticky residue from an earlier spill until it was too late. Down the corridor toward Uncle Shorty's room, each step of his rubber-soled work boots resounded in the quiet zone like ripping velcro. A nurse's head looked out from the station down the hall, frowning at the racket; curious faces peered from every room he passed.

Shorty's eyes didn't open. Radaker stood with his hands on his hips: *Too late,* he intuited. He sat by the window to wait, wondering why the old man had summoned him—certainly not to wish him a Merry Christmas. A sprig of plastic mistletoe hung over the doorway, no doubt prompting Shorty's race to beat Christmas out the door. He'd always disapproved of the holiday as frivolous; Aunt Carrie, before she'd died, had tried to sneak Earl a small Christmas gift when she could, a comic book, a cap gun.

Several times Radaker spoke his name, but the gray, sunken man never stirred.

Why *had* he summoned him? Radaker had read some stories, seen some movies; the idea of a deathbed revelation occurred to him, then kept nagging. Had Shorty known more about Earl's parents than he'd let on? The significance of the possibility was too much—too unlikely, he told himself—to consider.

Through the window he looked out over Hartsgrove. From the Court House on Main Street, he calculated where Rita's furniture store would be, farther down on the opposite side. Gwenda's place on Longview was hidden behind the crest of Irishtown Hill, where the steeple of the Catholic Church was just below eye level. He watched the town fade into darkness, lights appearing on the hillsides, chimney smoke trailing up, losing itself in the twilight. Stars slowly crept into the sky.

He whistled "Twinkle, Twinkle, Little Star."

Shorty never stirred. Just like the old man to summon a body to hear his last words, and then not utter a single one. He remembered endless evening hours of his childhood, woodstove steaming, Carrie knitting, Shorty listening to the radio so low Radaker could barely hear the "Hi-ho Silver!" The clicking of the knitting needles the loudest sound in the room. He gave the old man's shoulder a gentle shake, to no avail.

The light was low, the room dim. He gazed out the window. He dozed. He awoke and watched the stars growing brighter and brighter in the nighttime sky over Hartsgrove. He whistled *Like a diamond in the sky.*

The phantom hammer finally drove him from the vigil. The nurse said she'd call him if Shorty woke up; he hadn't said why he'd wanted to see Earl. Radaker walked down the long corridor, boots loudly ripping every step, echoing from the empty walls, tearing him away. What was the old man taking with him? Where was it going? Another vanishing.

What remained, what stayed with him, was the diamond in the sky. Maybe he'd been wrong. Maybe Rita was right. Maybe you don't— maybe you shouldn't—outgrow your magic, outgrow your mystery. Didn't he still believe his mother was making her way back to him? Didn't he still wonder what he was going to be when he grew up?

First thing next morning, he bought a diamond. Rita had always wanted one, but he'd always dismissed it as too extravagant. Well, he wasn't going to take it with him. He was going to leave it all here, one way or another. Magic, she wanted? He had a hunch a big old diamond, sparkling and expensive, would let loose plenty of magic.

He wrapped the little box in shiny blue paper, writing on the card simply, *I love you.* He didn't write Rita's name on it, thinking at the time it was because the card was too small.

Christmas Eve he set off to deliver it personally to Rita, Fuzzy or no Fuzzy. Snow fell steadily out of a black sky, and he had to drive slowly, his heart pumping in time to the beat of the wipers. He pulled to a stop in front of Rita's mother's on Pine Street; he didn't pull into the driveway. He didn't get out of his truck. The drapes on the bay window were open so the world could admire their tree—tall, full, shiny and fake. He could see them on the sofa, Rita, Tammy, then Fuzzy, apparently watching television—he couldn't see the TV. Rita's mother came to the tree, absently adjusting a strand of tinsel. The other three never glanced her way. They never looked at her, never looked at the tree, never looked at each other, never looked through the window to see Radaker in his pickup, watching them like fish in a bowl. Fuzzy sneezed, and Rita yawned. Tammy stood up and stretched. Rita and Fuzzy stayed on opposite ends of the sofa, staring straight ahead.

Radaker couldn't bring himself to get out of his truck. The thing of it was, it had nothing to do with Fuzzy, with the idea of confrontation, which had always made him uneasy. What it was was Rita's yawn. Her blank stare. It was the dull thump of the wipers, the artificial tree, the brightness of the living room, the shabby aluminum siding on the front of the house. Where was the magic in that?

He drove to Gwenda's. Her place was dark.

He drove to his office and pulled into the parking lot, tires crunching to a stop. A light shone from the window, in front of which sat Gwenda's car, covered with inches of snow. Across Route 302 the Tastee Freeze was dark, closed for the winter, and for some reason, at that moment, the image of hot fudge steaming off the snow came into his mind, and it occurred to him there was something a little magical about that. He looked up at the light on the pole at the edge of the lot, watching the big, fat flakes swirl and float through the glowing circle, and it was Christmas Eve. In the office window hung a sparkling star he hadn't seen before, something Gwenda had no doubt put there to celebrate the season all alone, and somewhere up in the snowy sky flew a jolly old elf and eight tiny reindeer, and he felt his heart as it quickened. And if this wasn't magic, if this wasn't magic, then nothing was.

Glitter and Grace

An assault was what it was, an onslaught of light. Jaw clenching, Charlie Grace watched from the window of his trailer as Emory Chestnut's place across the road lit up in fits and starts like a two-bit, snowbound circus: Santas and elves, reindeer and angels, carolers and candy canes, snowmen and Wise Men, the whole Nativity, an acre of gleaming capillaries snaking into a glistening script on the rise beside the house: *Merry Xmas To All!* Chestnut's Christmas display had been growing for years, along with his fame—and Grace's vexation—as pilgrims flocked from miles around, from as far south as Pittsburgh, as far north as Erie, to marvel at the glittering seasonal extravaganza. And to turn around, most of them, in Grace's driveway.

The light was bad enough, the omnipresent glow from which there was no escape in any corner of his trailer, the headlights prying through the curtains with irksome regularity, but the noise was maddening as well: the drone and whine of the cars, the slamming of the doors as the faithful disembarked to deposit their donations in Chestnut's begging box, the awe-filled voices through the windows rolled down for a better view.

Watching the Christmas glitter through his own shadowy reflection in the trailer window, Grace seethed. Ostentatiousness was bad enough—Grace considered himself to be a humble man; he was in fact proud of his humbleness. Ostentatiousness that held him hostage, that imposed itself upon his mind, body and soul was intolerable. And intolerable, to Grace, was not a rhetorical word.

His wife, Jean, came into the window, her reflection behind him, putting on her coat over her gray uniform dress, on her way to work. She was pretty, plump and plain, a Cajun gleam in her straight, dark hair. He watched her watching him stand in the window. "Like my daddy always told me," she said, "when God gives you lemons, make lemonade."

"I ain't thirsty," said Grace.

"You can turn off all the lights. You'll never even miss 'em. We can save a ton on our electric bill."

"I ain't laughing."

"Get over it," she said with a peck to his cheek.

"Easy for you to say. You ain't here all night when the circus is going on."

"Yeah. I'm just relaxing at the truck stop with my feet up, getting a pedicure."

He watched her leave with a wave through the window. Her taillights were barely out of sight when the little lightless motorbike pulled into his driveway, nearly lost in the glow of the Chestnut firmament. The slight, hairy figure of Bunny Boozer dismounted. Grace watched him turn to take in the Chestnut spectacle, saw the nearly palpable gawk, and it annoyed him how long Boozer stood and stared. Grace thought he might have to go and shake him, Boozer having wandered off again among the stars.

The tin door rattled open. "Charlie, how many light bulbs you suppose he's got lit up over there anyway?"

"Damned if I know, Bunny, but his electric bill's gotta be more'n what you make in a year." When Boozer didn't respond, Grace wished he hadn't said it, but he didn't let on. Instead he said, "Ain't you cold?"

Boozer, wearing only frayed and faded denim, shrugged. "Little chilly. Jean around?"

"She's at work," Grace said, and Boozer relaxed perceptibly. Grace removed his hat, the high cloth welder's cap he always wore—today's was a checkerboard pattern—to run his fingers through his long black hair. "You going looking for a job like that?"

Boozer bunched his eyebrows. Most of the left one was missing, along with half the teeth in his seldom-seen smile, losses redeemed by the reckless red growth of his hair and beard. "Why?" he said. "How should I be going?"

"Dressed up. You gotta make a good first impression, you can't go walking in there looking like a damn stumblebum."

"I don't know what happened to my suit."

"You can't lose a suit," Grace said. "You can lose your keys, or your lighter, or your mind. You can't lose a suit."

"I don't know what happened to it. Annie musta throwed it out."

"Before or after she threw you out?"

"What's the difference? I ain't applying to be no bank president."

"That's a double negative."

"You got that right," Boozer said.

Outside Grace scraped the windshield of his old Olds, gritting his teeth at the carloads of gawkers creeping down the road. Boozer, gaping again, said, "You know, me and Chestnut's second cousins."

"I was aware of that fact."

"So how'd he end up rich? And I ain't got a pot to piss in."

Grace said, "Life's a bitch and then you die," then grimaced, wishing he hadn't. But he didn't let on.

The Golden Steer, one of Hartsgrove's finer restaurants, was not a haunt of Grace's. Sipping a beer at the bar, he watched Boozer, at a table by the men's room door, laboring over the job application. Legs crossed tightly at the knees, Boozer's body was tensed as though assembling a bomb. In the dining room beyond the swinging saloon doors, at a table by the wall festooned with old bridles and saddles, sat Emory Chestnut, feasting with his wife, Dora.

"He come here often?" Grace asked Osborn, the bartender. Osborn was a burly man, overflowing his tight gold Golden Steer vest.

"Couple times a week anyhow," Osborn said. "Eats whole butter patties right outa the dish. Sprinkles sugar on 'em."

"Good. He can't have that heart attack soon enough."

Osborn grinned. "Love thy neighbor."

"Neighbor my ass. How'd you like your neighbor setting up a circus in your front yard?"

"I'd be pissed. But since he didn't, I gotta drive the whole way across town to see it. I probably been up there a dozen times."

"Probably turned around in my driveway every goddamn one of 'em."

Osborn laughed, then went to wait on Earl and Gwenda Radaker, regulars who'd walked in full of Christmas cheer. Boozer came up to the bar, application in hand. "What do you think, Charlie?"

Grace glanced it over. "I think it looks like a bunch of chicken scratches."

"I don't write all that good."

"All's you gotta do is be neat. And don't go crossing things off like that."

"I had to. I put the wrong address down. I put Annie's address down."

"Erase it."

"It's in ink."

"You shoulda used a pencil."

"They give me a pen."

"They oughta give you a damn crayola. Get another one and start over again. You can't go handing them something that looks like that."

Boozer labored on. Osborn came back to mix a rum and Coke. "This one here's for your neighbor. Wanna add anything special?"

"Do I ever."

Osborn nodded toward Boozer. "Little buddy's out of work again, huh?"

Grace nodded. "He's a real good cook. He cooks up at the club all the time."

"We got a chef, Charlie."

"I was aware of that fact. I'm thinking he'd be a great chef's helper."

"We got them too."

"Well, see what you can do, will you? He's conscientious and all that."

Grace tried to think of other good words to put in as Boozer labored on. Osborn said, "Is he all right? You know, healthwise I mean."

"Bunny? Nothing to keep him from cooking."

Looking up at the waitress bringing his drink, Chestnut spotted Grace at the bar. Grace smiled and waved. A dark red flush crossing his face, Chestnut sniffed suspiciously at his drink, putting Grace, admittedly prejudiced, in mind of a rooting hog.

Osborn lowered his brow and his voice. "He ain't got that queer's disease, does he?"

"Jesus Christ. Where'd you hear that?"

Osborn offered a vague shrug.

"He lived with Annie Bennett for five years," Grace said.

"Yeah, but she threw him out."

"Shit, if every man that ever got thrown out by a woman was queer, we'd have a big problem propagating the species."

"Doing what to the species?"

"Bunny ain't got no damn queer's disease. He don't have anything contagious."

"No? So what's he got then?"

"He's got the blues."

Grace and Boozer had been sitting at the bar of the Hartsgrove Rod and Gun Club two months earlier on a Saturday night when Boozer, out of the blue, had said, "I got lumps on my nuts."

In the happy weekend din, Grace wasn't sure he'd heard what he'd heard. Boozer repeated it, elaborating. Grace pushed aside his bag of Beer Nuts, which he eventually left on the bar in lieu of a tip. At some point in your life, it stands to reason, you reach the very peak of your youth and begin the long, slow (Grace hoped it would be long and slow) trek down toward the grave. Had that been his moment? Grace wondered, thinking back on it.

Buster Clover caught up with them in the Rod and Gun Club amid the clamor of country music, old time rock and roll, and Christmas revelry. The cement block cavern was brightened by the ten-foot Christmas tree on the far side of the dance floor, and by a string of white lights adorning the long soffit above the bar and circling the club seal, an ornate, crossed fishing rod and rifle.

Clover, big and lanky, sensed a story into which he could stick his long nose. He wrote for the *Hartsgrove Herald*, the town's weekly newspaper, and he was doing his obligatory annual piece on the Chestnut Christmas display.

"Sounds like you got a regular Hatfield and McCoy thing going on up there."

"Not hardly," Grace said. "Did he say that?"

"In so many words."

"He's my second cousin," Boozer said.

"He seems to think you're jealous," said Clover.

"*Jealous?*" Grace said. "Try pissed—all those goddam lights coming in my bedroom window."

Clover nodded. "You don't think it's pretty?"

"Pretty fucking tacky. I can't believe all those morons drive miles to see it. Get a life, man."

"I think it's kinda pretty," Boozer said. Grace shot him a frown.

"He said you had somebody call him up and say they were from *Time* magazine, and they were coming out from New York City to do a story—"

"He said that?"

"Of course nobody ever showed up. And he said—he *implied*—you knocked a ladder over when he was up on the roof replacing a bulb. Said he damn near froze to death till Dora let him down."

"That was wind. It was real windy that night."

"He also said you pissed 'Joy to the World' in his snow bank the day the photographer from the *Pittsburgh Post Gazette* was coming up."

"He accused me, and I said, why? Does it look like Dora's handwriting?"

"He didn't mention that," Clover said.

"Did he say anything about the money missing from his begging box?" Boozer asked.

"No," Clover said, expectantly. Boozer said nothing. Grace shook his head.

"Reminds me of when we were in college," Clover said. "We had this rivalry with a fraternity across the street from us. They always had this big, fancy light show, so one night we made this snow sculpture of a fist, flipping them the bird. Pointing right across the street at 'em. It was beautiful." Clover made a fat fist giving the finger with his right hand, holding his left horizontally at his wrist, snow-level. "Looked just like this giant reaching up out of the snow, pissed off."

"Cool," said Grace, nodding in admiration.

"Wow," Boozer said.

Conversations sloshed up and down the bar, laughter overflowing. Beside the jukebox, blaring "Jingle Bell Rock," life-sized cardboard cut-outs of four Pittsburgh Steelers of the seventies looked on, a Santa's cap on Mean Joe Greene. Someone had found a Cabbage Patch Kid doll for his daughter, but someone else topped that, having heard McCrory's was getting in a whole shipment of them on Saturday, just in time for Christmas. Meanwhile, the Herculean effort of dragging a two-hundred-pound buck two hours out of the woods was bragged, while two stools away, an affair involving a waitress and a dentist was rumored, and, just down the bar, Penn State's chances in the upcoming Aloha Bowl were assessed. Clover scribbled a few notes, Grace sipped his beer, and Boozer wandered off again, without ever leaving his bar stool.

Grace saw the nervous tic in Boozer's eye, involuntary, an atavistic alarm of prey, the same tic he'd seen last week when Boozer had told him about his hospital exam that morning. The doctor asked him to stand on a stool and drop his pants. Seven student nurses filed in solemnly to observe his testicles, to witness the rarity of a dual strickening.

Wasn't he embarrassed? Grace asked.

No, Boozer said, although the blood did rush to his face. And, oddly enough, not only to his face.

He was not embarrassed even when his penis had gradually begun to arise beneath their startled stares. Slowly swelling to full erection. A glorious cantilever, half as long it seemed as his own wiry self. They swore in clinical terms it had never happened before; it was in fact unprecedented. With other somber medical musings they filed out again, though he thought he heard the word *boner* being giggled down the hall as they left.

Boozer was proud in his own modest way, as proud as his wretched life would allow. He had, after all, made medical history.

And wasn't that the stuff of which miracles, such as Lazarus, were made?

In a field of darkly glowing snow, eerily reflecting Chestnut's acre of lights, Grace wondered if he'd been beamed magically into the heart of an aurora borealis. He and Boozer labored in the nocturnal stillness beneath a luminous low cloud ceiling. A grunt, a crunch of snow, the deep-throated hum of a distant truck climbing a Hartsgrove hill.

"Looks like we could use a little more snow up there around the head."

"I couldn't agree more, Mr. Grace."

"I'll give you a hand with the ladder."

"You hold, I'll climb."

"Absolutely, Mr. Boozer. I do believe you have the artistic touch."

"I do believe I'm drunker'n a fuckin' skunk."

Ghosts of breath vanished around their heads, though the heat of creation made them impervious to the cold of the early winter morning. Avid hunters, they were used to the outdoors, but there was a delightful novelty to the outdoors late at night, like a secret adventure. Like being a kid again, blissfully unaware of unemployment, bills and ill-nesses. Mortality. When love could be taken for granted, and planning and plotting were only games. When all that mattered was the work of your hands, the color of the moment.

"Do you believe in God, Charlie?"

"Not particularly. But I do believe I'll have another beer."

"More snow here."

"Yes sir, Mr. Boozer, coming right up."

They were beginning to feel good about their sculpture, a potential work of art. Certainly enough to knock the socks off all the Chestnut gawkers.

"You really don't believe in God, Charlie?"

"I'm really not sure."

"Then you're a, whatcha call it, agnostic?"

"No, I'm a dyslexic. I definitely believe in Dog."

"I'm serious."

"Well so am I, dogdamn it."

"You ain't the one with the cancer on his balls, Charlie."

God blinked, and the light was gone. The whole Chestnut acre went black in an instant, effectively vanishing. They waited, letting their eyes adjust, as the gray glow of the low cloud ceiling began to assume shapes and motion. Vague stirrings of heaven. Somewhere a dog barked for the good old days. From the center of the universe one moment, Chest-nut's glittering glory had gone to oblivion the next.

"Then the real question is whether or not *you* believe in God, Mr. Boozer."

"Well. I try. I try to just open up my heart and let the faith flow in like they tell you to, but I can't. I can't get it open. It's stubborn, like one of them clam shells. Did you ever shuck any clams? My heart just won't let me pry it open to let the faith flow in, and I'm afraid if I use a knife on it, I'll just kill it."

"And if you get your heart all pried open anyhow, what makes you think the faith'll just flow in like they say? It'll probably just gum all up like molasses."

"Just be my luck anyways. Get stuck with sticky faith."

"I do believe you need another beer."

"So do I, Mr. Grace. And I'm purt near out of things to believe in."

They toasted their work and sat in the snow, admiring their towering achievement. Grace worried about Boozer driving home wet in subfreezing temperatures through the hopefully copless back alleys of Hartsgrove on his unregistered, unlicensed, uninsured, unsafe and unlucky motorbike, a worry he quickly dismissed as irrelevant. A cold would be the least of Boozer's worries.

"Why do you think we were put here, Charlie? On this earth."

"That's easy. To hunt, fish, cook, eat good, drink good."

"And to fuck good too?"

"Sure. As long as it don't interfere with the others."

"You know why I think we were put here?"

"What's your theory, Mr. Boozer?"

"To live as long as we can."

A breeze suddenly swept over them, bringing with it a chill. The trailer door rattled open in the dark, Jean's voice calling, "It's half past two! What are you guys doing out there?"

"Male bonding," Grace answered with a chortle.

"Yeah," said Boozer thoughtfully. "It don't get much more male bonding than this here."

Boozer got going while the getting was good, setting off on his lightless motorbike, a noisy apparition, *Keep breathing!* his shouted farewell.

Five hours later, Grace awoke from a nonsense dream involving severed body parts and gutted bunnies, Jean shaking his shoulder. *"Char-lie, what is that in our yard? What did you do?"*

Grace rubbed his eyes as it all flowed back in a wave of happy expectation. He made his way to the window beside her, adrenaline alleviating his hangover.

"That's a *hard*-on in our yard!"

"Yeah," said Grace. "A *yard*-on."

"*Charlie!*"

"Looks even better in daylight."

Ten feet tall and splendidly shaped, it was a magnificent, realistic erection, complete with veins and testicles, positioned adjacent to a sprawling bush. Like a giant reaching up out of the snow, happy. And towering over Chestnut's.

"Our Mr. Boozer's quite the artist," Grace murmured admiringly.

"You're going to blame that on Bunny?"

"*Blame?* Hell no. *Credit.*"

"That thing's not staying in my yard," said Jean, the whole, clenched, five foot two of her.

"No," Grace agreed. "Not past April anyways."

"Charlie. My daddy's a preacher, remember?"

"In Louisiana, remember?"

"That's not the point."

"What is the point? Preachers don't get hard-ons?"

"Either that thing goes, or I go. Take your pick."

Jean had been gone less than an hour when Hartsgrove Police Chief Toole showed up. Grace thought he detected a certain reluctance on Toole's part to enforce whatever obscure ordinance he intended to enforce, perhaps even a glint of admiration in his eye as he took in the sheer artistry of the sculpture, so he made it easy on him, pointing out that Ruggles Road, between his place and Chestnut's, was also the borough line. He was out of Toole's jurisdiction. The discussion with Paine County Deputy Sheriff Twilliger, who arrived two hours later, took a little longer. To him, Grace insisted that the sculpture was a lighthouse on two storm-beaten rocks, symbolic of the guiding light of Jesus Christ, and meant to complement Chestnut's far gaudier (no pun intended) tribute to Him in the season of His birth. When Twilliger responded bullshit, he knew a hard-on when he saw one, Grace refrained from any number of sarcastic retorts, replying instead that he'd have to prove it in court, and that the ACLU would be all over him like white on snow.

Boozer didn't arrive till nearly dusk, just about the time Chestnut's lights came on, and the traffic commenced. But tonight he stood gawking not at Chestnut's display, but at the well-lit sculpture. Grace had fashioned spotlights to augment the illumination of the headlights.

The tin door rattled open. "Charlie, maybe we oughta put a wreath on it or something."

"How about an angel on top?"

Boozer ruminated. "Wouldn't that be, whatcha call it, sacrilegious?"

"Sure. Did you eat yet?"

"Not today," said Boozer. "Jean around?"

"We had an artistic disagreement. She went up to stay at her girlfriend Sally's."

Boozer, relaxing perceptibly, sniffed. "Man, what are you cooking?"

"Venison steaks and lobster." Grace wiped his hands on his sunflowered apron. "Pull the table and chairs over next to the window there."

For the occasion, Grace had marinated the venison steaks before broiling, serving them *St. Hubert* with a tart sauce of cranberry jelly, vinegar, and peppercorns. The lobster was boiled to perfection, accompanied by drawn butter, asparagus, and french fried potatoes. Wine was on the table. Admiring their craftsmanship, they feasted.

"Did you see that?" laughed Grace, mouth full, pointing out the window with his fork. "That guy damn near drove off the road."

"This steak is great, Charlie, where'd you get 'em?"

"Osborn asked me to keep 'em in my freezer for him. Ran outta room in his." Grace broke a lobster claw with a vicious crack. "Lobsters are on Jean. We were supposed to have 'em tonight."

"And so we are," said Boozer.

Car after car crawled by. Grace took off his high cloth welder's cap—today's was purple tie-dyed—to run his fingers through his long black hair. He thought he detected an even slower pace than usual, fewer daring to turn in his driveway, where they were forced to face the phallus. He savored the bile that surely would be boiling in the fat arteries of Emory Chestnut. Blubbery, rich bastard. Grace told Boozer about the three Chestnut phone calls he'd fielded that day, each more enraged than the previous, each containing threats more grave. Grace told him he'd built it so Dora could see what one looked like.

They toasted friends, food, drink and the hard-on, Grace admonishing Boozer to drink his red wine after a bite of steak, white after the lobster. He'd laid in a nice bottle of Mouton Cadet and a fine chilled Chablis in the ice-bucket.

"What about the beer?" Boozer clenched the fat brown bottle in his fist.

"After the potatoes or asparagus. Or when you're just taking a break."

They ate for an hour, stacked dirty dishes in the sink, then sipped after-dinner beers, watching from the darkened living room for another hour, then another, the crawling cars, the glowing lights, the glistening phallus, and the house of Chestnut for signs of aggressive activity.

The traffic seemed to thicken as the night wore on.

They sat in silence, in the harsh-shadowed glare from the lights outside. It dawned on Grace that perhaps the pilgrims would not avoid the phallus after all. Perhaps it would attract them instead. Maybe they'd created a magnet. He was not dismayed by the thought.

"If you build it, they will come. If you build it, *it* will come."

Boozer didn't laugh. Didn't utter a sound. Grace pried his eyes from the lustrousness beyond the window to the figure across from him buried in shadow. Boozer's face was frightened and pale, the tiny tic back in the eyes. One puff would send him whirling away like a dust mite.

"Jesus, Charlie, I'm scared."

Grace studied the face, thankful to see no tear, then turned away. Looking through the window to the other end of the cosmic seesaw where the fat bully sat grounded with all his scintillating wealth, leaving this frailest of playmates teetering terrified halfway up to heaven. Justice blinded by the glitter.

"Don't let on," Grace said. "Don't give 'em the satisfaction. You ain't the first unlucky bastard in the world, and you won't be the last."

Next morning, Grace was up early and alone. Jean had called, gruffly inquiring as to whether or not the snow sculpture—*that thing*—was still in her yard. Grace had gruffly inquired right back at her as to whether or not it was April yet. He waited by the window, unable to enjoy his *Gourmet* magazine, distracted by the towering phallus, and by Chestnut's unlit display, so bland and tacky in the gray daylight, and by car after car creeping by. Was it his imagination, or was traffic unusually heavy for a Saturday morning? He waited, not deceived by the quiet, by the stillness. The eye of the storm? He didn't know what he was waiting for, but he knew it was something, something was in motion; just as he knew that he was never peacefully at rest in his bed on a quiet night, that he was in fact hurtling through space on the wings of the earth.

Boozer and Clover arrived together, coincidentally, around noon, having had to fight traffic the whole way up the hill. It was already heavier than the evening peak.

"I'm impressed," Clover said.

"What the heck's going on?" said Boozer.

"The second coming?" Grace chortled. He loved his sense of humor.

It was all over town, Clover reported. Word had quickly spread last night through the bars, at least the ones sampled by Clover, which included the Green Lantern, Jum's, the Golden Steer, Bill's, the God and Run Club, the Eagles, the Oriental Tavern and the Pub Bar. And this morning it was all over Main Street as well. Reaction was mixed. Many were amused (mostly in the bars), many annoyed (mostly on Main), few indifferent. A polarizing event, appropriately, Clover noted. He wondered how, if at all, he could work it into his Chestnut display story.

"Just report it straight up," Grace suggested.

Grace tried to read the faces in the cars. He tried to judge where he stood, tried to guess what was in motion. Outside of the occasional carload of fist-pumping, cheering teenagers, it was a difficult task. Osborn and a couple of buddies passed by in his blue Pinto, waving and smiling, but most of the faces were inscrutable. Were they neutral, or was it the distance, the glass, the shadows, the reflections? Were they smiling? Frowning? Friendly? Hostile? Al Black driving by in his pickup, scowling out the window with a wave, only served to reinforce the futility, for Grace knew his buddy Al Black would wholeheartedly support his endeavor. It was just that he always scowled. Now and then Grace detected a passing camera pointing at the phallus. Now and then he detected Emory Chestnut peeking out his window, the one entirely scrutable face in the crowd.

Clover said, "I just talked to the Mayor."

Grace felt the stirrings of motion, wings beating air around his ears.

"He's been getting all kinds of phone calls, and not just from Chestnut. Every preacher in town's called him up. He's heard from Jim Geist, from Meg Allshouse"—of the Historic Hartsgrove Foundation and the WCTU respectively—"from the school superintendent, the Chamber of Commerce—you name it. He's been talking to the sheriff and the DA and the justice of the peace all morning. I guess some people are pretty pissed."

"So what?" Grace said. "What are they going to do about it?"

"I guess they're discussing all kinds of options."

A caravan of college kids passed by, honking loudly.

"Maybe we just oughta knock it down," Boozer said.

"That's one of the options they're discussing," Clover said.

"Bullshit," said Grace.

"We put it up so you could get rid of this here traffic bothering you," Boozer said. "Well it didn't work."

"*This* traffic ain't bothering me," Grace said.

"Well it oughta be," Boozer said. "It's worse'n what it was before."

Grace sighed. "You know, Mr. Boozer, that's your problem. You gotta look at the big picture. If that fat bastard over there can put up whatever the hell he wants no matter who it bothers, then so can we. It's called Freedom of Speech. It's called God bless America."

"Yeah," Clover said, "but they're gonna say there's a big difference between a joyful Christmas display and a frozen hard-on."

"I personally think a hard-on's a lot more joyful than a gaggle of tacky lights," said Grace. "And I bet your wife would agree with me."

"JINGLE BALLS, JINGLE BALLS!" someone sang from a passing car.

Boozer waved. Just past midnight, he and Grace sat in lawn chairs at the perimeter of the pool of light bathing the phallus. Jean, having returned home, was inside sleeping it off. Grace and Boozer sipped beers, marveling at the unseasonably warm evening, watching the traffic abate, immersed again in the aura of Chestnut's display and their own glistening creation, another night lost in lights.

Grace sat with his shotgun on his knees. "I can't believe you wanted to knock it down."

"I didn't really want to knock it down, Charlie. I just didn't want no trouble."

"What the hell's a little more trouble to you anyways?"

"Me? I ain't got no trouble. I got all God's love I can use, and all your beer I can drink."

"I thought you didn't believe in God."

"Well maybe not, but I sure do believe in your beer."

"One outa two ain't bad."

Reverend Johnston from the Methodist Church had called Grace on behalf of the Hartsgrove United Church Alliance to express their objections to his lascivious display in this holiest of seasons, to beg his understanding and cooperation, and to inform him that should the sculpture still be standing the next morning, Sunday conveniently enough, their male parishioners would protest en masse. Grace would be picketed. Grace said go for it. So he really didn't expect vigilante action tonight. Nevertheless, the shotgun was loaded, with birdshot.

Presumably safe from hostile activity, friendly fire was another story. Drunk and happy was how Grace had met Jean working in Louisiana ten years earlier, how they'd spent much of their time since, and how Jean's girlfriend, Sally, had brought her home tonight. Drunk, happy and forgiving. She swore in fact she'd never let another hard-on come between them, then laughed so hard she fell in the snow, where she made an angel. It had been all they could do to restrain her from joyfully embracing the sculpture, which, considering their relative conditions and the troubling warmth of the evening, might have resulted in total toppling.

"I don't care much for this heat, Mr. Boozer."

"Yeah. I'm afraid we're getting a little limp."

"Maybe God isn't on our side after all."

"God, God, God. Here we go again. Can't we talk about football or fucking?"

"I don't care much about football, Mr. Boozer. And everything's been said about fucking there is to say. If you have a new fucking thought, I'd love to hear it."

"Then maybe we oughta just pray for a cold front."

"Pray to who?"

"Good question."

A car hadn't passed in a quarter hour when they heard the heavy double bong of the Court House bell from down on Main Street. In the distance a drunken caroler found his way home, singing "Silent Night" at the top of his lungs, dogs protesting in unruly chorus. Chestnut's glitter had gone to black again, and the air seemed even warmer when Boozer finally left on his lightless motorbike with a wobble and a hardy *Keep breathing!* Grace noticed worrisome rivulets of moisture on the sculpture before he turned off his floodlights and made his way to bed.

Later he wondered if Boozer had indeed prayed for a cold front, for if he had, his prayer had been answered.

That day's weather in fact would be revisited time and again. The temperature had risen steadily from afternoon through the following morning, till a massive cold front slammed in with a sudden shock, loud and late, when Grace was crowded restlessly beside a snoring

Jean, and Boozer was curled shivering in his sleeping bag beneath his sister's stairs. The wind whistled, knifing through every crack and crevice at which it could pry. The atmospheric phenomenon might have been remembered in its own right, but given the change it wrought—or was alleged to have wrought—it became one of the most discussed weather happenings in the history of Hartsgrove since the flood of 1936. It would be debated in western Pennsylvania and beyond for years to come, from barstools and pulpits alike.

Divine intervention was argued. The possibility of meteorological miracles was entertained. What else could cause the warmth of a gentle trade wind to yield so suddenly to a savage jet stream driving its mass of polar air southward? An ice cold jet stream, the winds of which cut like a whetted chisel? Of course there were doubters. The debate centered not only on the possibility of divine intervention, but on whether or not any real change had occurred at all. For every person who argued the case of the miracle, there were two who dismissed the notion out of hand, as they would dismiss gossip—silly, irrelevant, the product of idle minds.

Grace, the principal witness, considered all the evidence. In a book at the library he read about El Niño, the climatic wonder behind all manner of worldwide meteorological mischief. El Niño originated off the faraway coast of Peru, where the Spanish-speaking natives held it in such awe as to name it for the other phenomenon born at the same time of the year.

El Niño: The Infant Jesus.

Car doors slammed him from his sleep. Hastily into his shoes, Grace headed for the window where the shotgun was propped, Jean stirring behind him. Sweeping aside the drape to the sunny blaze of the frigid morning, he saw men sluggishly assembling from assorted cars, drawn toward the sculpture as though by gravity, not protesting, not picketing, forgotten signs adroop on the crusty sweep of the snow. They gathered and stared. Others arrived, approaching with slow frowns, white breaths escaping them like blank dialogue balloons.

Grace watched their slow motion in puzzlement, watching in vain for something familiar, something expected. Had he awoken on another planet?

Outside, the jolt of the arctic air. No sound except the crunch of his steps. When he reached the congregation, he turned to face the object of their stares, his eyes squinted against the glare of the morning. The gleaming statue was a full foot smaller than the night before, yet larger than life, transformed utterly.

Later, he would try to reconstruct the most crystal clear moment of his life, but he could never be certain of the accuracy of the memory— how much was the actual emotion he'd felt at the time, how much had accumulated since, layered on with each reliving? But he thought he remembered, in that brief, intense instant, feeling as though he were the solitary focus of the vast, all-seeing eye of God.

For it seemed to Grace that his own uncomprehending eyes were staring into the face of Jesus Christ.

How long he looked he didn't know, but the face of the statue seemed to stare back with the serenity of a steady star until a shiver broke his gaze, and he found his welder's cap clutched to his chest. He looked around. All the faces mirrored his own, numb with incredulity.

The shell of shock that had frozen his mind was cracked by the sound of a sob. Grace turned to see Jean on her knees in the snow just behind him, staring at the statue, tears melting down her face.

The sob gave way to a sudden roar. Emory Chestnut in his black pickup, snowplow blazing like a saber in the morning sun, descended upon them, an avenging angel, hell-bent and bouncing high, destroying the statue in one fell pass, leaving nothing in his wake but the frozen rubble of wonder.

One week later, on Christmas Day, Grace visited Boozer. "I saw Clover up at the club. He was calling it the 'Resur-Erection.'"

"Dang," Boozer said. "I still can't believe I didn't get to see it with my own two eyes."

"Nobody did for long. About two seconds. Or two minutes. Or two hours."

"Jim Geist was up. He said it was Jesus."

"How does Jim Geist know what the hell Jesus looks like? I thought it looked more like Minnie Pearl. Emory Chestnut thought it looked like a limp dick."

"Well, Jim Geist said it was a miracle."

"That's the argument. There's the miracle camp and the anti-miracle camp. The bullshit camp."

"What camp are you in?" Boozer said.

Grace wondered. Unlike his wife, Jean, he'd slipped from the miracle camp, though he hadn't slid completely to the other side. He couldn't deny what he'd seen, how he'd felt—but he couldn't believe it either. He was hanging on to the fraying twine between the two camps, twisting in the wind, fingers aching. "It was a freak of nature," Grace said, "a cosmic accident. A happy coincidence."

"Ain't that what a miracle is?"

"Goddam it, Bunny, *I* don't know what Jesus looks like either."

Grace's words, his vehemence, caught them both by surprise. Boozer didn't answer, eyes beginning to falter, the tiny tic commencing, and they looked away from each other, out through the window to the snowy hills of Hartsgrove, settling on the clock in the Court House dome down below.

"Anybody else been up?" Grace finally asked. Being Christmas, the other three beds in the ward were vacant.

"Osborn stopped in yesterday. His uncle had some operation or something." Boozer shook his head, frowning with his eyebrow and a half. Slowly the frown lifted. "You suppose the doctor'll be in today?"

"On Christmas? Are you shitting me?"

"You suppose he'll tell me what they did with my testicles?"

"Hell, I can tell you that. I seen 'em hanging on the Christmas tree in the lobby when I came in, spray-painted silver. Didn't look half bad either."

Muddy Bottom

So there you are, just cruising along admiring the scenery, when a bird sneezes in Brazil, the load starts shifting, and suddenly it's all you can do to keep it on the road. Thursday Peggy came home from visiting our daughter Jenny in State College, and tells me Jenny's got something growing on her leg, something bad. Then Friday afternoon Mrs. Ishman tells me Bruner is missing.

"Russell, have you seen Douglas today?" she said. I was leaving my office at the newspaper on Main Street when I bumped into her.

I said, "Bruner?"

She said, "How many other Douglases do you know?"

She still sounded like my teacher, which she had been way back when. Mrs. Ishman was a good-looking woman, stern and gray, and today she was dressed more or less normally. Her blue skirt hung nearly to the sidewalk, and I was suddenly imagining a growth on her leg—the way things just pop into your mind like that. I'd been working on obituaries all afternoon—Libby Wingart, 103, slipped on a loose shingle repairing the roof of her chicken coop—but my heart hadn't been in it. All I could think about was Jenny's leg. Jenny's eighteen. Peggy said the thing was hot to the touch.

I looked at my watch. "He's not down at the studio?"

"No," she said. "It's closed." I didn't find that so odd. I figured he was just doing something a little wild and crazy (for him), taking a day off just for the hell of it. Spring fever maybe. What was odd was Mrs. Ishman on Main Street in the first place. She didn't mingle all that

101

much. Even odder was her smile: a quick little twist of her red lips that sent a glitter across her eyes, gone again just as fast. Every time I saw it, it took me back thirty years to trigonometry class, where she'd taught us, Bruner and me.

"Maybe he's just playing hooky," I said.

"Douglas? I don't think so."

"I don't know. He seems a little middle-aged crazy lately."

"You have no idea."

"I don't?"

"I tried to call him Wednesday night after you'd all left, but he wasn't home."

Wednesday evening four of us had met with Mrs. Ishman at her house, planning our thirtieth high school reunion; she was our class advisor. I wondered why she'd tried to call him, but I didn't ask. "Was he around yesterday?"

Mrs. Ishman thought for a moment. "I don't believe so."

Marvin Eshbaugh came out of the Western Auto, three doors down, just past Sandt's Drugs. He'd been two years behind us in high school and had worked in the Western Auto ever since. His jeans were too tight—he thought he was still as skinny as he had been back in school—and he was carrying a brown paper bag.

"Hey, Marvin."

"Hey Buster," he said. "Mrs. Ishman?"

"You seen Bruner around the last couple of days?" I said.

"Lemme think." Marvin gazed intently at the Court House dome, scratching his scraggly goatee. "Nope."

"Strange," I said.

"Not really," said Marvin. "I probably ain't seen him in two years."

Marvin grinned. Mrs. Ishman said, "Marvin, go to the office." Then she was gone. We watched her cross Main, heedless of the traffic, which was heavy, vintage Friday afternoon, three pickups for every car. Marvin said, "You got twenty-two cents I can borrow, Buster?"

I didn't ask. I handed him a quarter. Marvin fished in his pocket, handed me three pennies, thanked me, and walked away. I nodded at

Milo Shreckengost who was looking bored while his wife, Gussie, window-shopped at Crooks Ladies Apparel. I'd taken two steps in the direction of Bruner's photography studio when it felt like somebody whacked me in the back with a baseball bat.

My back is a thing of mystery. About once a year it decides to go out on me, no matter how religiously I've been doing my stretches, no matter what my weight is—it's fluctuated considerably over the years, though generally on an upward trend—and no matter the circumstances. Sometimes I give it good cause, like twenty years ago moving an old iron stove up the cellar steps, but other times I can be completely innocent. Like crossing my legs at my desk—or walking down Main Street. You just never know.

I baby-stepped into the house, sweating despite the fact that it was only forty-five degrees out. Peggy looked up from her sewing machine. "Haven't been doing your sit-ups, have you?"

"Neither have I," I said. Grabbing a package of frozen peas from the freezer—I keep meaning to get an ice pack—I hobbled into the TV room, lowering myself to the edge of the sofa, then onto my nest of afghans and pillows on the floor, where I sleep.

Peggy followed as far as the doorway. "You could give me a hand," I said.

She applauded. "Maybe you should call the doctor." She says that every time.

"Why?" I slipped the peas behind me. "He'll just tell me I threw my back out." I say that every time. The doctor told me ice for the first twenty-four hours, then heat. I thought of Jenny's leg, of the heat in that.

"Maybe he'll give you something for it."

"I have some muscle relaxers. Would you get them for me? In the shoe box on top of the refrigerator."

She hesitated, arms crossed, just long enough to let me know she wasn't at my beck and call. "I don't see them," she called from the kitchen.

"In Jenny's old antibiotic bottle," I called back. "Did you hear anything else? Did you talk to her again?"

"No. Not since this morning. They won't have the results for a couple days."

She came back in, handed me the bottle. "Thanks," I said. Did she think they were chewable? "Could you get me some water?"

"Anything else?" she said with an edge.

"I can't take them without water." When she brought me the water, I asked her to hand me the remote. It was only over on the end table, but it might as well have been across town. I figured I'd better preface my next request. "Bruner seems to be missing. Nobody's seen him in a couple days." I thought I was being overly dramatic at the time, but it was for a good cause.

"Dougie? How do you know?"

I told her. That was good for the phone, the phone book, a pencil and paper, an extra pillow. "Buster, I have to finish Margie's dress in time for Easter." Margie's our niece. "Anything else?"

I thought for a second. "How about a hand job?"

"Help yourself," she said, leaving. We hadn't had sex in probably two or three months. At least not with each other.

I'd managed to hobble on down to Bruner's place, which had indeed been closed, not that I'd doubted Mrs. Ishman. It had been closed yesterday, too, according to John Mertz, who runs the print shop next door. I called Bruner's sister Marcia, then his next door neighbor up on Thompson Street who hadn't noticed Bruner's car the last day or two, then Judy Cable and Ron Allshouse, who'd been at the reunion meeting with us. I tried Donnie Reinsel, who gave him banjo lessons, but I couldn't get a hold of him. No one had talked to Bruner since Wednesday, and he hadn't mentioned any travel plans to anybody.

I called the Hartsgrove Police, the Paine County Sheriff, the State Police, and the Hartsgrove Hospital. Nothing. No reports about Bruner, no unidentified charred corpses. "What's for supper?" I called.

After a second, Peggy yelled, "Peas!"

My stomach had been hollow all day anyhow, thinking about Jenny, and I'd meant to drive down to the Quik Stop and grab a couple of hot dogs to tide me over till supper, but Mrs. Ishman and my back had waylaid me. I went over every detail of the Wednesday night meeting, trying to recall exactly what Bruner had said, how he'd said it, how he'd acted, but all I could come up with was normal. His mood had seemed light enough, he'd been full of quips, the usual banter—nothing to suggest anything wrong. I was wondering if my back was ready for another move yet—the first twenty minutes of ice was about up—when Peggy came in.

The first thing I noticed was the two meatloaf sandwiches stacked on a plate, and the bottle of Miller High Life—I'm a fool for meatloaf sandwiches. Then I saw she was wearing a little nightie, no underwear, and a look on her face halfway between sheepish and wanton. Her nipples were hard as candy kisses.

You just never know.

I fell asleep. Muscle relaxers, orgasms, full stomachs, a couple of beers will do that to me. I woke up around four a.m., alone. I mean alone. You're always alone, when you stop and think about it, even with somebody else, locked inside your own skull with your own babbling brain, your own tightly wrapped little self. But daytime, other people, all the distractions, tend to minimize it; the middle of the night magnifies it. That's why God invented sleep.

Still, there are different kinds of alone at four a.m., too. There's the kind you don't even notice, like after a bellyful of beer at the club, or maybe a road trip up from a late Pirates game. Then there's the opposite kind, like when you're just getting up, maybe to do your chores on the farm, like I did for years when I was a kid. And this kind, when you feel empty and scared and wish to God you could go back to sleep because you don't want to be alone with nothing but black mysteries like cancer and missing friends.

Clicking off the TV, I stood gingerly, jamming my feet into my shoes, leaving them untied. My cane was in the corner behind the sprung recliner. Hobbling out to the kitchen, I glanced up the stairs; no sign of

Peggy, only dark and quiet. Our sleeping arrangements have nothing to do with the rarity of sex—I was still mystified by the meatloaf rendez-vous—but with my bad back; I need something firm, she prefers soft, very soft. I like to keep the TV on all night, she likes it dark and quiet. There's probably a hundred other things. It's evolution: All the different little reasons get all snarled up till you never know just how or why you end up exactly where you do. You're just there, and you take the mystery of it for granted.

The kitchen was faintly lit by the streetlight through the window. I took two aspirins, two more muscle relaxers, found my back brace on top of the medicine cabinet in the little downstairs bathroom, ate a to-mato standing over the sink. Putting on my coat, I tapped my cane like a blind man out the back door, across the patio in the chilly night air to my car.

Bruner lived on the highest hill in town, not far from the hospital. His car was gone. Across the way, the far hillside was black, invisible, mapped by random spots of white light, a poor imitation of the sky. Orion was low, just above the horizon where the red light pulsed from the top of the water tower over past Longview Hill.

I thought of mornings when I was a kid, heading out to the barn for my chores. In winter and spring, I tracked Orion—I didn't know the name of it then—sinking toward the horizon, and on warmer spring mornings, like this one, I'd stop to take it in. At the time—I was maybe ten—I thought no one else on earth had ever noticed the peculiar for-mation of those stars, and I can remember getting goose bumps as I had the oddest feeling that someone was about to whisper a great secret in my ear.

The door was unlocked. "Doug? Bruner?" Nothing.

It was a small house with a large, enclosed porch, a wall of win-dows. There were no curtains, and the streetlight outside by the hedge gave me plenty of light. The hardwood floor of the living room was scattered with little rugs like pools of black; bookcases took up two walls. A table and desk formed an L, a computer on the table next to a little lamp with a green glass shade. I turned it on. There were pictures on the walls, old prints of Hartsgrove scenes, and a corkboard with snapshots, a calendar, notes and notices tacked to it. I checked those out first: a doctor's appointment Thursday, "Fiddler on the Roof" at the high school on the twenty-ninth, bill due dates, meter readings; ordinary, everyday notes. I lifted April and looked at May. He'd circled the fifteenth, the date we were going to the John Prine concert in Pittsburgh.

One of the snapshots on the corkboard caught my eye. I tilted the lamp for a closer look, a chill crossing my back. It was a picture, maybe ten years old, of Bruner and Mrs. Ishman. They were standing in front of a fence and a tree. In the background was a lake. I tried to read the pose. Leaning shoulder to shoulder, heads close, they were in a no-man's land between intimacy and companionship. It could be read from either direction: intimates moving apart for the pose, or companions coming together. Either way was puzzling.

It occurred to me he was a stranger.

Who was he? He wasn't from around here. He'd moved up with his family from Maryland when he was a sophomore in high school and had trouble fitting in at first. He was tall, soft, freckled and clumsy. He had a big nose and defenseless eyes, long lashes and pale hair that seemed too insubstantial for a head so large. But he was smart. By his junior year he was editor of the school newspaper, the *Beacon*, and a damned good one, despite a few lapses we never let him live down: One time he edited one of Plotner's stories—James Plotner, another one of our buddies, was his sports editor—changing "three-yard line" to "third-yard line."

His father, a manager at Sylvania, had died not long after the Hartsgrove plant closed—cancer. When Bruner and his sister were away at college, his mother moved back to Maryland. But after teaching history for twenty-five years at Penn State—where Jenny is now, and one of the reasons why—Bruner came back to Hartsgrove, even though his mother is still living, in Maryland. He'd become an avid photographer over the years, and when Myron Knapp died and his photography business came up for sale, Bruner thought it was too good to pass up. Knapp's

father and grandfather had run the place before him, and it was a trea-
sure trove of local history—history and photography, two of Bruner's
main interests. Probably what we had most in common, besides school,
was our interest in the history of the area. I was just about the only one
still around; most of our other friends have scattered.

That's the nature of Hartsgrove. Usually the farmers and blue collar kids stay put, while the ones who go away to college stay away. For
the last three-quarters of a century, since the last of the local fortunes
was made in gas or timber, Hartsgrove has been the victim of a brain
drain. That's why there's not a single fern bar in town.

Headlights flashed through the room, a car pulling in beside mine.
I went to the porch. A cop got out of his cruiser, started toward the
house—I recognized the waddle of Officer Deemer. He flashed his light
on me through the window. I waved.

Inside, he said, "Jesus, Clover, you'd make a lousy cat burglar."

"So would I," I said.

"What are you doing up here?"

"Wanted to see if Bruner was home."

"Ain't you the one reported him missing?"

"Not exactly."

"So where's he at?"

"Still missing," I said.

Mrs. Ishman lives in a little log house on the side of a hill three miles
south of town on Black Road. Black, not coincidentally, is her maiden
name. On the hills and hollows beyond her place are several ramshack-
le farms belonging to various Blacks and their relations, mostly Coni-
fers and Shugars. Mrs. Ishman's great-great-great-grandfather, Isaac
Black, cleared the original farm around 1810.

Orion had sunk behind the hill, and the sky was getting blue in the
east. Despite the early hour, it didn't surprise me to see the light in her
kitchen. It wouldn't have surprised me to see Bruner's car in her driveway for that matter, but I didn't. That didn't surprise me either. Nothing was surprising all of a sudden, because nothing was predictable.

She opened the back door, the kitchen door, before I knocked. "Russell?"

"I thought you might be up."

She pulled her purple robe tighter across her front. "I can't ask you in. I'm not dressed."

"Neither am I," I said, then felt stupid.

"Have you heard something about Douglas?" She ignored the cane I was leaning on as pathetically as I could.

"No. I was just up at his place. Looks like he hasn't been there in a day or two."

"Then why are you here?" Mrs. Ishman wore her brusqueness like a new Easter hat. She could gut a deer, but Lord help the farm boy who'd come into her class wearing a shoe tainted by manure from his morning chores.

I told her I wondered if she'd heard anything else about Bruner (she hadn't), then asked her about the snapshot, told her I was curious, and I thought for a moment I was back in class and had asked a stupid question. In the back of my mind, I realized how silly it was for a man going on fifty to be withered by his teacher's glare, but there was nothing much I could do about it.

Nothing but hobble back out to my car after she'd shut the door in my face.

Night was melting down around the shapes of the hills and trees. I'd have to get my coffee at home. I was more curious than ever about the snapshot, even though I realized it probably had nothing to do with Bruner's whereabouts. It just pisses me off when I don't know something.

Four blocks down from my place, I passed the Darius Litch House, just across the street from the Pub Bar. I've always appreciated the irony of two of the town's most venerable institutions—an old nursing home and a seedy bar—sitting in a staring contest all these years, but they've coexisted, in one form or another, ever since the town went wet again after prohibition. Peggy's Uncle Roy is one of the residents of the Darius Litch House, as is Alton Ishman, Mrs. Ishman's husband. He spends most of his time wandering the halls—I see him there when I go with Peggy to visit Uncle Roy—repeating nonsense syllables in a sort of a chant: *nun, nun, nun, nun* . . . He doesn't recognize anyone. He was a good singer in his day, a member of a barbershop quartet that sang at church suppers and club benefits. Then along came Alzheimer's. I wonder if, in what's left of his mind, he's still singing.

At home, I started a pot of coffee and took the package of peas from the freezer. I stopped short in the doorway of the TV room beside the ironing board. Peggy was curled up in my nest on the floor. I tiptoed back out to the kitchen.

What did she want? A cuddle? My back and my brain were in no condition for cuddling. Cuddling, if necessary at all, should take place immediately after sex, not twelve hours later. Then again she might have wanted something more—like a conversation. Even worse.

I snuck out. I was easing the door shut so I wouldn't wake her, then figured what the hell, and let it close. Five hundred years from now, who was going to know the difference?

That was one of our running punch lines. Bruner, Plotner and I, and some of the other guys we hung around with, like to keep a good gag going for decades. Say for example I might have a few beers and get serious; I might confide that I couldn't remember who I was when I got married, that my life twenty-five years ago couldn't be any more remote than if it had been someone else's. And say I went on, wondering if it isn't supposed to be better, if there isn't supposed to be more—that's about the time I'd hear, "Five hundred years from now, who's going to know the difference?" It didn't pay to get too serious.

Of course, if I'd gotten even grimmer, maybe wondering what life's all about, then they might use a different running punch line, one reserved for especially ponderous occasions. We stole it from an old *Peanuts* comic strip back in high school, the one where Charlie Brown pours his heart out to Lucy for three panels before Lucy, staring off into space, says, "You know, we've had spaghetti three times at our house this month."

The idea of Bruner and Mrs. Ishman an item seemed so absurd to me, I doubted that could have been her inference, the reason for her brusqueness. Plotner's parents still live in town, and when he comes back every couple of months to visit, we go out for a beer. One of the questions he always asked me—another one of our running punch lines—was whether or not our buddy Bruner had come out of the closet yet. No one's ever seen him with a date.

Of course that includes males as well as females, so we didn't assume he was gay. If anything, we assumed he was asexual. In high school we hung out at Les's, a dilapidated joint down by Potters Creek bridge. It was Lester Chitester who'd introduced pizza to Hartsgrove, and every night the place was packed with kids who flocked there every night because the place was packed with kids. It was dingy, sparsely furnished with battered benches, crates and chairs, the Pepsi was ice-cold, the pizza hot and cheesy, the jukebox loud, and the hormones rampant. We watched Linda Pence dancing in the din one night. Never mind that she's since gained a hundred pounds, her ass was absolutely magnificent then. I commented worshipfully on that fact to Bruner, who noted with his wry grin, "Yeah, but think of what comes out of it."

I couldn't imagine Bruner in the act of sex with anyone, male or female, himself included. I'd seen him attempt dodge ball in gym class. He was graceless, a non-physical person. He was a mind, not a body.

Going down the rickety steps to the basement apartment on Mabon Street where Donnie Reinsel lives, I remembered Doodle O'Hanlon had lived there once upon a time, a decade or two ago. Odd how history keeps walking through this town, everywhere you go. O'Hanlon was an old rummy with a good heart that quit on him one Christmas Eve. He gave away his prized possession, went up to the jailhouse and died. His prized possession was Molly, his old cat, and he'd given her to Jenny.

I remembered all this in the time it took to hobble down the steps: the look on Jenny's face that morning when she woke up and found

Molly beside her in her bed, the other Christmas gifts that delighted her, the Barbie dolls, the long slender legs of the Barbies, like Jenny's little legs when I used to wash them in the tub, slippery, muscular, perfect little legs. Perfect: cystless, tumorless, cancerless, every molecule exactly where it should be, exactly what it should be.

I figured I'd be waking Reinsel up, but I was wrong. His brown, glossy eyes were like little mirrors. "Buster?" He wore an unaccountable grin. He also wore his battered old cowboy hat, scuffed old cowboy boots, and a silly yellow bathrobe in between.

"Did I get you up?"

"Just got in," he said, still grinning. "Ain't been to bed yet." I never know how to take his grinning spells, which might come from stupidity, booze, drugs, friendliness, or all of the above.

So I grinned back. "Got a minute?"

"Shit, take a load off." He noticed my hobble and cane. "Got a hitch in your git-along."

I told him about my back. He commiserated, sprawling obscenely on the sofa, a yellow-green plaid thing with wooden arms. I picked the straightest, hardest-looking chair. The little room was bright with the morning light through the bare window and stank of stale cigarette smoke. He didn't seem too concerned about Bruner.

"Probably out somewheres getting laid," he said.

"Bruner?"

"Sure. Probably shacked up somewheres with one of them cute little coeds he's always telling me about."

"*Doug* Bruner?"

"How many other Bruners do you know?"

"Yeah, but Bruner doesn't strike me as much of a . . . "

"A cunt hound?"

"I was going to say a ladies' man."

"Hell, don't let ol' Doug fool you. He likes to eat pussy as much as the next man."

"Bruner?" Reinsel was obviously drunk or high or both, maybe permanently. He was ten years younger than us, but looked older; he'd been ridden real hard. I panned for facts: He hadn't seen Bruner since Sunday, when he'd given him a two-hour banjo lesson up at his place. Bruner hadn't been acting any differently. He hadn't mentioned any travel plans, except for the John Prine concert next month.

"Listen," Reinsel said, "if he don't show up by then, can I have his ticket? I'd love to catch that dude in concert."

Reinsel being Reinsel, I ignored the insensitivity of the question. I started to tell him there were probably tickets still available, I could check into it, but when I looked up he was passed out, head back, mouth open, snores billowing forth.

The Rod and Gun Club—aka the God and Run Club—serves breakfast on Saturday and Sunday mornings, but not until nine. I still had an hour to kill. At the Quik Stop, I picked up a coffee and a couple of egg and cheese muffins to tide me over, and headed out toward Coolbrook, where the old farm used to be.

The Coolbrook Road rolls over and around the hills, two lanes of plain blacktop full of swerves, curves, dips, waves, and wrinkles. At one time it had been a trail through the forest, then dirt wagon tracks between freshly cleared farms, gradually growing wider and muddier as the farms grew in size and number. In the thirties, Governor Pinchot promised to get the farmers out of the mud and covered it and a thousand others like it with gravel. Plotner's grandfather was on the crew that blacktopped it back in the forties. Plotner and I had hitchhiked this seven-mile stretch a hundred times when we were kids going to Little League practice in Hartsgrove, and we'd probably smacked every road sign on it with a rock. Where the road crests a hill about two miles out of town, you can see the hospital and, just below it, the steeple of the Catholic Church above the trees; they look about an inch apart.

Mrs. Ishman seldom smiled. In the snapshot with Bruner, she's wearing a smile of sorts, a pleasant, companionable expression beside Bruner's goofy grin. As I was rounding the Halfway Turn out by Nosker's farm, her other smile came back to me, the one I saw, or thought I saw, on Main Street yesterday when she told me Bruner was missing.

The trigonometry class smile: Standing in the classroom by the cast-iron radiator, a splash of sunlight on the blackboard behind her, she's wearing a flowery blue dress, which the frames of her glasses match perfectly (she had interchangeable plastic frames to match her outfits), and on her face, just a twist of her lips, bemused, almost cruel. She'd just asked a question, maybe about the properties of sines and cosines, an advanced question. It was the way she always smiled when she asked a question that no one could answer.

I cruised by our old farm—the barn tumbled down, the house bleak and abandoned, the yard overgrown with weeds. I passed the old schoolhouse a mile down the road—now the Coolbrook Social Center—and took a left out toward Weed Run, to circle back toward Hartsgrove. I've heard of runner's highs, though I've never experienced one, having successfully avoided jogging all my life. This was a driver's high, caused by the easy cruise and the clarity of the sunny dawn, the depth of my focus, the width of the countryside and the memories. I felt hypnotized, detached, balanced on the rim of the moment. I felt as though at any second I would be able to plunge my hands into cool, dark secrets, and drink my fill.

Midway between Coolbrook and Weed Run, the road curls down a steep hillside through the woods to the old iron bridge over Muddy Bottom Creek. On either side of the bridge, the shoulder of the road widens. No one was parked there now, but in a few days when trout season opened, half a dozen cars would be, fishermen in floppy hats and waders making their way up and down the banks of the creek. I pulled over, got out to stretch my back.

Why the creek is called Muddy Bottom is a mystery. It's clear as iced tea, the bottom mostly rocks. I have my own theory: Where the bridge passes over it, the creek is wide, the bed sandy, shallow enough to be easily forded. My guess is that in the old days before the bridge was built, travelers in wagons and on horseback made a muddy mess of it, and "muddy bottom" originally referred to the crossing—to the road itself—not to the creek.

I took a pleasant piss off the bridge into the water, rapid and high from the spring thaw. Along the banks and beyond, streaks of snow striped the floor of the forest where the sunlight seldom reached. Standing in shadows, I watched the dawn reaching down toward me, the bare trees across the top of the far hillside silver in the morning sun. I was still high. I got back into my car, headed toward Weed Run.

At our twentieth reunion ten years ago, we'd decided to go tubing the next day, from Hartsgrove down to Bethel on the Red Bank Creek. We'd done it a few times in high school. It seemed like an excellent idea at the time, in the loud, smoky lounge of the Holiday Inn, when we were all drunk. We tried to talk Bruner into it. "C'mon," I said, "it'll be *fun*."

Bruner said, "Isn't that what they told the Christians to lure them into the Coliseum?"

"I can almost guarantee there'll be no lions."

"It isn't lions I'm afraid of. It's raw sewage."

Plotner said, "What's a few turds among friends?" which for some reason struck us as quite hilarious at the time.

"You're right," Bruner said. "I number quite a few turds among my friends."

We kept at it, but Bruner wouldn't budge, which didn't surprise me. I doubted he owned a swimming suit. The idea didn't seem quite as excellent the next morning, but we went anyway, six of us; after a few hairs of the dog, it wasn't so bad. Floating downstream, I'd imagined what it must have been like a century before when the creek was a public thoroughfare—so designated by the state legislature—and logs were rafted down it every spring to the Allegheny River, then on to Pittsburgh. For over a hundred years, lumbering was Hartsgrove's heartbeat. The history books say that most of the sawmills closed down around 1910 because the timber was gone. It's back now.

We'd left three cars in Bethel, and I ended up driving back alone. Dazed by sun and beer and suddenly sentimental, I pulled over where the road veered close to the creek about halfway back to Hartsgrove. My old classmates were scattering back to their homes far away, but I was feeling just as nostalgic for the old rafters and lumbermen of another era, some of whose descendants undoubtedly were at the reunion. Rafting had been a dangerous profession, a splash of adventure across the past of a place best known for its brawn, not its brains. Standing on a bank overlooking the creek, I tried to picture the hearty, rough-hewn men with bearded faces, steely eyes, callused hands, riding their unruly cargo down the raging stream. At that particular moment, Bruner came bobbing placidly around the bend.

He was wearing peach-colored bermuda shorts and a long-sleeved white shirt with a button-down collar as he floated toward me on an inner tube. He had on a floppy blue hat, sunglasses and a glob of white on his big nose. Sunlight glittered off the water. As he drifted closer, I noticed everything was not quite as placid as it seemed: His toes gripped his flip-flops as rigidly as his fingers indented the sides of the tube, and his jaw was clenched. It occurred to me he didn't know how to swim.

He hadn't noticed me standing in the trees. When he was just a few yards away, I said, "Bruner! Nice day for tubing, eh?"

I still believe I saw air between him and the tube. Rocking, he spun slowly around, ripples widening away. A few yards downstream, when he was turned toward me again, he grinned. "Raise the drawbridge!" he said in a meek shout, and floated away, still spinning slowly.

Just before Weed Run, I took the left back toward Hartsgrove. I was on automatic pilot, cruising with a sense of urgency, heartbeat pulsing in my elbows. I felt prickles in my legs, points of heat. A cosmic thread materialized between Jenny and Bruner; I was certain he was fine, that he was visiting his mother, maybe a museum in Pittsburgh, maybe even out getting laid, and that if indeed he was fine, then Jenny would be fine too. By the same token, if the growth in her leg was benign, if she was all right, then he would be too.

The prickles in my legs and the memory of Bruner bobbing on glittering water in peach-colored shorts contained everything I needed to know—if only I could decipher it. I held the image, the sensations, like a kid holding a soap bubble on the tips of his fingers, eagerly searching the shimmering mystery, knowing that at any instant it would pop, unable to bear the weight of itself.

Somewhere between Broadacres Farm where the barn by the road says *Chew Mail Pouch Tobacco—Treat Yourself To The Best* and burnt eggs at the God and Run Club, the bubble burst. Nothing had been revealed.

Six hours later, Meryl Fenstemaker followed my route, driving from his place near Coolbrook over to his brother Melvin's just north of Weed Run. I found this out the next day. He noticed a little red Ford Escort parked by Muddy Bottom Bridge when he went by, thinking nothing of it. He and his brother worked on Melvin's John Deere all afternoon, replacing the rings, a big job. Melvin's wife cooked them up a mess of spare ribs afterwards, and they sat around the woodstove talking for quite a while over coffee and blueberry pie. Meryl didn't head home till after ten. When he noticed the Escort still parked by the bridge, it didn't seem quite right; he decided to call the sheriff. The car turned out to be Bruner's.

There were no signs of foul play. Boy Scouts, firemen and other volunteers searched the area, but couldn't find a clue. There are miles and miles of woods up north of Hartsgrove, some of it pretty rugged, and Muddy Bottom Creek runs right through the heart of it. About fifty years ago, two little girls—old Luke McCracken's daughters—went berrying in the woods up near there, and were never seen again.

Bruner was seen again. Wilber Bish—who said he was out for a walk, but who was probably poaching trout—found his body about five miles upstream on Tuesday.

The news spread like a cloud of gas. By Friday afternoon, I'd heard a dozen different rumors. Bruner had slipped on a rock, bumped his head and drowned; there were several variations of this, the "clumsy" theory. He'd simply gotten lost in the woods and died of exposure was one. Heart attack was another. Suicide, however, was the consensus: by pills, by exposure, by razor, by a plastic bag over his head. No one suggested gunshot. He'd committed suicide because he'd been despondent over a girlfriend leaving him, a boyfriend leaving him, the impending bankruptcy of his business, illegal shenanigans from his Penn State past about to be revealed—blackmail.

Marvin Eshbaugh had his own theory when I bumped into him on Main Street Friday afternoon. My back was feeling better by now, almost as good as it was a week before when I'd talked to him and Mrs. Ishman on that very spot.

"I figure he found out he had AIDS and just decided to go up in them woods and lay down and die," Marvin said.

"We'll probably never know."

"Why not? Ain't they doing an autopsy?"

"No," I said. "They're not."

"I thought they had to."

"Apparently they don't. No reason to suspect foul play, and his mother refused to authorize one."

"His mother? I didn't even know he had a mother."

"She's in Maryland. She's going to bury him there. She had him cremated."

"Without an autopsy? She can't do that." Marvin's eyes and goatee were elongated indignantly.

"She already did."

"There oughta be a law."

"No signs of foul play. I talked to the sheriff, and I talked to Bish. Bish found him."

"I know," Marvin said. "That crazy old loon. He probably conked him on the head for his money."

"His money was still on him. Will said he was all laid out on his back with his hands crossed over his belly, like he was just taking a nap." I didn't tell Marvin the rest of what Will Bish had told me. He told me Bruner wasn't wearing anything but his boxer shorts. The rest of his clothes were neatly folded in a pile on top of his shoes under a nearby tree. I'm sure he'd wanted to be naked for whatever job he had to do, but just couldn't quite bring himself to go all the way.

■ ■ ■

The Darius Litch House is a mansion originally built in 1878 by Darius Litch, who owned the biggest sawmill in town, up on Potters Creek where the dam is now. After Litch died, the place was a hotel for quite a few years before it became an old folks' home when the county went dry in 1916. All the original, fancy woodwork's still there, and the ceiling in Uncle Roy's room must be twelve feet high, the drafty old windows taller than a man.

Uncle Roy has a headful of dry, spotted skin. He asked me—for the fourth time in twenty minutes—if I'd known that Bruner fellow. "No," I said, "neither did I."

Peggy glared at me. The first three times I'd told him yes, I'd gone to school with him. "Musta been about your age," Uncle Roy said.

"Oh yeah," I said. "I went to school with him."

"Went to school with who?" Uncle Roy said.

Peggy was annoyed. It hadn't been a good week. Tuesday, when the news came in about Bruner, I'd gone straight to the club from the office, and had come home around midnight to find the dining room table still set, candles, her best china, a bottle of wine, a cold roast on a platter smelling like grease. She'd had good news from Jenny; the tests were negative. She hadn't heard about Bruner.

I gave Uncle Roy a kiss on his dry, spotted head, and told Peggy I'd meet her in the parking lot. In the hallway Alton Ishman was twitching his hand down the wall, chanting, "Nun, nun, nun, nun."

"Mr. Ishman?" I said, sticking my face in his. "How you doing?"

His eyes were vacant, evasive. "Nun, nun, nun, nun," he said.

Waiting in the car, I watched the Pub Bar across the street; business was booming. I decided against walking over for a beer. It was about time for the Friday night fights.

I thought about the last conversation I'd had with Bruner alone. It had been in this car. I'd given him a lift to the first reunion meeting at Mrs. Ishman's in January. He didn't like driving in the snow, and we'd had a couple inches that day. Afterwards, he'd invited me in to shoot the shit, and I'd asked if he had any beer. No, but he had some sherry. I passed.

It had been a black night. We watched the red light pulsing on top of the water tower over past Longview. Bruner asked me if I'd ever heard that we—humans, he meant—use only a very small percentage of our brains.

"Why, yes," I said. "Especially in your case."

He went on, ignoring me. Every single experience he'd ever had was still in his brain, he theorized; the memory was not lost, only the ability to access it. He wondered what else might be in there, inaccessible. What, exactly, is transmitted in the chemicals that make up semen and egg? He speculated that God might have somehow imbued us with His spirit—the soul—and that it had been transmitted down through all the millennia with every single act of reproduction. And wouldn't it contain all the answers, the reasons for existence, the secrets of the universe? In other words, we might hold everything there is to know. If only we could *reach* it.

He paused, and I looked over at the big nose of his silhouette, his long lashes blinking as he studied the pulsing light beyond the edge of town. I said, "You know, we've had spaghetti three times at our house this month."

Across the street a ruckus broke out. Two men were locked in combat in the parking lot of the Pub Bar, the crowd pouring out behind them, cheering. One of the combatants was flabby and shirtless, the other skinny and quick. The crowd surrounded them and I couldn't see a thing, and I was debating whether or not to stroll on over for a closer look when a rap on my window made me jump. Mrs. Ishman was standing beside the car. She looked sterner and grayer than usual, her lips redder, her coat long and somber.

I rolled down the window. "The picture you asked about," she said. "It was taken in June of 1987, in Saratoga Springs, New York. Douglas and I had just won the ACBL bridge tournament there. We were both quite happy and proud of ourselves."

"Bridge tournament? I didn't even know he played bridge."

"Then you really didn't know him all that well, did you?"

"How long have you and him been playing bridge?"

"How long have he and I been playing bridge?" she said. "Since Alton became unable, which has been what? Over ten years now. Of course his skills were declining a good while longer than that. Douglas was a wonderful partner—he got such a kick out of calling me the dummy. I think that was the only reason he liked to play with me in the first place."

"And you went to tournaments."

She nodded. Almost wistfully, I thought, if such a word could ever apply to Mrs. Ishman. "They were delightful getaways. How I looked forward to them."

For a moment, the sky opened. It was a revelation, a mystery solved, with all the attendant relief. Then, just as quickly—this all took about a tenth of a second—the clouds were back. *Nothing* had been revealed. I said, "Why do you suppose he did it?"

"I have no idea, but he's proven to be a great disappointment to me. I believe it was a very selfish, weak, inconsiderate act. The act of a coward."

"Don't you think he was just . . . I don't know, tired? Lonely?"

"Douglas doesn't—didn't—know the meaning of the word *loneliness*."

"Isn't that a little harsh?"

She gave me the schoolteacher look. "The two particular options we're discussing here, Russell—understanding and unforgiving—are not mutually exclusive."

She turned to go. "Wait," I said. "Can you sit down for a minute? Can we talk?" I thought I was back in class again, and had asked a stupid question again. I said, "Where were the other bridge tournaments? Did you play in Hartsgrove too? Did you . . . *socialize* a lot, beyond bridge, I mean?"

She leaned close, her red lips twisting into that smile that glittered for an instant across her eyes. Then she said, "Five hundred years from now, who will know the difference?"

I watched her walk away, watched the Darius Litch House swallow her whole.

You just never know.

PART THREE

■   ■   ■

Strauss the Butcher

Strauss stations his kids strategically around the perimeter of the house to alert him in case Dottie, his mother, tries to escape. His wife, Sally, dubious, waits in the car. He positions Angie, eight, at the corner of the garage by the sprawling rhododendron that's beginning to blossom purple. Aaron, ten, he places by the big maple in back where Billy's swing used to be. Then, for the first time in a long time he notices the rope, buried in the limb where he tied it fifteen years ago when he put the swing there for Billy, his brother, to play on. Billy was only three then, twenty years younger than Strauss, and he didn't have a dad to put up a swing for him. Now the rope's choking the limb. He tried to get it off one time, but it's in too deep. Now the rope says, *Look what's happened to Billy! Look what's happened to Billy!*

Aaron isn't listening. Air rifle at the ready, he says, "Want me to pick her off if she tries to get away?"

"Very funny, wise guy."

Angie says, "What am I supposed to do if she comes out this way?"

Strauss says, "When in danger, when in doubt, run in circles, scream and shout."

"Very funny, wise guy," Angie says.

The house is small, in need of paint and repair, on the south side of Hartsgrove near the woods, and Strauss enters it like a visitor to a museum. It's the house where he grew up, filled with the artifacts of another era: the patch on the wall near the baseboard where his father kicked a hole before he found better ways of coping, such as leaving; the ironing board by the yellowed curtains of the window; the heaps of magazines, mail, newspapers, sweaters, coats, cushions, blankets, laundry, whatever his mother hasn't put away, which is nearly everything. And Aunt Carol high on the shelf. Though she died before he was born—barely—he's lived with his Aunt Carol all his life. Now he's more than twice as old as she was then. Her picture's on the walnut bookcase, occupying a place of honor, cleared of clutter, no knickknacks, dolphin figurines, pink Beanie Babies, no other pictures or books within a certain, sacred radius. For years it sat on a doily on the television, back when the television was a piece of furniture instead of a plastic box. It's Aunt Carol's high school picture, her senior portrait, black and white, taken the year she was killed, the same year Dottie was married and Strauss was born. She was the baby of the family, the darling, pretty, smart, popular. She was murdered, the story goes, by a janitor who worked at the school.

Dottie's locked herself in the bedroom. Strauss uses his MasterCard to lift the hook, about the only thing he ever uses it for. She's sitting on the bed in gray sweats, her eyes casting plastic daggers. Her skin has an uneven translucence, dark patches under her eyes, and though her hair is still blond, it's losing interest fast. She clutches the bedpost with both hands. "I told you I'm not going."

The bravest mom in the world. Strauss remembers a crisp Halloween night, he was ten, his mother standing on a chair on Pearsall's porch, stretching up to unscrew the single lightbulb, the beacon protecting Pearsall's farmhouse from mischief and mayhem, from glass-soaping, corn-peppering, toilet-papering. Halloweening was a serious Hartsgrove sport. Buddy Strauss and his best pal Marvin wait in the shadows of the woodpile in a state of high tension and adoration. As the first flung handfuls of cow's corn rattle the windows, old man Pearsall charges from the door, shotgun in hand. And they miraculously escape, Dottie driving helter-skelter over the bumpy country road, headlights off, making good their getaway. Now the bravest mom in the world clutches the bedpost with no hope of escape.

"Do you want to get cleaned up, or you do you want to go like that?" Strauss says.

"What part of 'I'm not going' don't you understand?"

"I'll carry you if I have to."

"You'll have to."

Strauss employs the fireman's carry. Dottie's put on a few pounds, but he doesn't mind; somebody has to watch out for her, and that's what broad shoulders are for. "Buddy!" she says, struggling. "Put me down. I don't *want* to go."

"Yeah, yeah," Strauss says. "Nobody wants to go to a funeral." Especially to a funeral such as this.

"Look at Daddy and Grandma!" squeals Angie in delight, pointing from the corner of the house. In the front seat of their yellow Grand Prix, Sally only rolls her eyes, shaking her head at the pair of them. Aaron runs around the house, air rifle blazing, *pow, pow, pow*. Strauss feels his mother sigh. He smiles and waves at all the rubber-necking neighbors.

Strauss and Billy were never very close, particularly not over the past few years when Billy had become a druggie, a drop-out, a delinquent. Strauss tried, but Billy kept him at arm's length, stealing from him only when necessary, when asking and begging didn't do the trick. Strauss keeps a journal listing everything Billy owes him, which he'd intended to show him someday, after Billy was grown up, mature, when they could laugh it off together. Now that'll never happen. Dottie couldn't keep the kid in line. There was no dad to do it. No one but Dottie knows who Billy's father is. She said it was nobody's business but hers, that she and Billy could get along just fine without another man.

She was wrong. Strauss went to his mother's one afternoon when he was just home from the army and found Billy, not quite three at the time, roaming the house by himself. Dottie was asleep—passed out—on her bed beside the crib from which Billy had escaped, the smell of booze on every snore. Just after noon. He sat on the couch to keep Billy company. The living room then was just as cluttered, Aunt Carol watching unperturbed from atop the TV, and right in the middle of the room was a big basket of laundry. The ironing board stood by the window where it always stood, where it stands to this day, sunlight gleaming off the iron that sat point up on its haunches, poised to topple and impale a two-year-old head. Billy wouldn't come to him. He didn't know him. Wearing only a diaper, he kept going back to the basket of laundry in the middle of the room. Every time Strauss picked him up and brought him to the couch, talking to him, pointing to pictures in the magazine, Billy got up and went back to the laundry basket. Standing on the floor, he leaned down into it, resting his head in the fresh clean sheets and towels and underwear. It must have been warm, Strauss decided, must have smelled nice. Though at the time, all he could think of was an ostrich.

As he drives across town toward the funeral home, Dottie sulks in the backseat between the kids. Angie stares out her window, Aaron out his. Nobody's looking at Grandma. Sally drums her fingers nervously, absently, on her purse. The backseat occupants might be hostages, but at least Sally is his accomplice, for which Strauss is grateful. She's a skinny woman, as tall or taller than him, depending on their shoes, her hair somewhere between blond and brown and gunmetal gray, depending on the light. She's an office manager at the glove factory, and they've always enjoyed a compatibility in plotting, but these waters, he knows, are uncharted.

Passing the South Side Market, Strauss wonders if Otto has heard about Billy yet. Then he thinks silly question. By now, there's no one in town who hasn't.

Otto Schwabenbauer is in his seventies, a crusty old German with thinning white hair and a jaw like the prow of a ship. He owns the butcher shop, the South Side Market, famous for its meats, for Otto is the only real butcher in town. He befriended Strauss years ago, when Strauss was in grade school and used to walk down to the market for free suet to feed their backyard birds in winter. Otto gave him work.

They needed the money; Dottie had left the nursing profession to become a waitress and a drinker.

Long mornings Strauss remembers, long, dark, cold mornings—he likes to remind his own kids of those mornings, no hot oatmeal made by his mother, no morning cartoons, not like kids nowadays. They were lonely mornings, Dottie's snore, a piece of dry white toast and water. Then trekking down the hill—generally through bitter cold winds, at least in his retellings—to the South Side Market, before Otto came downstairs from his apartment above the shop where he still lives to this day with his wife, Gretchen. Strauss's first chore was to sweep the floor and mop it, with soap and steaming hot water, then to scrub and disinfect the butcher block and all the cutting surfaces, even though Otto had already done so at close of business the night before. Otto was a stickler for cleanliness. Strauss loved the pungent, hot, clean smell on a cold winter morning. He would wash the glass surfaces and shelves and stock them, careful to rotate for freshness, keeping the older cans in front, the newer in the rear, then put on the coffee pot for Otto and his customers. Finally came the heavy step on the stairway and Otto, with a smile, always with energy to spare, infectious energy, and a good word to send his young charge off to school. *Cheer up*, Otto would say. *Things could always be worse. At least when you had your tonsils removed the doctor didn't mistake them for your testicles.*

After high school Otto began giving him more meaningful chores, teaching him how to sharpen his knives and blades, the rudiments of meat cutting. But Strauss was eighteen and restless. To Otto's dismay, he joined the army.

Dottie threw a going-away party for him in early June. It was the first time Otto was ever in their house, and it made Strauss uncomfortable. It didn't fit. It didn't help that Dottie seemed determined to embarrass him, dancing with his buddies, not just dancing but jitterbugging, not just jitterbugging but jitterbugging with Joey Fawcett. Strauss was vigilant, watching for the telltale smirk on Joey's pasty face, but if Joey's intent was patronization and ridicule, he never tipped his hand. Otto seemed to be having a fine time. Drinking beer from his big ceramic stein, he sat at the kitchen table close to the keg, smiling and tapping his foot in time to the music, chatting with whomever came by, which was a steady stream, given the proximity of the keg. Gretchen had stayed home; she normally did, for she'd never been inclined to learn the language, so socializing was not high on her list, which seemed to trouble neither of the Schwabenbauers a great deal. But Strauss thought he knew his mentor well, and he could see through Otto's façade to the lurking discomfort.

Otto stayed till the party was all but over and they were down to four, all sitting at the picnic table in the backyard enjoying the dubious fragrance of a smoldering mosquito coil. Joey Fawcett lingered too, infatuated with Dottie, and too drunk for discretion.

"Otto," Dottie said, cigarette flaring. "I want you to confess. What *really* goes into sausage? You can tell us your dirty little secrets, we're all friends here." Her speech was a flourish of slurs.

Joey giggled. "I can tell you about *my* sausage."

"Be quiet, Joey. I was asking Mr. Schwabenbauer a serious question." She giggled.

"My sausage?" said Otto, ignoring the double entendre. His voice boomed, accented but slurless. "Or supermarket sausage? My sausage contains nothing but good cuts. Fine, pink meats. My sausage, not like the supermarket kind that gives sausage the bad name, my sausage is no relative to my garbage can."

Strauss, nauseous, had to excuse himself. When he returned from the bathroom ten minutes later, everything was different. Joey had slithered away, and Dottie was asleep, head on her arm on the picnic table, snoring along with a chorus of crickets. Otto sat quietly watching the stars. He shrugged. "Sausage bores her."

"Sorry," Strauss said. He started to say more, but Otto put a finger to his lips and frowned, the same frown he employed when Strauss returned a knife to the wrong slot. He stood, patting Dottie's hand, then he put his arms around Strauss, the first and only time he ever embraced him. Otto was an amazingly solid presence.

"Make your mother proud," Otto said.

■ ■ ■

"Did you know there are over five thousand sausage recipes in the world?" Strauss asks no one in particular. No one in particular responds. Otto always told Strauss that if the taste of his sausage didn't dance a polka on his tongue, it wasn't good enough for his customers.

Strauss sees motion in the mirror. "Ma? What are you doing?"

In the backseat Angie says, "Grandma!" Aaron says, "Oh, gross!"

Sally turns. "Dottie? Dottie! She's taking off her clothes."

Strauss pulls over. Turns around to see Dottie blue and saggy in her underwear. "Put those back on."

"No." Her chin is up. "I told you, I'm not going."

Strauss looks at his wife, at her stricken pallor. Sally says, "Mom, you certainly have a unique method of crisis management."

"I try to think outside the box," Dottie says.

Strauss sighs. There are times when his shoulders don't seem so broad, when he feels as though he's collapsing beneath the weight of her—when he feels like shaking her, walking out, leaving her to her own childish schemes. Like now. But always he comes back to Otto. What would Otto do?

"Okay." He pulls back into the street. "Have it your way."

"What are you doing?"

"I'm thinking you'll be the life of the party in your underwear."

Just before he and Sally got married ten years ago they went to his mother's one afternoon and found Billy and his friend Dickie Kennedy sitting on the stoop. Billy was holding a baseball bat, the bat Strauss had given him for Christmas, a wooden bat. Though Strauss isn't much of a baseball fan—football is his game, the Steelers his team—he knows enough to scorn aluminum bats.

"Trying out for Little League?" Strauss considered it unlikely.

"Naw," said Dickie. He had black hair, black eyes and sloping shoulders, a head taller than little blond Billy. "We're on guard."

"Uncle Jack's paying us a dollar," Billy said, "to keep all the riff-raff away."

"*Riff-raff*?" Sally said. "Where did you hear that?"

"What does riff-raff look like?" Strauss said.

"Uncle Jack," Billy said.

"Uncle Jack looks like riff-raff?" Strauss had no idea who Uncle Jack was.

"No," Billy said impatiently, "Uncle Jack told us to keep the riff-raff away."

"How can you keep it away if you don't know what it looks like?"

"We'll know it when we see it," Dickie said.

"Riff-raff, riff-raff, riff-raff," Billy said. "Riff-raff."

"We gotta see Ma," Strauss said.

"We're not supposed to let *anybody* in," said Dickie.

"He didn't say anything about Buddy and Sally," Billy said.

Dickie glowered. "This better not cost me half a buck."

Strauss stepped past them. The door was locked. He turned and frowned toward Sally. "Ma?" he called. He knocked once. "Ma? Me and Sally have to talk to you about the wedding." Sally wanted to talk to her about the dress Dottie was planning to wear, a delicate discussion concerning cleavage in which Strauss did not plan to participate.

Sally had told him that morning, "If anyone's going to be showing any cleavage at my wedding, it's going to be me."

"But you don't have any," Strauss had pointed out.

"I'll muster some up," Sally had said, squeezing her boobs together. "I'll rise to the occasion."

Dottie appeared at the living room window, holding the curtain before her. "Can we talk later?" Her cheeks were flushed, mellow, interrupted. A man's voice grumbled, not too loudly, though Strauss thought he heard the word *dollar*.

"God damn it," said Dickie. He spat on the stoop.

Billy dropped the bat, which rolled off the step with a hollow rattle. He stared at the living room window, at the empty curtain his mother had left behind.

■ ■ ■

Strauss left Otto not long after that. When he'd come home from the army the old German had welcomed him warmly. He'd made Strauss his apprentice, to teach him his proud profession. "You become Master Butcher like me," Otto had told him, "and you will never worry for someplace to work. People will always have to eat no matter what."

Otto was like family in those days. He wrapped gifts of meat—roasts and chops and steaks and sausages—for Strauss to take home for Dottie to cook, though Strauss usually ended up preparing them himself. Sometimes Otto dropped off his gifts in person, though often as not no one was there to receive them. Every day he asked: *How is your mother? Is Dottie taking care of herself? How is Billy doing at school?*

Strauss learned much in his five years with Otto. He learned about the anatomy of a cow, a pig, a sheep and nearly every other animal in the food chain. He learned to assess the quality of meat, how to cut and debone it, the proper tools to use ("It fills me with horror," Otto said, "to see someone cut their meat with a serrated knife"), the proper position to hold the knife. He learned the tools of the trade—the bone ax, cleavers, bone saws, machines to cut, saw, crush and grind—and how to use them safely, the Kevlar gloves and aprons. He learned how to cure meats and make sausage, how different spices complemented one another, the proper way to work the meat. "Meat is the right working temperature," Otto said, "when it feels like your fingers will fall off your hands from the cold."

Late on a dark January afternoon, Strauss told him he was leaving. It hadn't been an easy decision; he was fond of the old German, grateful for all he had done for him. But the Golden Days Supermarket had expanded and was looking for a butcher, someone young and capable; it paid more than Otto paid, and the Meat Department manager, Ralph Serafini, was older than Schwabenbauer, so the chances of moving up were good. Strauss mentioned the money, his growing family; what he didn't mention was that, fond and grateful as he was, Otto and his market were becoming claustrophobic. He was twenty-eight and felt the need to move on, to explore, to leave behind Otto and his circle of regular customers, balding Mrs. Ferraro, dumpy Mrs. Battaglio, Mrs. Shingledecker and Mrs. Scheafknocker who always shopped together with their little wire cart.

Otto splayed his hands before his bloody apron. "Here you become a Master Butcher. You want to leave instead to become a mere meat-cutter? A meat-wrapper?" Strauss slumped a bit. Otto gestured toward the display cooler, his sausages, his cured meats. "To have your own place, to be the boss of yourself, to have your own customers who love what it is you make for them to eat—that is happiness. That is a good feeling no money can buy for you."

But for Strauss it was too late. He'd smelled the new car smell, and now he had to close the deal.

Otto read this on his face. "Okay. Okay. Leave if you think it is best."

"Of course I'll give you notice—is two weeks enough? I can give you more."

Otto shrugged. "You can leave tonight," he said.

They are still good friends, Strauss and Otto, but no longer apprentice and mentor, no longer confidantes. They still see each other now and then at the supermarket when Otto comes in with Gretchen to purchase his groceries, now and then at Dottie's when Otto drops off his gifts of meat, as he continues to do to this day. When Billy turned ten, Otto offered him Strauss's old job, but Billy hadn't the slightest interest and declined, declined rudely, dismissively, even after Otto called upon Strauss to intervene. It was to no avail, nor were Otto's repeated offers down the years. Strauss makes it a point to stop at the South Side Market once or twice a month to buy Otto's sausages or cured meats, to chat and reminisce. But the chatter never rambles like before; Strauss has left the nest. Otto no longer shares his secret recipes and techniques, seldom imparts his nuggets and pearls.

After ten years of Golden Days, it's the nuggets and pearls Strauss misses the most.

■   ■   ■

Midmorning and sunny, hot for May. Not a proper day for a funeral, much less for the funeral of someone so young. The viewing is at Guth's, which is overflowing, and Strauss has to park well down Jefferson. The second he stops, the kids are gone as though shot from the car. Aaron crosses the street, climbing the bank to the sidewalk as Angie wanders behind, bending to pick up a pebble. They both have black curly hair and swarthy complexions, favoring their father, not their fair-skinned, skinny mother. Sally stares through the windshield, watching her kids. Her parents, Gus and Maggie, a banker and retired receptionist, are staid and dependable, as squat and solid as their brick house with the flower boxes beneath the windows up on Cherry Street. Sometimes Strauss thinks Sally enjoys being along for the ride. Other times, like now, he's sure she'd rather be having tea and Oreos, doing crossword puzzles with her mother.

Hooking an arm on the back of the seat, he turns to face Dottie. She sits in her underwear, arms crossed, still shooting for defiance, though Strauss detects a tremble in her jaw. "Ma. Put your clothes back on. We have to go in and you know it."

"I know no such thing."

"There's a girl in there dead and Billy was involved. We have to pay our respects. It's what we have to do."

"Billy could never have done such a thing."

Strauss looks in her eyes, never breaking his gaze, until a cloud crosses her face.

"Believe me, I don't want to go in either," Sally says, "but it's the right thing to do."

Always do what is right. Another of Schwabenbauer's credos. "What about when Aunt Carol was killed?" Strauss says. "Wouldn't you have wanted the family of the man who killed her to be sorry? To show they cared?"

"I wanted them dead," Dottie says.

Four years ago Strauss went over to his mother's to help take her old refrigerator to the dump. Billy was there, still living with her then.

His blond hair was thatched and matted, unwashed, and his small, square, handsome face was dirty as well. It was before bits of his eyebrows went missing where he sometimes wears safety pins, back when his eyes still showed some depth. It was a muggy August day, and Strauss noticed the hooded skull inked on Billy's skinny bicep when he raised his arms to push. "That's not real, is it?" Strauss said, nodding toward the thing.

Billy was annoyed. "Hell, yeah."

Strauss grabbed and rubbed. "You dumb little shit. What would possess you to put something on your skin you can never get off?"

Billy said, "Ma?"

Strauss said, "Did you know he got a tattoo?"

Dottie hesitated, a silly smirk overcoming her face. "I don't think they're so bad, Buddy. Some of them can be very pretty."

Billy was laughing by then. Dottie too. "Show him yours, Ma!" Strauss looked from one to the other, shaking his head, smiling in spite of himself. Now Billy's skin is crawling with crude tattoos. Now Dottie sits in the back seat half-naked and lost in thought, stalling, light years from delight, hoping the world will go away. The butterfly and flower are blue on her shoulder, sagging and sad.

When Strauss was five his father skipped town. He sent cards, birthday and Christmas gifts for a while, but they slowed to a trickle and stopped. The image that remains in Strauss's mind is of a muscular man in a white tee shirt, surrounded by cigarette smoke. It didn't seem to trouble his mother a great deal; she blamed herself. She blamed the murder of her sister Carol, ever since which the capacity for homemaking had eluded her; *unglued* was a term she used, a fine term. It was as though gravity had lost its grip.

Before he left, his dad taught him to fish. Strauss loves fishing to this day, loves it even more than he loves the Steelers, getting away on a sunny spring afternoon—usually Tuesdays now, his day off at the Golden Days—to his trout pool near the mossy boulders in the woods a few miles up the Sandy Lick. Aaron is following in his footsteps—

even Angie is showing an interest, though she prefers soccer, an abomination of a sport in Strauss's mind, a feeling he tries to hide from her. Aaron often goes fishing by himself, at the bottom of Hartsgrove where the three creeks converge, standing along the bank with the other, older fishermen, his floppy hat and waders, his rod and reel and creel all replicas of his father's gear.

Strauss tried to teach Billy. But Billy was more interested in skipping rocks across the water, an amusement not conducive to successful angling. The last time he took him Billy was about twelve, Aaron about four.

"Dad! He's scaring the fish again!" Aaron yelled. Strauss was trying his luck upstream from the flat pool above the rocks, beside a stand of laurel. Billy said, mocking, *"Dad! He's scaring the fish again!"*

"Billy. Hey, I told you. If you don't want to fish, go downstream. Don't be throwing rocks up here. Me and Aaron are after the big one—aren't we buddy? Moby Trout."

Because Strauss was too far away to see him roll his eyes, Billy rolled his entire head. Aaron said, "Yeah! The big one! Moby Trout!"

Billy started to make his way downstream. Aaron said, "Dad—can I go too?"

"Go where?"

"With Billy."

"He's going to skip rocks. I thought you wanted to catch the big one. Moby Trout."

"I want to skip rocks."

Strauss sighed. "Sure. Go ahead. Billy—don't take your eyes off him. Understand?"

"Yeah," Billy said. "Don't worry."

He watched them pick their way downstream, around the bend, then he cast his line again. He could hear them, not far, Billy's instructional tone, Aaron's giggle with every successful skip. Strauss watched the shadowy form of a six-incher knife through the cloudy pool. Eased his line back. Wondered if his father were still fishing. How were the streams in South Carolina? What did he fish for? Trout? Catfish? This was what fishing was all about: the sounds of his son and brother, the birds, the buzz of bugs, the warm air, the mystery of the murky stream. The memories and the plans. The best part of fishing had nothing to do with the fish. Trout was fine and flavorful, his father's favorite, but not Strauss's; it couldn't compare to a prime-cut, well-aged steak. Otto had indoctrinated him far too well into the joys of meat. He wondered if his father still smoked Luckies and, when he got a bite, if he still threw his cigarette in the stream with a *fsst* sound. He heard Billy laugh, loud, then Aaron's high-pitched wail.

Downstream through the trees in a rush, he found Aaron soaked and crying, Billy laughing, rolling on the bank holding his stomach. "He pushed me in!"

Billy quit laughing. "I did not! He fell!"

"Did not!"

"Did too!"

Strauss knelt by his son. "What happened?"

"He pushed me!"

"I did never!"

Strauss looked at Billy; Billy looked him in the eye. Strauss looked at Aaron. Aaron looked at the ground. "I slipped. I was trying to step on the rocks." A string of slippery rocks led across the stream.

"Then why did you blame Billy?"

Aaron's lip came out in a powerful pout. "He laughed!"

Janey Geer is the girl in the coffin. She was fifteen, a dark-haired, wide-eyed girl, slow, learning-disabled. Strauss remembers seeing her from behind the counter in the Golden Days, trailing her mother down the aisle, her hand reaching out as if she were afraid to lose touch, walking behind her, hand reaching out, almost like the blind. There'd been a party in the woods above the dam on Potters Creek, drinking and drugs, and somehow, some way, Janey had ended up dead. Hanged from the limb of a tree. Strauss couldn't imagine why she'd have been there in the first place, though the rumors suggested she might have lied to her mother, might have had a crush on a boy who was there, might have threatened to snitch about the drugs, that Billy and his friend, Dickie Kennedy—the only two still in custody—might have intended only to scare her when everything went out of control.

Guth's is thronged with mourners, including dozens of her class-mates. The line to pass by the coffin trails around the walls of the high-ceilinged, soft-carpeted room. Rows of chairs filled with friends and relatives face the coffin. Thick fabrics in deep colors mute the quiet conversations. Strauss, Sally and Dottie enter the room at the rear of the line. Dottie is wearing a dark blue cotton dress, for Strauss and Sally convinced her to go home with them and change, where he allowed Aaron and Angie to stay. Dottie is doing the right thing. At a price. She's brittle with apprehension. For his part, Strauss feels precarious stirrings in his bowels. Sweat breaks out on his face.

He stands taller, tightening the muscles of his abdomen, willing himself stronger. For that is who he is, a butcher, a tough guy, a good father, a Steelers' fan. Otto's apprentice.

Dottie and Sally clutch his arms. "Why Potters Creek?" Dottie whispers.

Strauss knows what she means. It had already occurred to him: Both Janey Geer and Dottie's sister, his Aunt Carol, were murdered along Potters Creek. "Because that's where the kids party," Strauss says. "Just a coincidence." But he's not so sure. He finds himself wondering if somehow there isn't a connection, something in the waters of the creek, something in the air of Hartsgrove.

Faces begin to notice and stare, a few at first, then more and more till it seems as though every eye is upon them. He doesn't know them all by name, but it's difficult not to know someone who lives in a town the size of Hartsgrove, and nearly every face is familiar, and not a one seems friendly. Sally's parents appear for hugs; Gus, heavy, with a neatly trimmed gray beard, and Maggie, heavier, her shiny black hair clenched from a recent perm. Across the room against the floral back-drop by the coffin stands a tall man with a beard wearing an ill-fitting suit beside a woman with limp blond hair—Janey's parents, Dave and Deb Geer, whom Strauss knows casually from evenings at the Rod and

Gun Club; or the God and Run Club, for the old spoonerism has never felt more appropriate. Fat Father Siebert from the Episcopal Church stands by the Geers. The sweat on Strauss's face gets clammier, pooling on his forehead. There seems to be a sphere of space around them in the crowded room. One by one he picks out the people he knows—Serafini, his meat department manager, Melissa Allgier who buys center-cut pork chops, Buster Clover who works for the paper, Charlie Grace with whom he's had a few beers, his old pal Jitterbug Joey Fawcett with the pasty face just as hairless as it was in high school. Neutral faces for the most part, though a few brows dip in what he can read only as hostility. Then he spots Otto Schwabenbauer standing across the room amidst a group of friends and customers. Strauss and Otto make eye contact. Otto starts his way.

"Things could always be worse," Strauss whispers to his mother and his wife. "At least you don't have a cactus growing out of your butt." Another Ottoism. There was a time, long ago, when it made Strauss laugh out loud.

It makes Dottie laugh out loud. "Cactus," she gasps, trying to hold back, clutching Strauss's arm, but the laughter won't be denied, clawing its way out, tears and snot into the bargain. "*Cactus*," she squeals, even louder, her knees nearly buckling. Strauss stands still and somber. Sally clutches his other arm, shaking her head into his shoulder. Dottie laughs on. And see the faces now, how they stare.

A damp, moonlit night a year and a half ago, November, unseasonably warm, patches of wispy fog. Strauss driving slowly over the back country road saw the car stuck in the muddy pasture below when he crested a hill above a darkened farm. He was returning from his friend Marvin Barber's house, where he'd spent the evening playing Monopoly and drinking beer. Marvin, laid up with a badly broken leg from his four-wheeler's encounter with a hidden stump, thought faster was better in all things and the convalescence was driving him crazy.

Someone was behind the car pushing, someone else gunning the engine, tires whining. Coming down the hill, Strauss recognized the multi-colored fenders of Dickie Kennedy's old Ford, and saw his little brother, Billy, behind it. He stopped in the road and got out, maybe fif-teen feet from the mired Ford. "Runs better on the road!" he called.

"Strauss!" said Billy. Dickie rolled his window halfway down. "Dickhead was taking a shortcut!" Billy was quite drunk.

"Need some help?"

"Naw," said Dickie. "We can get it."

"Easy for you to say," Billy said. "Sitting high and dry behind the wheel. Dickhead." Strauss stepped onto the yielding earth of the pas-ture. Closer, he could see Billy swaying, splattered in mud from head to toe. Strauss had to laugh. He stopped and laughed and pointed, crying, "You look like an African American," and laughed even harder, know-ing how they both detested the term, preferring the racial slur.

"You just gonna shit your pants," Billy said, "or you gonna help me push?"

"I'm not pushing," Strauss said. "These are good clothes. I'll drive."

The door didn't open. Dickie was glaring through the half-open window. Then Strauss noticed motion, looked closer and saw the dogs. In the back, three or four, maybe more, different breeds and colors and sizes he couldn't make out in the dark.

Strauss looked from the dogs to Dickie to Billy. "What's this?"

Billy gave a grand gesture. "Strays. We're trying to find 'em good homes."

Dickie opened the door and squeezed out. He'd been tall for his age at ten, but hadn't grown an inch in the seven years since, though he'd lifted weights to compensate. He wasn't smiling, tense as Billy was loose. Yin and yang, just as they'd always been. Big white dog eyes in the back of the car. Strauss opened the door and out they clambered, eager and excited, jumping up, romping about, jumping up again, be-ing dogs, spreading the mud and the joy.

"God damn it," Dickie said, edging closer to Strauss. Strauss turned his back and left them there. He never knew how they got out of the field. At last glance Billy was chasing a German Shepherd toward the tree line, stumbling, falling face-first in the mud, Dickie attempting to pick up a collie.

Soon afterwards Strauss read an article in the paper called "Dealing Dogs," having to do with medical research labs, with ill-treatment and experimentation, with two hundred to eight hundred dollars per pup, with an epidemic of pets missing from the Hartsgrove area. This was when he began to fear that Billy was lost.

Otto Schwabenbauer picks his way with purpose through the crowd toward Strauss, homing in down the beam of his vision, his eyes never breaking contact, heedless of the mob of mourners. Dottie regains her composure, her bright crimson face all that remains of the meltdown, a flush shared in full by Sally and Strauss. Gradually the mourners look away, resume mourning.

His old friend and mentor wending his way toward him with such dogged determination causes a revelation. Strauss is doing the right thing; he has always tried to do the right thing, to accept and live by the rules, but Billy, his little brother, his own flesh and blood, has never. Strauss often wondered why. Twenty years of course could account for much, the difference between growing up in the sixties and the eighties, but it couldn't account for everything. They'd both had the same feckless mother whose development had been arrested in 1960, so that wasn't it either. Which left the father factor. Strauss is not worldly, has never seen an inner city except for glimpses from the Parkway driving through Pittsburgh to Three Rivers Stadium, but he nevertheless has an impression of anarchy in the urban ghettoes attributable to the lack of father figures there, and now, seeing Otto bearing down, he's sure of it. Billy had no father. But Strauss had Otto. Otto the solid and wise, the dependable and permanent. That, Strauss knew with sudden clarity, was the difference.

Otto arrives, his focus fixed. But when he raises his arms to embrace him, Strauss realizes that Otto's eyes are not locked on him at all, they see beyond him, he is not reaching to embrace him at all, he is reaching beyond him.

To Dottie.

Painting Pigs

Goosey goosey gander where shall I wander,
Upstairs, downstairs, in my lady's chamber.
There I met an old man who wouldn't say his prayers,
I took him by the left leg and threw him down the stairs.

It annoyed Al, the ancient imperative that compelled everyone in a barroom to look up at the door of the place when it opened, but what annoyed him even more was when they didn't look down again. Like today, when he walked into the Pub Bar this lovely May afternoon, a day of warm, delicious air and crisp contrails decorating a high blue sky, a day he sensed he didn't deserve. His fly was not open, he was not bleeding, but still they stared. It didn't make sense. But since when did anything make sense? The idiotic redundancy of the name, *the Pub Bar*, didn't make sense. So far, Bogie Zimmerman, the owner, had resisted the urgings of Al and his drinking buddy Charlie Grace to rename it the Pub Bar Tavern, but he was weakening. In the lopsided trajectory of his life—the quick climb up, the long slide down—Al Black had always savored nonsense, and he wondered if it were that, the pure nonsense of the staring faces, the idiotic name, that had summoned the old nursery rhyme into his head. He'd never heard it as a child, of course—his own mother and father were not the nursery-rhyme-reading sort. The first time he'd heard it was a few years ago, his daughter Deb reading it to her daughter, Janey, reading it to her from a book of nonsense verse— nonsense verse!—an entire book of the stuff! Who'd have guessed? But of all the verses, it was goosey goosey gander that struck closest to home, for he could never think of this particular nonsense poem without the other bit of nonsense coming to mind, the nonsense his Granddaddy Black had told him about when Al was a child at his knee, Granddaddy Black's own version of a bedtime story: the story of a gander who'd had his head yanked off, and lived to tell about it. It had been his Granddaddy Black himself, in fact, who'd done the yanking, back in the days when men were men, and blood sport was commonplace, but that was another story. That was another ancient imperative.

"What the hell you looking at?" said Al, making his way to the bar. He scowled. Having pulled a good number of his teeth with pliers over the past few years, his face was ready-made for scowling. Reluctantly, eyes turned away. Begrudgingly, elbows bent, whispers resumed.

Sitting next to Charlie, Al put his five dollar bill on the bar, but Bogie didn't budge. Bogie was wearing the same limp white shirt and clip-on bowtie he always wore presiding over one of the seedier joints in Hartsgrove, a town with more than its share of seedy joints. He and Charlie still stared, regarding Al with an odd aura of expectation.

"What the hell's the matter, you run out of beer? Gimme a shot too."

Bogie, a sour look on his hangdog face, drew and poured. "Wasn't that Janey Geer kid some relation to you?"

Shot poised before him, Al licked his lip. "Janey Geer's my grand-daughter. Why?"

Bogie and Charlie looked at each other, then looked away. Bogie washed a glass. A game of eight-ball broke out behind him, balls clacking loudly. Al licked his lip again, glancing in the overcast mirror behind the bar to see all the eyes scrambling away. "Why?"

"The question of the hour," Charlie said. Charlie Grace was aging oddly, his long hair half jet-black, half pure white, though it wasn't always easy to tell. He usually wore a high cloth cap, the type favored by welders, his on-again, off-again profession. Today's was a purple floral pattern.

"What's that supposed to mean?" Al said.

Charlie shrugged. "I guess you been away."

"*Why?*" Al said, with considerably more emphasis. He looked at all the somber faces in the barroom, then back again to Bogie. "Why did you say *wasn't?*"

"Al, something happened," Bogie said.

"I guess you didn't hear nothing yet," said Charlie.

"What happened?"

"Janey up and got herself killed," Charlie said, and everyone leaned another inch away from Al.

He treats his old pickup rudely, clattering and slipping up the hummocky bricks of White Street toward his daughter Deb's house on Rose Hill. If he can get there fast enough, it won't be true. Clamminess breaks out on his forehead, spreading down his neck, under his arms. She's there. Janey. Rounding third base—the only time she ever rounded that base in her life—like an awkward angel after her accidental hit, pudgy in her powder blue softball uniform, the light of the miracle on her pure, wide face. He feels heat. The fury is banked in the furnace, growing molten, ready to erupt. She was *his* granddaughter, *his* blood. Whatever had happened to her had happened to *him* as well. Someone, *something*— he tries to wring blood from the steering wheel—would have to pay.

Deb's place was filled with long faces, most of them unfamiliar. Everyone looked up when he came in, which annoyed the hell out of him.

"Where's Deb?" His lack of teeth made the spittle fly, especially when he was emphatic, which also annoyed him.

"She's up in her room," a skinny, gray-haired woman said.

A fat-cheeked woman with a fat-cheeked baby said, "She wants to be left alone."

Al scowled. "Then what the hell are you doing here? Get out! All of you! Out!" There was hesitancy, questioning glances. "*Go!*" he yelled, punching the air, and the hesitancy vanished in the scramble for the door.

He headed for the stairs. *Upstairs, downstairs, in my lady's chamber.* One of his rules held that no one he'd brought into this world was entitled to keep secrets from him. He didn't knock. Tow-headed Deb, thin and gaunt, was curled on the bed; they were both a mess, her and the bed.

"Big Al," she whispered.

"What the hell happened?"

"You're frothing."

"Deb, what happened?" he said more slowly.

"They killed her, Daddy." Her eyes were dry hollows of black and white, peering over the pillow she squeezed. "They killed my baby."

"Who?"

The police were still investigating. A bunch of kids had gone to celebrate spring at the clearing in the woods up from the dam on Potters Creek yesterday. There'd been drinking and drugs, a long day full, and somehow, some way, Janey had ended up dead. They were still trying to get to the bottom of it, though the police had told her one thing: It hadn't been accidental.

"What did they do to her?"

Deb's eyes squeezed shut. She shook her head.

"What was she doing out there? What'd you let her go for?"

"She just wanted to fit in. That's all she ever wanted."

He dropped to the chair by the side of the bed, sitting on a heap of laundry; Deb was the same housekeeper her mother had been. "Why didn't you call me up?"

"You know why. You'd just get drunk and cause trouble."

"Cause trouble? Me? Don't you think the goddamn trouble's already been caused?"

She sat up, wearily. "Easy, Big Al."

"I want some answers!"

"You want some blood."

"God damn right!"

She handed him a picture. "Remember when you used to paint pigs on their bellies?"

He remembered. Ten years ago maybe, but a lifetime really. Just before he'd lost the house, just before he and Louise, Deb's mother, had split up. The family gatherings had been a lot bigger then, before Al's son and his wife had become estranged from the family, before his other two daughters had moved away with theirs. He remembered rooms full of people, floors full of giggling kids, grandchildren, nieces, nephews, neighbors, friends, laughing and drinking, reading nonsense poems, singing nonsense songs, roughhousing, wrestling—and painting pigs.

Al had invented the game. He'd pick a victim and announce, *I'm gonna paint a pig on your belly*, and the chase was on. The victim was held down by the other kids, Gramp's accomplices, and amidst much giggling, screaming and squirming, the belly was bared, the painting commenced. Magic markers were the favored medium, difficult to wash off, and they always tried to wash them off, wash away their shame, immediately. And within the hour, one of the accomplices had become the next victim, the last victim the newest accomplice. "I always used the belly button for the pig's nose," Al said. "Outies worked the best."

"Janey would never let me wash hers off."

"Do tell. I never knew that."

Deb lifted her knees, resting her head there, yellow hair falling limply. He looked at the picture again. Janey was maybe six in it, about the time of the pig-painting parties, a smile with two new teeth too big for her mouth, her forehead high, her eyes wide, set apart: *learning-disabled*—an expression new to him at the time. He would never use the word *retard* again.

"Where's she at?" he said.

"Down at Guth's." Guth's Funeral Home on Jefferson Street.

"Where's Dave? Did you call Beth and Barb?"

Deb's husband, Dave, was down in his cellar workshop, her sisters and their families were en route. Her mother, Al's ex, Louise, was flying up from Florida, where she'd moved after the split nearly ten years ago.

"I threw everybody out," Al said.

"I know. I heard you."

"I'm going too. What do you need? What can I do?"

"Just don't do anything stupid, Big Al. Please?"

"Al," Officer Shick said, "don't do anything stupid. Or you'll end up right down there behind bars with the rest of 'em."

Al paused in the doorway of the police station as he was leaving. "That supposed to be a deterrent?"

"Al, you heard me. Don't do anything stupid."

Six kids were in custody. Shick hadn't told him much more than that. The State Police were handling the interrogations, and they should have it pieced together within a few hours. What had apparently begun as horseplay had escalated, veered out of control. No specifics, no why, no who. In these days of high school murder and mayhem, what did anyone know? Just troubled kids, mean kids, bored, restless, drunk, drugged-up kids who'd probably been victims of abuse themselves.

Al longed to show them the meaning of real abuse.

He stood five foot eight. He'd earned the nickname *Big Al* in high school, on the offensive and defensive lines of the first Hartsgrove High School football team to have a winning record in twenty years, and the last for another twenty. There were still chinks missing from his right forearm, bits of flesh left on the teeth of opposing linemen foolish enough to challenge his "forearm shiver." He married the Homecoming Queen, Louise Hulse, when they were both sixteen. Each lent a confidence to the other that neither had. He took correspondence courses, teaching himself surveying, then civil engineering, caught on with the coal companies, prospered, bought a big old house, remodeled, had four kids, leapfrogged up the social ladder till he was rubbing his leisure-suited elbows with lawyers and doctors at the country club. Then the coal business went down the toilet, and the drinking—which had given him his brashness, his edge—caught up to him, overtook him; *Big Al* all the while, as the nickname spiraled slowly downward, away from respectful.

At sixty, he had the same broad, sloping shoulders, much of the same muscle, but his stomach had morphed from washboard to watermelon.

Driving past the Court House, he peered toward the basement jail, seeing no signs of life. He drove down to Memorial Park by the confluence of Hartsgrove's three creeks, where the broad green baseball fields unfolded in the late May sun. There was a skateboard facility, a curving plywood structure, by the fields near the tennis courts, intended to keep the kids off the streets.

He figured more than six kids had been at the clearing yesterday.

The facility sat idle, but the parking lot of the adjacent Sylvania plant, long since closed, was crawling with them: a dozen kids, maybe more, fresh from school, skateboarding, biking, rollerblading, all strut and swagger and noise. *Goosey goosey gander where shall I wander—* Pulling up in their midst, Al climbed out.

His scowl made room for a snarl. Kids—baggy jeans around their asses, underwear showing, earrings, nose rings, nipple rings, ball caps backwards, all badges of their ignorance. A couple looked familiar. One was a dead ringer for a man whose name Al couldn't remember, but he remembered sitting next to him—must have been the kid's father—years ago at a businessmen's banquet, the exchange of words, the embarrassing mashed potatoes incident. Anger flushed through him. "Hey! Any of you little bastards out at the clearing yesterday?" A spray of spittle sparkled in the sun.

"Who wants to know?"

"Why, it's Big Al!"

"Big Al! Big Al wants to know!" A rollerblader swooped toward him, the sun at his back. A kid on a bike sling-shotted a trailing skateboarder at him. "Hey, Big Al! How they hanging?" They began buzzing him, laughing. *There I met an old man who wouldn't say his prayers—* Sunlight burned at his brain, a poker raking across the smoldering heap of coal, flames leaping out. Muscle memory took over. Al was on the gridiron again, protecting his turf. A kid with greasy hair escaping his backwards cap zeroed in on a skateboard—*I took him by the left leg and threw him down the stairs!* Bracing himself, Big Al flipped a forearm shiver into the kid's face with perfect grace and timing, the skateboard flying, the kid tumbling. Al noticed a bloody tooth in his forearm just before his bad knee gave way to the wheel of a bike behind him. His cheek warm on the blacktop, his knee hot with pain, he saw a skateboard heading toward his face, front wheels rearing like an angry horse.

Al sees the ghost of his Granddaddy Black. By the red boards of the barn, the horse rears and stomps at his shadow. Above them, hanging from a pole by its feet is a large bird in full panic, feathers flailing, punishing the air. The horse retreats in a dancing canter some distance before turning and commencing its gallop, and the rider—the young man who is Al's grandfather—strains high in the stirrups, extended, reaching like a child for forbidden fruit as he passes beneath the bird. The gander hanging from the plank, head and neck greased with lard, evades the clutch of the rider, and the horse circles, stomping and snorting, galloping again toward the bird, hooves pounding the dirt in time to the lunatic beat of the shouts and laughs and claps of the men looking on. Al is not clapping or laughing, he is small and scared, and he knows he is not really there. The gander begins to tire, drooping toward the passing, groping fist, and on the third pass, the fist finds the head, the grip is sure, the twist violent, and the head departs the body with a dull snap, red blood flying in the sunlight. A deep-throated cheer from the watchers, at the same instant the gander's feet come free, and he falls awkwardly to the ground in a flutter of wings, landing on his feet.

The gander lives! His death flurry ebbs and dwindles, and soon he swaggers about the barnyard like a rooster, headless, feathers glistening at the top of his serpentine neck. The horses in a semicircle prance fitfully in place, their riders slack-jawed with wonder. The gander struts to the pounding of their hearts. He nears a horse who whinnies and rears in fear. He beats at the air with his wings, lifts off the ground a few tentative times, then races unerringly through the circle of men and animals, past Al, past the barn, toward the pasture, taking off, lifting into the sky, flying straight toward the woods, over the trees, away.

Goosey goosey gander where shall you wander?

Al's granddaddy opens his clutched fist, staring at the glassy-eyed head of the bird. He holds it toward his wide-eyed grandson. A drop of blood falls blackly through the air.

An antiseptic odor. A nurse shakes his shoulder, insisting he awaken. He refuses. He remains Little Al, sitting at the feet of his Granddaddy Black, who is not a ghost at all. He is a memory, an old man with tobacco-stained lips and a misshapen face, where the cheekbone shattered years before by the kick of a mule never properly mended. It is 1943. He is telling his grandson, not for the first time, the true story of the Headless Gander, a legend more than sixty years in the making—the last time the sport of gander-pulling was ever practiced on the Black farm, or anywhere else, to the best of his grandfather's recollection, in all of Paine County.

"Let's hear your story," Officer Shick said, standing beside Al's hospital bed. Al came around. Groggy, he told him, listening to his own voice: how he was set upon by a pack of unprovoked young hooligans. How could Shick not believe him, with Al's granddaddy there to vouch for the truth of it?

"That's not the way they told it," Shick said. "The one kid's down the hall."

"The one that bit my arm?"

"Listen, Al. I know you got problems with your head, and I don't just mean the concussion. I can call it your word against theirs. But don't go pushing your luck."

Al lifted himself on his elbows, the load shifting painfully in his head. It was dark outside. Below, the lights of the town lay sprinkled across black hillsides; Hartsgrove Hospital was on the highest hill in town. Louise was standing beside his bed where Officer Shick had been. Had he slept?

"You look like hell," she said. So did she: Shock, grief and travel had compounded the wrinkles, fat and gray of age. And on the wide, deep shelf of her bosom, on the yellow, Floridian blouse, the likes of which Hartsgrove had seldom seen, lay the remnants of her latest meal. The Homecoming Queen was dead.

"Nice to see you too, Weezle."

"What do you think you're doing?"

The surge of anger hurt his head. "Trying to find out what the hell happened."

"Why?"

"*Why?* If you gotta ask that . . ."

"Al, this isn't about me—or Janey. It's about you."

"Me?"

"You were never there for her. This is just some misguided attempt on your part to compensate for your neglect when she was alive." Her years of therapy were showing, in her amateur diagnosis, in her calm, unnatural voice that irked the hell out of him.

"*I'm* not the one who moved a thousand miles away."

Her nostrils flared in disgust. "You might as well have moved a million miles away."

"Bullshit."

"Al, the last thing Deb needs right now is to have to take care of another kid. Do you think you can behave yourself?"

"I went to all Janey's softball games."

"I doubt it. And when you *were* there, you were so drunk you embarrassed her."

"She knew I was there. Where were you?"

"I couldn't be there, and you know it. You might have tried to kill me again."

His face melted to a scowl. "I still don't remember that."

"You wouldn't." Her hand remembered at her throat.

He stared at his own hands for some time. Rough, callused hands, like his Granddaddy Black's, powerful. If he'd tried to choke his wife, if he'd meant indeed to kill her, wouldn't he have succeeded? But then maybe he did. Maybe he did, and then, afterwards, maybe she flew off to Florida. Where was the truth of it, where was the myth?

The sun crested Longview Hill, streaming in the window. Al looked out; the first light hadn't yet touched the town below, still cupped in darkness. He dressed. Throwing his bloody bandage in the wastebasket, he covered the gash with his cap, bill pointing forward, and walked down the hushed hallway. There was no cartilage left in his bad knee, which throbbed nearly as painfully as his head. Looking in every room, he found only one patient under eighty, a kid sleeping with his mouth open, a gap where his front tooth should have been. Asleep, he looked closer to five than fifteen. Unclenching his fist, Al hobbled out.

"Where do you think you're going?" The night nurse was frumpy, fat and familiar.

"See a man about a horse."

"Al, you get right back here—that's a bad concussion."

"I'm immune to 'em by now." He'd lost track after his first ten or so.

"Al! We won't be responsible."

From the pay phone by the Emergency Room, he called Charlie Grace for a lift. He couldn't tell if Charlie was still up, or already up, though since he was between jobs, it was probably the former. "You look like hell," Charlie said when he got there.

"So folks keep telling me."

"What happened?"

"Kid tried to decapitate me with his skateboard."

Charlie laughed. "Punks."

Al eased into the wide front seat of the old Buick. On the floor at his feet was a scattering of *Gourmet* magazines. He didn't ask. "Let's take a ride out to the dam."

When Charlie hesitated, Al looked over. Charlie said, "Ain't you going to fasten your seat belt?" Al scowled, and Charlie laughed again.

He parked at the dam, and they walked across the footbridge, over the steaming water. Fresh daylight filtered into the woods as they made their way up the trail toward the clearing. A light mist rose from the melting dew that soaked their boots and the bottoms of their jeans. Al ignored the pain in his knee, Charlie ignored Al's hobble.

A plump young rabbit dashed across the path, and Charlie mimed firing at it. "Shoulda brought my shotgun."

"Me too," Al said.

"Yeah. But you'd be after more than rabbits."

Al grew away from the pain. He felt as though he were watching them from a tree. He was at a loss as to whether to attribute the out-of-body sensation to the concussion or to the circumstance—a dawn visit with a man wearing a pink plaid welder's cap to the woods where his granddaughter was killed.

The clearing was littered with natural debris, rocks, logs and stumps, as well as with the waste of campers and partiers: broken glass, beer cans, butts, wrappers, assorted trash. A sour smell arose from the soggy campfire ashes. Al stood, hands on his hips, breathing in the smell. Charlie kicked through a pile of rubble behind a log. It was hushed and wet and violent, red sunlight slashing down through trees.

"Aha!" Charlie said. "I thought so." Bending, he plucked up a plastic six-pack binding, three heavy blue cans drooping down. "Kids are stupid. Want a beer?"

Two cans cracked open like snakes hissing. Charlie stood staring at the solid limb of a maple spreading over the clearing. Al joined him. They each took a long drink of beer, eyes never leaving the limb. "Did you know this place used to be a resort of sorts?" Charlie said.

"Do tell," said Al.

"There was a dance pavilion, a road, about a dozen private cottages. Rich folks."

"When was that?"

"Cloudburst washed it away in 1911. I read about it in the paper."

They stared at the raw spot on top of the limb, where the bark was broken away. Where a rope might have been tied to hang something heavy.

Al said, "Did you ever hear that story my granddaddy used to tell, about the Headless Gander?"

"Who hasn't? A rural urban legend."

"Do you believe it?"

Taking off his cap, Charlie ran a hand through his black and white hair. "Hell yes," he said. "I've bore witness to miracles myself, with my own two eyes."

After a bracer at the Pub Bar—they met Bogie unlocking the door—Charlie dropped him off at his truck. It still sat where he'd stepped out of it on the Sylvania parking lot, door still open. Driving past his dumpy room in the Union Apartments on Main Street, Al headed south. Two miles out of town, the road curved down a hill under a railway bridge, the abutment scarred and indented like his Granddaddy Black's cheek. It was the site of at least three fatalities he could remember without trying. Approaching it at sixty, his grip tensed; he resisted the magnetism again, the lure to take it on, to see how tough it really was, to spit in its face.

Three miles out of town he turned onto Black Road. Past Mrs. Ishman's, past the Conifer's and Shugars'—all cousins of some distance or other—Black Road curled down through a hollow where a cluster of trees stood beside the old farmhouse. An outbuilding near the road had caved in on one side, overcome by creeping ivy, vines and bushes, so it looked like a building of boards and leaves. The barn beyond was abandoned, decaying. Other farmers, relatives mostly, worked the fields now. The house was still solid, though the paint was faded to patches, and the clenched shingles of the roof had taken on the green hue of mildew.

He smelled the frying bacon from outside, where the old dogs lay on the porch drooling. In the kitchen, his mother bent like a question mark over the skillet; seeing Al, her face filled with wary delight. Behind her, his father sat before his plate, fork in hand.

It took him a moment to recognize his son. When he did, his invisible eyebrows arose, opening his face to an emphatic blankness. "You got any alcohol on you or in you, you can turn around right now." The old man, hard of hearing, always barked.

"None to speak of." Al's breath mint was lost in his toothlessness.

"Good. You look like hell."

"So do you."

The old man laughed, and slapped the table.

"You want me to fix you a plate?" his mother said. Hard of hearing too, she compensated contrary to her husband, by talking too softly.

"He don't want a plate," the old man said, "look it how fat he is."

"Why he ain't fat at all."

"Nothing for me, Ma. Just some coffee."

"He don't want a plate, but I could sure use one. In this lifetime."

"Hold your horses, Mister." This the old man didn't hear.

Crossing the black floorboards, Al took a mug of coffee to the table, where the red flowers on the oilcloth had long since faded to pink smears. He told them about Janey.

The old man took it personally. "I don't know no Janey Geer."

"She's your great-granddaughter," Al said.

"Never heard of her." The old man fairly shouted.

"You remember her, don't you, Ma?"

His mother stood by the stove, where she always stood while her husband ate. She cocked her head. "Janey Geer, Janey Geer. Wasn't she the sweet little retard?"

"She ain't the one used to teach Sunday School out at Rassleton?" the old man said.

Al shook his head. "She was only fifteen."

"She ain't the one married Wilbur Shugars?"

Al shook his head. His mother's voice came in low beneath the volume of his father's, like a spy plane under radar. "He don't remember anything, Al—that's why he never calls you by your name. Why, he can't even remember to die."

His folks weren't dead on the kitchen floor, being feasted upon by the dogs. That was one reason he'd come out. The shotgun he kept upstairs since he'd lost his house was another. And there was a third reason: Al hobbled out to the barn.

The old man limped along, using his cane, though it seemed to Al that his own knees were worse. His father had never subjected his to football or brawling. They didn't discuss their walk to the barnyard, they didn't speak at all. The old man made no plans; he had nowhere to go, and all day to get there.

Al tried to remember painting the pigs on Janey's belly that she didn't want her mother to wash off, but he couldn't. All the pigs he'd painted on all the squirming, giggling little bellies were the same in the distant fog. No single pig stood out. He remembered watching Janey round third base with the winning run once—the only time it had ever happened, as she was an indifferent, infrequent softball player, who handled a bat like a two-by-four. The glow on her face ignited that one time by her teammates' hugs and cheers had lasted all evening long. He remembered holding kids—grandchildren, nieces, nephews—on his knee when they were infants and toddlers, tickling, talking, playing, singing, but he couldn't pick out Janey in his memory. The kids were as indistinguishable as all the pigs he'd painted.

A barn cat skulked across their path; the old man swung his cane, grazing it, the cat scampering off with a slinky hiss.

Al had lived with cruelty all his life and had thought he understood it to be a natural, human thing, simply the flip side of kindness. But he was wrong. He was baffled. There could be nothing on the other side of this coin. He didn't know what to do now that the fire had gone to a slow smoldering. The three options that had settled upon him were unsatisfactory: Take his twelve-gauge and throw some fear—or some buckshot—into the hearts of some deserving young punks; take on the railway bridge abutment and see who was really the better man; or go to Janey's funeral tomorrow, and weep like a child.

Or, none of the above.

"So this is where they used to pull ganders," Al said. He and the old man had walked around back of the barn, where he hadn't been in forty years. It didn't seem to be a setting fit for a legend. It was overgrown, nearly impenetrable. The rusted corpse of a John Deere and the bare skeleton of an old Hudson sat ensnarled in creepers and vines, while bald tires, ancient appliances and assorted debris lay mostly hidden by the undergrowth. In the musty smell from the barn, there was no distinction between what was dead and what was waiting to die. The barn boards were warped and weathered gray, many missing altogether. Al cleaned it up in his mind. He cut away the undergrowth, plowed the adjacent field over to the tree line; the barn boards were new and fitted and whole again, a deep red hue. He pictured where the pole must have protruded, where the unfortunate bird had been tied. He imagined the horses and riders, the bearded farmers in denim and wool.

He could see it as clearly as the dream last night. Where had it come from after so many years? Why? Had Janey brought it to him? How much had been the true memory of his grandfather's story, how much invention? Who had invented it? He saw the snorting horse, the desperate flurry of the gander. Standing there in the hot May sun, a baggy tee shirt over his watermelon gut, Al became his muscular young granddaddy on the galloping horse, stretching, reaching for the evasive head of the bird. The old man stared with him, at the same spot on the side of the barn. Was he seeing it too? Al felt the muscles in his back go taut. He bounced and swayed on the prancing horse. It was all he could do to keep from reaching up with his right arm, grasping for the head of the fowl, trying to get a grip, trying to take hold of the elusive nature of whatever this thing had become.

The old man said nothing. "So this is where they used to pull ganders," Al said, louder.

"They done what?" the old man said. "Who?"

Early next morning, two contrails crisscrossed the blue sky high over Hartsgrove. Emily Ungar, eight, on her way to buy a quart of milk for her mother, was taking a shortcut down by the softball field below the Golden Days Supermarket, where the Sandy Lick met Potters Creek to form the Red Bank. Studying the white X high in the sky, she didn't notice the man sitting in the bleachers till she was very close to him. "Hey, kid," he said.

"Hey, Mister," she said. "What are you doing here?"

"Just sitting here not watching the game."

"What game?"

"That game right there. The game that nobody's playing."

Emily Ungar stared at the empty infield.

"It's a perfect day for not watching a softball game, don't you think?" the man said.

"If you say so."

"I might just sit here and not watch 'em play all day long, unless they don't go into extra innings. The toughest part is not knowing which team not to root for."

"You're weird, Mister."

The man had an odd, hollow smile. He rubbed at his knee. "You think so? Well, you'd probably be weird too if somebody grabbed you by the left leg and threw you down the stairs."

Emily Ungar hurried away.

Later that day they buried Janey Geer. Hundreds of folks showed up, most of her classmates, many weeping, including the boy with the missing tooth. Charlie Grace was there, wearing a jacket that covered his thumbs, a tie and a welder's cap with yellow daisies; Janey had liked daisies. Bogie Zimmerman, his hangdog face sad and flaccid, was there in his limp white shirt and clip-on bowtie.

Big Al, however, was not.

Louise was hardly surprised. Her arm around Deb was a rigid embrace, no comfort, as all she could think of was Al. "You didn't really think he'd be here, did you?" she said to Deb and her other daughters in her calm, unnatural voice. "He couldn't grieve like a normal human being, he's too macho for that. I'm sure he's out getting drunk for her, for Janey of course, not for him. That would be the manly thing to do."

Deb squeezed her thumbs in her fists. "Mother, you've got something on your shirt," she said, watching Louise brush at a breakfast crumb encrusted on her bosom. Deb loved her parents, both of them, but she didn't have time right now. She had to grieve, to think of Janey, her little girl, not to think of how much she wanted her mother to hurry back to Florida, her father to hurry up and kill himself, to get it over with.

Officer Shick was there. He wanted to be on hand in case Al did show up. It was a volatile situation. Big Al was a loose cannon, and besides all the kids, Strauss was there too, Strauss the butcher, along with his wife and his mother; Strauss's kid brother was one of the suspects, one of only two kids still in custody.

Snuffy Guth, the funeral director, took Officer Shick aside and told him his place had been broken into last night. At least he assumed so. There were glass shards inside the cellar door, the small pane nearest the lock broken. But nothing seemed to be missing; there was nothing, really, there to steal. He didn't even know whether or not to report it.

"Anything disturbed?" Shick said.

"I'm not sure. Kind of hard to tell. Mrs. McManigle might have been a little tilted, and there was a floral basket crooked in by Janey Geer. But nothing to speak of."

Because he was on his mind, Shick immediately thought of Al, but dismissed it again just as quickly. One small pane of glass wasn't up to Big Al; he would wreak considerably more havoc than that. "Let me know if anything turns up missing," Shick said with a shrug.

Janey Geer looked perfectly at rest. Everyone thought Snuffy had done a wonderful job on her, all things considered. She was laid out in the black skirt and white blouse she'd worn to her cousin Brenda's wedding, where she'd wondered if she'd ever be a bridesmaid. She'd doubted it, since her flower girl dream had never come true, so she'd decided that the bridesmaids weren't all that pretty anyway, especially Marla Ewing, who was too bony.

Janey's wide eyes were peacefully closed, her expression placid, though her lips seemed a bit apprehensive. Her broken skull was cushioned in the soft, satin pillow, and the rope burns on her neck were invisible beneath the powder.

Snuffy of course didn't inspect every square inch of his premises, let alone every square inch of everything there. How could he? Why would he want to? So he—or anyone else—never noticed the third button on Janey's blouse, the edge of which was not quite completely clear of the buttonhole, a condition Snuffy would never have tolerated. And so it followed that no one ever thought to open her blouse. It never occurred to anyone to look at her belly, and thus to behold—lo and behold!—the wonderful pig painted there.

Bad Actors

When it becomes apparent that Cookie isn't going to die for them just yet, restlessness settles over the family. They fidget and shuffle, scratch, stretch and yawn. Linda, Norman's mother-in-law, leans forward, holding the hand of her father, Cookie, while her brother Eddy strikes a similar pose on the other side of the bed. "We love you, Cookie," says Linda.

"Don't eat the liver!" says Cookie, delirious, his eyes unfocused and darting.

No one responds until Eddy, moments later. "I'm hungry."

Linda's three daughters—Ginger, Rosemary and Amber—nod vaguely in sleepy agreement, Norman noting a certain sisterly synchronicity.

Norman is married to Amber. He says nothing himself, though his stomach feels hollow as well. Pulse ticking across his clammy skin, he feels uncomfortable, self-conscious, as though they're all bad actors in a soap opera deathbed scene. His and Amber's daughter, Samantha, sits dozing on the big chair in the corner, while Benny, Rosemary's one-year-old, naps in his car seat on the floor.

Amber is the youngest of the sisters, Ginger the oldest, Rosemary the most immature. They couldn't be less alike, and the more Norman is exposed to their mother, Linda, the more suspicious he is of their paternity. Amber is dark and deliberate, often reminding Norman of Pooh's pal Eeyore. Ginger, also known as Big Red, is an executive who drives a new Mercedes, while Rosemary, a bartender, is dirty blond and usually high. Rosemary keeps glancing his way, as though remembering. Or as though trying to decide whether or not to reveal what she's remembering. Norman's been avoiding his in-laws for two years, ever since the unfortunate incident with Rosemary, but Cookie's impending demise has forced them all face to face.

Eddy announces that the truck stop serves breakfast all day. Norman magnanimously offers to stay with Cookie. Everyone's reluctantly all for it.

Norman's motive is far from unselfish. Every time Rosemary glances his way he holds his breath. He finds himself holding his breath often, her glances as frequent as they are inscrutable. He could use a break.

Linda says, "Dad—we're going to go get something to eat. Norman will be here with you." She's a woman who still believes in the blondness of her hair, gray roots be damned.

"We'll be right back, Pop," says Eddy, who wears a Hawaiian shirt and smells of stale booze. His brush cut is graying and thinning, giving him a frayed and fringed appearance.

"Hang in there, Cookie," Ginger says. "We'll see you in a little bit."

Rosemary says, "Don't die till we get back, Cookie."

"Jesus," snaps Ginger. "You're one dumb fucking blond, you know it?"

"Don't say that in front of the kids," Amber says in her deliberate drawl.

"Don't say that in front of me," Linda says. "I don't like to hear shit talk like that."

"What?" Rosemary says. "Like he's not going to die?"

"The toilet's overflowing!" says Cookie. "The toilet's overflowing!"

Norman sighs in relief when they're gone. He straightens his tie, settling into the chair in the corner by the head of the bed, the only soft chair in the room. It's facing toward the television high on the wall, not toward Cookie, but that's fine. Norman might be on deathwatch, but there's no law that says he can't watch from the corner of his eye. Taking the remote from the windowsill, he turns on the TV. He craves distraction; he had to get up early and drive eighty miles this morning, abandoning altogether his own life, his overgrown lawn, his broken garage door, his precarious pile of paperwork at the mercy of his bored, prowling cat, Frankie. Norman mutes the TV; after all, he is on deathwatch.

He finds a football game—Penn State, Toledo. Penn State losing. *Penn State losing to Toledo?* They should be having Toledo for lunch; Toledo's on the schedule just for practice. "Holy Toledo," Norman says.

Cookie mumbles behind the oxygen mask, held in place by straps around his ears. His ears are big in the first place, and when the straps began to irritate them, a nurse inserted padding. What remains of his hair is gray and stiff, his skin gray too. The grayness, the flappy padding, the hose drooping from the mask, all form an elephant caricature in Norman's mind, and he empathizes all the more with the old man, his dignity in shreds. "Do you believe it?" Norman says, thinking Cookie must have been responding. Cookie strings together some syllables that register with Norman as *Believe it or not*. Or maybe *Boy is it hot.*

The old man becomes agitated. Norman becomes worried. In wanting to be alone, he hadn't considered Cookie's condition. When he isn't unconscious he's delirious; who'll restrain him? Linda and Eddy had to hold him down once when he tried to get up; his gown flew open when he flipped the sheet, exposing his puny, blue penis. Norman locates the call button.

Cookie relaxes. Norman tries. A few syllables later, Cookie's mumble subsides, his eyes fluttering shut.

Toledo scores again. What's wrong with this picture? Norman is overcome by clamminess. The drive from Slippery Rock that morning seems ages ago. He should be home keeping an eye on the kid cutting his grass, he never mows under the lilacs. The spring from his garage door had sprung, shooting across the garage—someone could have been killed. Had the guy shown up to fix it? How much would he charge? What if Rosemary blurts?

Holy Toledo. Norman closes his eyes. Breathing the antiseptic sourness of the hospital, he falls into a fitful nap.

When he awakens, his brain is thick and sticky. The room seems darker. He looks out the window. Clouds have moved in, and the town below—the hospital is high on a Hartsgrove hill—seems still, too still, like a photograph. When he turns from the window, Cookie is staring at him, his eyes oddly focused. "She was a *cock* tease," he says.

Norman frowns, sighs. He doesn't want to hear it. Whatever it is. Call it delirium, call it what you will, but Norman suspects it's all true; delirium is nothing more than all the sins and secrets of a lifetime being tumbled in the dryer, falling out the open door, running around the room disguised as hallucinations. He couldn't care less if this old man ever had his puny, blue cock teased. Where's the nurse? Isn't it time for his vitals? Where the hell is Amber? Do they think he's a damn babysitter?

"I killed her," Cookie adds, clearly.

"What?" Norman looks at the TV. "Yeah—Penn State got killed."

Cookie shoves the mask aside. The strap pulls his ear straight out. His hospital gown droops, exposing his bony shoulders, biceps like gray lumps of modeling clay stuck on sticks. His eyes fix on Norman. He doesn't seem delirious. "I didn't mean to," he says, "but I killed her. There was this rock, just *sitting* there."

"Killed who?" Norman says.

"That Siebenrock girl. The one they were all looking for."

"You *killed* her?"

Cookie nods, earnestly, lucidly. "She said she was gonna tell, I panicked, wham, bam, boom, it just happened. The girl was a *cock* tease."

Movement in the doorway, where Samantha has stopped, bewildered. She comes running to jump on Norman's lap, digging him with her knees. "Daddy, what's a cock tease?" Linda appears; seeing her father's gown and mask in disarray, she hurries to his side. "What's wrong? Is he okay? What happened?" The others file in in a flurry, wearing similar masks of concern, until Rosemary, bringing up the rear, weary and bored, lugging Benny in his car seat.

"I won't say she had it coming," Cookie says, "but it came all the same." Annoyed by Linda fussing at his gown, he swats at her hand.

"What came all the same, Dad?" she says, fussing at his mask.

Cookie's eyes flash around the room. "The ides of September!" His gaze falters and flutters, losing its grip, flitting away.

Norman, struck dumb in his soft corner chair, watches Cookie sink back into delirium. What can he do? What can he say? What do you say to a family whose beloved, dying patriarch has just confessed to murder? Norman's heartbeat fills his throat.

But no one asks. Samantha takes up the remote, channel-surfing at the speed of light, and Benny begins banging on a bedpan with Rosemary's keys.

"I think he's going to be a percussionist," Rosemary says. Benny garbles along.

"That's not funny," Ginger says. "Take the keys."

"Oh shut up," Rosemary says.

"You shut up," says Amber.

"Kids," Linda says, "can you just behave? Please?"

"Yes, Mother," they say in unison, giggling.

Cookie bolts up, saying, "God have mercy!" then drops back down to his deathbed. Certain this is it, Linda says, "We love you, Dad."

"They're praying," Cookie says. "They're all praying. It's a *cult*."

"Who's praying, Dad?" Linda says.

"*Praying*!" Cookie says. "Candles! Chanting! Mumbo-jumbo!"

"Do you suppose he's remembering something?" drawls Amber.

"Right out there in the hallway!" Cookie says. "Doctors! Nurses! Specialists!"

"Cookie," Linda says, taking his hand again. "Dad—you must be imagining things."

"Maybe he dreamed something," Eddy says.

Rosemary says, "I want some of what he's taking," and the conversation yields to a chorus of sighs. Rosemary and her drugs are a sticky issue.

Norman scarcely hears through the buzzing in his brain. He seems to be out of step, on a different wavelength, a different frequency entirely. Straightening his tie, he clears his throat. "Anybody ever heard of a girl named Siebenrock?" Linda and Eddy look at him, as do the sisters in turn, Ginger, then Rosemary, then Amber.

Linda says, "Why?"

"Cookie said something about some Siebenrock girl."

"There was this Siebenrock girl who was killed," says Linda. "Back in high school."

"Carol, Carol Siebenrock," Eddy says. "She was three or four years ahead of me. Blinky Mumford killed her, the janitor."

"Why?" Linda says. "What did Cookie say about her?"

Norman stalls. From his lap, Samantha says, "What's a *cock* tease?"

Norman met the Darling girls in turn, inversely as it turned out, to how well he knows them now. Ginger he met first, when they were students at Slippery Rock University, where Norman still works to this day, an Admissions Counselor in Freshman Services. Ginger was two years ahead of him. He noticed her his freshman year, the confident way she navigated the campus with long, self-assured strides, seldom bothering to make eye contact with anyone. He admired that. On a cool October morning of his sophomore year, she approached him after their Organizational Behavior class in Eisenberg Hall, the first and only class they ever shared. "You're Norm—Norm Bowley," was not a question.

"Norman," said Norman.

"I'm Ginger Darling. Don't you find it astonishing that one of the basic elements of the bureaucratic structure is that promotion is based on technical competence?"

"Not at all."

"But it defies the term 'bureaucracy' as we know it." The epitome of eye contact—she virtually pinned him in place, red head tilted for emphasis. He blinked first, retrieving his jacket from the back of his chair. "Can we walk together?" she said.

Across the quad toward the upper campus, a breeze rattled leaves from the trees in a soft shower. He was noncommittal as she disputed virtually all the basic tenets they'd been studying, even that organizations are governed by rules and regulations. The personality and character of the leaders—charisma—was the real power within any organization, not rules and regulations. Though skeptical, Norman finally bit.

"Don't you think Weber was describing an ideal?" he said. "Something to strive for in the real world, not necessarily the real world model?"

"Oh goody," she said. "There is someone home."

"Beg pardon?"

The clock chimed from the tower up in Old Main; she grasped his shoulder. "I love how you always wear a tie. That's special. Are you seeing anyone now?"

"Nothing personal, but that's personal."

"Of course it is, but I have another class. Are you seeing anyone, or not?"

He wanted to say no, no, he wasn't seeing anyone now, but he couldn't bring himself to. It was simply none of her business. Ginger said, "I was seeing someone, but he graduated. I need to see someone else. *Soon.* I was hoping we could make an arrangement."

"What kind of arrangement?"

"You know what else I like about you? Your Adam's apple. It's very big. You know what they say about men with large Adam's apples, don't you?"

"Are you implying what I'm inferring?"

"I *love* that!" she said with a bright-eyed smile. She pressed a scrap of paper into his hand, her phone number. "I live off campus—call me. *Soon.*"

He watched her stride away toward Vincent Hall, never glancing back.

Her first floor apartment was behind a deep, shady porch on a quiet street not far from campus. Two days later, a girl answered the door when he knocked. "Ginger's not here."

"I just talked to her this morning."

"My sister's weird." Recognizing the dirty blond hair, round cheeks and gap between her front teeth, Norman realized he'd seen this girl on campus, with Ginger, though obviously eclipsed. "I'm Rosemary. She wanted me to tell you she made an arrangement with somebody else. You should see the Adam's apple on this guy."

She grinned her gap-toothed grin, but he wasn't sure if she were making fun of him or not. "Your sister is very rude."

"Weird, rude, whatever. Big Red can't be bothered. She's a girl in a hurry."

"What about you?"

"I can be bothered. I'm not a girl in a hurry. I'll split a joint with you or something, but we're not doing any *arrangement*, if that's what you're thinking."

"What *arrangement* are you talking about?"

"You know perfectly well. Did you bring the rubbers like she told you to?"

His face darkened. He didn't say a word. Rosemary grinned. "How many?"

"I bought a dozen. They're cheaper by the dozen."

"Wow. Cheap rubbers." Her face brightened. "Let's blow 'em up and scotch tape 'em to the ceiling."

"Now let me get this straight—*Ginger* is the weird one?"

He was surprised at the liberation, the catharsis, unleashed by the creation of the Trojan Constellation, as Rosemary dubbed it. They fell in together immediately, giggling like kids as she stood on the kitchen table, arranging the inflated condoms around the light fixture, Norman handing her strip after strip of tape, directing the placement.

Years later, he realized that first hour together was when his and Rosemary's relationship as pals—he'd assumed it was mutual—was set in concrete, even though he remembers at the same time checking out the curves and crevices beneath her baggy sweatshirt and jeans, a dichotomy to be sure, but one he dismissed as entirely biological. They were buddies, their relationship born in mischief, nurtured in companionable co-conspiracy, its future course fixed at the instant of conception.

Or so he thought, right up to the day he married Amber.

Rosemary introduced him to her kid sister in September of the following year, his and Rosemary's junior year. Ginger was gone, graduated. Standing in front of Patterson Hall on a slick, muddy Monday, Norman couldn't believe that lethargic Amber, her dark hair and big, teddy-bear eyes, was from the same gene pool as Ginger and Rosemary. Later, meeting their mother, Linda, only deepened his suspicions.

"My little sister's all bummed out," Rosemary said. "Our parents are splitting up."

Amber looked at Norman with a question on her face, took two steps forward and buried her forehead in his shoulder. This before she'd ever said a word to him.

"See?" said Rosemary.

Glancing down at the top of Amber's head, Norman never moved a muscle. Finally, stepping back mechanically, she looked at him and said, in a drawl, "Do you like to cuddle?"

Rosemary shook her head at her little sister's naivety, eyeing Norman's reserve, his blue blazer, his spiffy Windsor knot. "Does he look like he likes to cuddle?"

Amber's head bobbed a slow nod. "Yes." And Norman felt a melting sensation.

They were married four years later in Hartsgrove, the Darlings' hometown. Never had Norman detected anything resembling jealousy—or undue affection—on the part of Rosemary during those years, the years he dated Amber, hung out with Rosemary. Sarcasm sure, but that was just Rosemary's way, always had been, always would be. The morning of his wedding, he was tying his tie in front of the mirror in his room at the Holiday Inn. It was a bright morning, drapes open to a green, ferny bank behind the hotel. Rosemary, visiting, was bored, sitting on the bed behind him, idly clicking through television channels—or so he thought. Looking up in the mirror, he saw her watching him.

"There he is," she said. "Unavailable as all get-out."

Even then, the implications of that remark took a long time to set in. After they did, for the rest of his life, the term *blind spot* took on a whole new dimension.

Half a block down from the Court House on Main Street, the Paine County Historical Society resides in the Blood Building, built in 1878 by Josiah P. Blood, Esq., according to the little green plaque on the brick wall. Apropos, thinks Norman. He's gotten away by himself, letting the family have their turn on deathwatch. He did his shift.

By all accounts, at least by all of which he's aware, Cookie led a decent, ordinary life, the one anomaly having been his change of professions about halfway through—why he left teaching to become a carpenter all those years ago is anybody's guess. Why he continued to wear his jacket and tie even after entering a blue collar profession is also anybody's guess, though Norman, who also prefers the dignity and defense of a jacket and tie, could easily identify with that particular quirk.

He doesn't have to search. At the mention of the name, the curator, a gum-chewing, rosy-cheeked woman named Verna, pulls a folder from a file cabinet.

Carol Siebenrock, seventeen, went missing in September 1960, and wasn't found for over a month, when her decomposed body was pulled from Potters Creek. Her skull was fractured. It was an unusually wet fall and the creek was a torrent, so there was no telling where she might have been dumped. There's a picture of her wearing her cheerleader's uniform and a bright smile. Herman "Blinky" Mumford was convicted on circumstantial evidence, the most damaging piece of which was a pair of Carol's panties found in the janitor's closet in the school basement. Verna tells him Blinky Mumford died in jail many years ago.

The Road Trip Lounge in the Holiday Inn—Ginger calls it the Road Kill Lounge—is loud, dark and smoky, but Norman needs his scotch, and

Amber has stayed in the room with the kids. "He told me he killed her," Norman shouts. "That Siebenrock girl."

"He told us his feathers were on fire," Ginger shouts back.

"What he actually said was his 'fires were on feather,'" Rosemary points out.

"I don't know," yells Norman, shaking his head. "He seemed very lucid, not delirious at all. It sounded to me like a deathbed confession."

The music stops just as *deathbed confession* rings out. Nearby patrons glance over, curious, but Eddy, hustling pool across the room with his Hawaiian shirt now totally open, and Linda, dancing with a burly man in a leather vest as if she were sixteen, didn't hear.

"Confession is good for the soul," Rosemary says. Norman tries to read her eyes. Another song comes on, thoughts, words flailing to stay afloat above the decibels.

"Confession sucks," Ginger says. "Confession is like opening a little door to your heart and watching all the rats and snakes slither out."

"Sheer poetry," Norman says.

"Poetry has no place in this conversation," says Ginger.

"I have nothing to confess," Rosemary says. "All the dumb things I do are right out there."

"Oh?" Ginger says. "Who's Benny's daddy?"

"Go fuck yourself," Rosemary says.

Ginger laughs, turning to Norman. "What about you, Norman?"

Norman goes clammy. Even though he's done the math a hundred times and is fairly certain Benny's not his, the question seems like an accusation to his muddled mind, before he realizes it isn't. He tightens his tie. "I was raised Catholic. We had to confess every week."

"My God," Ginger says. "What could you possibly have to confess every week? Or are you allowed to use the same sins over and over?"

"Impure thoughts," says Norman. "That sort of thing."

"Have you ever had an impure thought?" Rosemary asks, her face blank.

"No," says Norman, bluffing. "Never."

"Don't you have to confess how many times you jack off every week?" says Ginger.

Rosemary says, "Do you leave your necktie on when you jack off?"

The music stops just as *jack off* rings out, nearby patrons looking again. This they find more amusing than *deathbed confession*, as do Rosemary and Ginger.

"So you don't think Cookie killed anybody?" Norman says.

Fickle hilarity. Rosemary assumes her customary posture, back hunched, fingers thrumming nervously, waiting for the next bad thing to swat her. Sipping a glass of flat beer, she looks as though she doesn't want to be here, or anywhere else. Ginger sits poised like a volcano, waiting to swat the next bad thing. Her vodka is straight, clear and expensive. "Let me put it this way," says Ginger. "If I believe Cookie killed that girl, then I'd have to believe that doctors and nurses were practicing voodoo in the hospital hallway. I don't think so. Not today."

Ginger wanted to show off her new condo in Pittsburgh's Squirrel Hill district, so she threw a party on a hot summer night two years ago. Amber, knowing Norman's aversion to parties, was willing to go alone, but this time Norman wanted to go. He was curious. Since they'd left Slippery Rock, he'd seen less and less of Amber's sisters, never both together since his wedding; according to Amber, they were heading in opposite directions.

After graduation, both had taken office positions in small Hartsgrove businesses, from which Ginger had gone on to climb the corporate ranks of an express delivery company in Pittsburgh, while Rosemary, a series of jobs later, was tending bar at a run-of-the-mill Hartsgrove restaurant. Her descent, according to Amber, attributable to drugs.

Norman missed his buddy Rosemary; at the same time, he wondered if he'd ever really had a buddy Rosemary at all. After her remark on the morning of his wedding, he'd thought about their Slippery Rock moments together, moments spent in what he'd assumed at the time was companionable ease: when he'd look up from his book to find her watching him, when she'd laugh too hard at his poor pun, the tank tops she wore braless, the careless glimpses beneath her skirts in unguarded moments of repose. *Blind spot.*

As for Ginger, he was curious to see her latest lover's Adam's apple.

The condo was modern and flawless, an airy space of hardwood, glass and sharp white walls—Big Red showing off again. Norman fortified himself on the high ground, an easily defensible corner of the bar in the open kitchen area, within reach of the bottle of Chivas Regal on the counter. From there he could look safely out upon all the chatters chatting, the dancers dancing, the minglers mingling, Ginger chief among them. Amber tried her sluggish best to keep up with her big sister, returning like a homing pigeon to Norman's corner with increasing frequency as the evening wore on. Rosemary, underdressed in a shapeless blue summer frock with a faint stain on the front, helped him defend his corner, matching him beer for drink, excusing herself to the bathroom or deck—also with increasing frequency as the evening wore on—returning each time with glassier eyes.

By the time the place cleared out, they were drunk, which did nothing to discourage them from another cocktail at the bar in the kitchen. Norman liked Ginger's boyfriend John, a tall man with glasses, a shiny face and, sure enough, a large knob on the front of his throat, because he seldom smiled, had little to say. Ginger showed them her new tattoo, a butterfly on the back of her shoulder, hidden by the top of her cocktail dress. "Ain't it a beauty?"

Amber said, "I like it."

Norman nodded. "Nice."

Amber said, "You don't like tattoos." Norman shrugged.

"What's the matter with tattoos?" Ginger said.

"Will you still love it when you're seventy?" Norman said. "It's still going to be there."

"Roe, show him your tattoo," Amber said.

"I'm not showing him my tattoo."

"Go on," Ginger said.

"Just the top of it," said Amber.

"What kind of tattoo?" Norman said.

"It's a rose . . . " Amber said.

" . . . sprouting out of her bush," said Ginger.

Rosemary stood, pulling her blue dress up, pushing down her panties, a wiggle to her hips, a tilt to her head, displaying the red rose rising from her brown bush.

Ginger looked at Amber.

Amber said, "Why don't you just get naked?"

"Okay." Rosemary slid her panties all the way down, her dress dropping, then stepped out of them. Picking them up, she put them on her head like a do-rag.

"You still have your dress on," John pointed out. Norman didn't like the tight, flushed glow on John's face, the same flush he felt on his own. "You stay out of this," Ginger said.

"I guess I'm a little drunk," said Rosemary.

"I guess you're a little slut," Amber said.

In the awkward silence, Ginger looked away, sipping her vodka. Rosemary slipped the panties from her head, balling them up in her fist, looking around as though trying to remember where she was, and why. Amber glared.

"The party's o-ver," Norman began to sing, but no one was amused. They went to bed soon after that, Ginger and John in the master bedroom, Amber and Norman in the guest room, Rosemary on the sofa bed in the long, wide living room. Norman couldn't sleep. Amber's anger, which he chalked up to her drinking, stayed with him—though not, apparently, with her, asleep within seconds. The bright noise of the party stayed with him too, mingling with Slippery Rock–Rosemary memories, all impressed upon the image of her silky, lovely, larger-than-life bush, the magical pubic triangle. He had to go to the bathroom. That was his only intent.

But he saw her in the living room asleep on her side, her back to him, the sheet not quite covering her. He couldn't be sure in the shadows what, if anything, she was wearing. He stood and stared. The blond hardwood floor gleamed, the wide windows displaying the lights of a Pittsburgh hillside. The magnetism was irresistible. When he climbed in behind her, she was awake, though she didn't turn, didn't look. "Norman?" she whispered. "What are you doing?" He said nothing, pressing close to her back, his hands exploring her, her small breasts, her backside. She wore a silly, baby-doll nightie, nothing else. "Go away," she said. Norman didn't. He was senseless with the buzzing in his head, and he kept feeling and exploring and pressing, and finally he was inside her. "Don't," she whispered. She was passive. He finished. He waited, but she never turned around. For the longest time, she never said a word. Finally she whispered, "Amber's going to kill us."

Later, remembering, he decided she'd been crying. He wasn't entirely certain, but it seemed, at least in his memory, as though she had been, and so he interpreted it the only way he could: She *hadn't* been entirely passive. There'd been motion, participation, on her part. The rest of that night, in his dreams, the next day, the next two years, he decided she'd been a willing partner. They had made love. He had not forced himself upon her. Her reluctance, her passivity, he attributed only to Rosemary's fear of hurting her sister. Although, as time went on, now, he began to see that perhaps it might be the other way around.

Light seeping around the hotel curtain. Two kids in the far bed, naked limbs askew, Amber in the near bed snoring softly, a gentle donkey sound. *Eeyore.* Norman sways, as though afloat, his brain brimming with echoes of music too loud. Maybe the fourth scotch was not a good idea. Nor those that followed. Undresses, teetering, hanging his smoky clothes on the wooden hangers with the metal nooses, careful not to rattle, unknotting his tie, pressing the wrinkles with his thumbs, draping it neatly over the rod. Cookie, gray old man with bony shoulders. His puny, blue penis—impossible to imagine as a deadly weapon. Norman's own, young and heavy, and rising up. Rosemary's gap-toothed grin. Gone. Mother-in-law dancing like a slut, her girls out smoking pot in Ginger's black Mercedes, beneath the green water tower looming like a flying saucer, HARTSGROVE across it in big, black letters.

Was this the room? Where he'd stayed for his wedding? Tying his tie in front of this very mirror where the shadow now undresses? Reaches toward it, falling short. Maybe this one, this very mirror. *There he is. Unavailable as all get-out.*

Climbing in bed with a jostle, hoping to awaken Amber. When he doesn't, he rolls, bounces, coughs, to no avail, so he finds her nipple playing hide and seek among the bedclothes. "Norman. What are you doing?"

"Won't take me a minute."

"You'll wake up the kids."

"Roll over."

"*No.*"

"Please?"

"What got you so horny?"

"I had nothing to do with it."

"Well, neither did I."

Blood throbbing in his ears, he stares at the darkened ceiling, in the direction his erection is pointing. Sees Rosemary shrinking before his eyes. *How many cocks would a cock tease tease.* . . . He squeezes his, a happy handful, an instrument of love, not a weapon. No more gap-toothed grin. Touches Amber's hip, a plea, but she wiggles away in a final refusal.

The room takes a slow twirl. Grabbing a sheetful of Amber's shoulder, a solid, white thing, he says, "Come on."

"*No.* The kids."

"Cookie told me something today. While you were all out at lunch."

"What did Cookie tell you today while we were all out at lunch?" The drawl. He thought she'd never arrive at the end of the question.

"He said he killed that Siebenrock girl. He told me he killed her."

Amber rolls toward him, led by her large eyes astonishingly white in the dark room. "He told me his feathers were on fire."

"But this was different. He was thinking clearly."

"So now you're a doctor?" Scorn in the whites of her eyes, she turns, rolling away.

Norman gets busy, lifting her nightie from behind. The Rosemary position.

Amber reaches back, grabbing him hard. Whether the grip is a promise or a threat becomes quickly apparent with the sinister twist she applies. "Keep your hands to yourself," she whispers with a hiss. He holds his breath till she lets him go. "Go to sleep."

But it's a long time before he does.

Cookie died when no one was watching, in the middle of the night, possibly at the same time Norman was in the bathroom jacking off. Cookie had sneaked away, in Norman's mind, lending credence to his confession. Who but the guilty sneaks away?

They gather in Rosemary's apartment, the downhill half of a shabby duplex on East Main. It's a cluttered, anti-Ginger condo. They gather around the rickety kitchen table, the wing of which is warped. Faces all somber and hollow, Linda's eyes red, though Norman can't tell if she's been crying, or is merely hungover. She and Uncle Eddy went to the hospital at four a.m. to meet with the pastor and the funeral director. Conversations are stilted and hushed, dealing mostly with arrangements, with what has to be done. Outside, through the window, early sun sifts through morning fog. When Norman returns from the bathroom, they look up at him, five faces staring as one. Linda says, "What's this rumor you're spreading around about Dad?"

"I'm not spreading anything around. He said he killed that girl."

"And you believe it?" Her coffee cup tilts on the warped board.

Norman clutches his tie. "Why would he say it if it weren't true? On his deathbed yet."

"Oh," says Eddy, "maybe because a stroke had made mashed potatoes out of his brain?"

"He was *hallucinating*," Linda says. "He said doctors were chanting in the hallway."

"He said his feathers were on fire," Amber says.

Rosemary says, "He was out there orbiting Mars, man."

"It was a long time ago anyhow," says Linda. "What difference does it make now?"

"It's all water under the bridge," says Eddy.

"Of course there were rumors," Linda says.

"But nobody ever really believed them," Ginger says.

"They convicted this other dude," Rosemary says.

"And besides," says Amber, words rolling slowly over the hush of the room, "the girl was a cock tease anyhow, okay?"

They stare at Norman, the jury still out. Norman cinches his tie.

Driving down East Main, he turns by the Borough Garage at the bottom of the hill, following the dirt road two miles back through woods to the waterworks, where a dam crosses Potters Creek. Beneath the dam is the Dr. William Darling Memorial Park, a swimming hole with a concrete beach and a picnic area among the pines. The family has gathered there before, in the park named for an ancestor. Legs rubbery, heartbeat bouncing, Norman makes his way to an isolated picnic table near the creek, watching the water flow. In a pavilion near the parking lot, a family is having a cookout. Waders splash in the water. A couple strolls past the waterworks holding hands. Downstream, on a footbridge across the creek, a man and a boy stand in floppy hats, fishing from the bridge. Norman stares at the creek, at the scene of the crime.

Cookie was a fisherman. Norman remembers him touting all the fat trout there for the taking in Potters Creek.

Hot September sun soaks his back, and he takes off his jacket. He watches the water flow, over the dam, under the bridge. He watches it ripple and run, seeing how clean the rocks shine underneath. He can't look away from the water, like a gruesome wreck, watching the spellbinding wrinkles and winks, picturing Carol Siebenrock floating there forty years before, motionless, decomposing, her cheerleader's skirt wavering in the water, while Cookie Zufall was teaching his class, writing on his blackboard, eating his lunch, correcting his papers, screwing his wife with impunity. While Blinky Mumford was sweeping the halls, mopping the floor, killing time, waiting to be swatted. The sweat on Norman's back turns to ice.

Downstream comes a cry from the footbridge, where the boy in the floppy hat yanks a thrashing trout through the air, the man cheering the fish's death throes, clapping the boy on the back.

Motion catches his eye, black and dreadful. Norman spots a spider creeping toward him along a rotten crevice of the picnic table, and he bolts in fear. He and Rosemary have always been terrified of spiders; Amber, on the other hand, always squashes them with glee.

Bye Baby Bunting

D*aveman the Caveman* his wife, Deb, had taken to calling him, for all the time he spent in the cellar. He'd never had a nickname in his life, and he wasn't particularly fond of this one. Not that he suspected Deb cared. Their indifferent coexistence was becoming an art form.

The cellar was unfinished. Mortar dust crumbled from the damp stone walls, dusting the cobwebs and the packed dirt floor. Dave's workshop, through a doorway under the stairs, had once been the root cellar beneath the kitchen. Over the worktable a lightbulb hung beside a high, ground-level window, and a tattered easy chair sat in the corner. Around the floor, up the walls, on the far reaches of the table, sat twenty-odd dollhouses, many of which had been finished at one time, but never quite the way he wanted, never quite good enough, before being cannibalized for the next model. His workshop suited him fine— except for the cat, the little pain in the ass forever invading his territory. Mr. Whiskers for his part saw no reason why the cellar, his hunting grounds—for he was an excellent mouser still—should not be exclusively his domain.

Dave was in the cellar when the call came in. Just after dark, early June, rain splashing mud outside the window above his worktable. He was repainting the trim around the interior living room windows of his current dollhouse, using a tiny brush at impossible angles, a tedious job for which his callused roofer's hands had little patience.

He heard the phone ring, then Deb's step on the cellar stairs. She was still wearing her blue lab coat from the hospital, and her limp yellow hair needed washing, though he noticed only from the corner of his eye. She put her hand on his shoulder like an old pal, watching him work.

"Lorrie called," she said. Lorrie worked with her in X-ray. "She heard on the scanner some kid's lost in the woods out past Chapel Cemetery. They got volunteers going in looking for him. She knows you hunt out there."

He withdrew the tiny brush, dabbed it in the paint. "Oh yeah?"

She withdrew her hand. "In case you feel like getting out of the cellar."

He listened to her climb the stairs. He heard a grumble from Mr. Whiskers, saw him crouched in the dark corner beneath the table, watching his every move. The cat held him in utter contempt, a feeling that was utterly mutual. Dave refused to accord Mr. Whiskers the dignity of the name—bestowed by his daughter, whose cat he'd been before she died—so he called him *Whiskers* when he was in a charitable mood, or *Mr. Shithead*, or, simply, *you little pain in the ass*, when he wasn't. For his part, Mr. Whiskers enjoyed leaping upon the worktable, timing his leaps for maximum disruption. Occasionally their disputes became physical. Dave was known to sweep Mr. Whiskers rudely off the table, while the cat was known to swipe at Dave, usually when the element of surprise was on his side, at an exposed ankle or arm, often drawing blood. On those occasions, Dave gave chase, and if he were able to catch him—a more frequent occurrence now that Mr. Whiskers was getting a little long in the tooth—took him by the scruff of the neck and bowled him across the cluttered cellar floor toward a distant corner, scattering any miscellaneous debris that happened to lay in the way. He couldn't quite bring himself to wring the little bastard's neck, or take him for a one-way ride in the country. He had, after all, been Janey's cat.

It took him five minutes to clean his brush, seal the paint can, cat-proof the tabletop. Upstairs he put on a flannel shirt over his black Harley tee, laced up his work boots, selected the camo trucker's cap he judged most rain-resistant. Took the keys to his pickup from the little tabletop. "Okay," he said to Deb, who was standing by the kitchen sink, arms folded.

"Come here," she said. Dave crossed the kitchen. "You're still wearing your potato chips." She brushed at his bushy brown beard.

"Thanks." He almost kissed her on the cheek. She almost waited for him to.

"Good luck," she said, turning toward the dirty dishes.

He drove to the Rod and Gun Club, parked in back, away from the street, walked in shaking rain from his hat, sat at the bar, ordered a Rolling Rock. She'd never asked where he was going. Let her assume what she would. The Pirates were on the TV above the bar, the beer was cold, there were pickled eggs in the jar by the cash register. His evening was pretty much planned.

He'd lost a kid once. No one had helped him search.

One of the customers at the bar was his father-in-law, Al Black, who returned Dave's nod by way of greeting. Al scowled, but it was nothing personal; it was his natural expression. Business was slow for a Friday, a couple of young couples playing pool. Missy was tending bar, but she didn't chat either, only brought him his beer, took his money, and returned to the scanner beside the pickled egg jar, where she stood listening, her back to Dave. A message crackled out of the little black box, but he couldn't make it out. Missy was wearing jeans, flimsy denim. She had a gorgeous ass.

The sound on the game was low. The others watched it like a fire. Dave listened to the announcers' murmur, the sporadic crackle of the scanner, the pool balls' clacking, the chatter of the players. The beer was going to his head. He found himself staring outright at Missy's ass, watching how when she moved, the denim clung. When she went into the kitchen, he found himself equally hypnotized by the second hand on the big, bright, Iron City Beer clock on the wall above the bar. The game he couldn't bring himself to watch. His beer was empty, even though it seemed he'd been there for only a minute, so he ordered another when Missy returned.

She slid the bottle toward him. "You hear about the Gilhousen kid?"

"Tim Gilhousen?" A member of the Club, younger than Dave. Nice enough guy, a truck driver, quick with a laugh.

"Yeah. His little boy disappeared in the woods up behind their place this afternoon. He was out playing with the dogs, they went inside for a minute, bang, he's gone, him and the dogs."

"How old is he?"

"Three, three and a half."

"That's a shame. Hope he's all right."

"There's a bunch of people out looking for him."

Dave drummed his fingers on the bar beside his change. "Hope they find him."

Missy said, "Don't you hunt up in there? Out past Chapel Cemetery?"

"I hunt up in there, yeah. A lot of people hunt up in there."

Al's scowl deepened. Missy went back to the scanner, facing Dave now so he couldn't see her ass. He watched the second hand on the clock. He should ask Al why he wasn't up there searching for the Gilhousen kid if he was so concerned, but he knew the answer. Al's knee was bad, so bad he couldn't walk anymore without a cane. Couldn't even hunt anymore. Couldn't do much of anything anymore, except drink. Dave sometimes wondered what kept his father-in-law going, but he supposed he knew the answer to that, too. It was Janey, Dave's lost kid. His daughter—Al's granddaughter—had been killed three years before by a bunch of drunken, drugged-up kids, two of whom turned out to be remorseless, real punks, the ringleaders. They'd gotten off on manslaughter, ten to fifteen years. Big Al, it was assumed by most who knew him, was determined to live long enough to impose a more realistic sentence when they got out.

Dave, for one, didn't think he'd make it. He watched his father-in-law order another shot and beer, watched him suck the shot in a single gulp into his nearly toothless face, saw the grimace, like taking bad medicine. Dave seldom thought of the punks, except when he saw Al;

sometimes Janey was so gone it was as though she'd never been there. How she'd loved Al, back in the days before he'd gone to seed, back when he'd been loud and friendly and funny.

Dave thought he'd been a good father to Janey, a strict, no-nonsense father, sure, but a good one, trying to do the right thing. He was staring at the second hand again. He remembered Janey's hand going around in circles. She'd been slow, learning-disabled. The habit began just after she was born, died with her fifteen years later, her hand going around and around in little circles against her mother's skin, her leg, tummy, back, never stopping, as if to stop would be to lose her.

Taking a gulp of his Rolling Rock, he grimaced like Al. Tasted like piss. Must have been a skunky batch, that happened now and then at the God and Run Club, probably forgot a case in the corner, let it sit a few months going bad. What the hell. He didn't much care for baseball anyway. Gathering his change, he left without a word, without a nod.

Main Street was deserted, stores closed, rain pelting the bricks of the sidewalks. His wiper blades were shot; he'd been meaning to change them. He turned down Pershing Street, over the bridge past Proud Judy's, deciding not to stop there, too many cars, too many kids, too loud. Heading out toward Irishtown, he pulled in at the Pub Bar, hesitated, pulled out again. It was Al's hangout, probably his next stop. Down Mill Street by the creek, he headed south, out of town. Up the big hill past Chapel Cemetery, he turned left on Shugars Road.

He didn't know exactly where Gilhousen lived, but he didn't have to. In front of the garage, up and down the dirt road, were a dozen pickups, two Hartsgrove Volunteer Fire Department trucks, three State Police cars. Pulling in behind the farthest, Dave stepped from the cab and heard, through the drumming rain, the hum of four-wheelers from the woods.

Three men stood in the drive backlit by the spotlight on the garage. He recognized the fire chief talking to a man he knew he should know, and a state cop he'd never seen. "No luck yet?" he said to the chief. The light was in his eyes, rain dripping from the bill of his cap.

"Not yet. Nothing."

"What's the plan?" Dave said.

"Got a lot of guys searching on four-wheelers, a few fellows in there on foot."

"Folks keep straggling in," said the cop. "Like you. Trying to point 'em all in different directions."

"I don't get the four-wheelers," Dave said. "How they gonna hear the kid yelling?"

The chief shrugged. "Figure he'll make himself seen, if they get close enough."

"Hope so," the other man said.

"What if he don't?" Dave said.

Across the yard, a woman stood under the porch light. Dave recognized the shadowed face of Gilhousen's wife, the kid's mother. She held a phone at her waist, like a cocked pistol, pointed toward the black woods beyond the yard.

Taking his flashlight from his glove box, Dave climbed the roadside bank, crossing a field next to the backyard, then into the woods. The flashlight cast a feeble beam against the dark. Fog had begun to come up. Could have brought his heavy-duty lamp, if only he'd known he was coming. The trees offered little shelter from the rain, which slapped the leaves louder than his steps, louder than the sound of the four-wheelers. The carpet of decay underfoot was soggy and slippery, the wetness filling him with a raw, fecund smell.

Up the hillside through the woods he followed a meandering trail, around undergrowth, thick patches of laurel and saplings, the same trail a deer would follow. Or dogs. His flashlight faltered, then brightened again, and he realized the battery wouldn't last. He'd have to conserve. He'd have to turn it off, walk in the dark. He could memorize the path to the beam's end, turn the light off and walk it, turn it on again to memorize the next piece. Dave fixed the route in his mind: around the low branches, past the thicket, through the trees. Avoid the fallen log to the left. Clicked off the light.

For a second the shattering of the rain was thunderous, the blackness complete. A surge of panic, sudden blindness. Turned the light on, then off again just as quickly. He could do this. Took a breath, a step. Hesitantly, following the trail in his mind, heeding the sogginess underfoot, one step at a time, slowly, then a bit faster. He hadn't gone ten feet when he slipped and fell.

Switching on the light, he saw the rock, now exposed and shiny where his boot had slid away the leaves. Standing, he made his way to the log, sat. Turned off the light. Couldn't see his hand in front of his face. He tried, waving it there. Might have seen a motion, blacker than the rest of the blackness. Nothing hurt, and he was no wetter than he had been before. Drenched was drenched. On the log, he stretched his leg, wrung some water from his beard. And asked himself, what the hell was he doing here?

"BILLY!" he yelled.

Nothing but the drumming of the rain, and, lower now, more distant, the sound of the four-wheelers. What was he doing here? It was a no-win situation. But then weren't most situations? If no one found the kid, if a bear found him first, if he fell, hit his head and died, then certainly the kid—if he'd lived—would have grown up to find a cure for cancer. But if they rescued him, just as surely he'd grow up worthless, probably into some drug-addled punk like the ones who killed Janey. Or worse, a lawyer.

He rubbed his hand in little circles on his drenched thigh.

He stood. He was here. He was where he was. Maybe there was a good reason, maybe there wasn't. The trick was not to think about it. The trick was don't try to convince yourself of anything, one way or the other, because you can never be sure when you're lying. Unzipping, he pissed into the dark, splattering louder than the rain. Then he turned the light back on.

The fog was thicker, bouncing back a brightness that blinded him for an instant. The forest was frozen on the other side of the light, indistinct, like an idea of woods, not like the real thing at all. Nothing was like the real thing at all. "BILLY!"

He memorized the next piece of path, turned the light off, tried

again. He'd been in the woods all his life, even at night a few times—
the time they took his little brother's friend snipe hunting. He could
handle it. He was a hunter. He'd bagged a buck—at least one—every
year since he was nine. How different could hunting and searching be?
Breathing the fog, the wet smell brought an icy feeling, and he began to
feel a chill, the heat leaving his body. Tripping, he stumbled but didn't
fall, made his way to the spot he believed to be the end of his memorized trail, turned the light back on. Surrounded again by the glimpse
of unreal woods, swirling in ghost-colored fog.

"BIIIL-LYYY!" This was how he climbed the hill.

Down the other side, the sound of the four-wheelers was only a
suggestion. More distant now? Or had they gone in, maybe found the
boy? Or was it just the rain, heavier, louder, drowning out the other
sounds? How far had he come? How far would he go? Walking in the
dark, tripping, stumbling, frequently falling, ignoring the bruises, the
scratches from the branches he walked into face-first. He saw his father-
in-law, his hollow face sucking whiskey, saw his snarl, his accusing
eyes. Knew Big Al blamed him for Janey's death. Knew Deb did too.

He walked in the dark to the end of the trail in his mind, turned on
the light, yelled, memorized, walked in the dark. A mile, two miles into
the woods, he judged, maybe an hour since he went in.

Stopping at the edge of the blackness, he flashed on the light. There
stood a man, watching him out of the fog.

The flashlight nearly bounced from his hand, his skin caught in a
clutch of chills. The man was standing ten feet before him, under an
evergreen canopy funneling rain like a waterfall. He held an umbrella
over his head. He was wearing a white shirt beneath a vest that failed
to close over his big belly and chest, where a prominent cross was displayed. A frightened, lost look on his face. It took Dave a moment to
recognize him.

"Francis?"

"Dave?"

"Jesus Christ, you scared the shit out of me."

"Boy, am I glad to see you."

"What the hell are you doing out here?" Dave moved closer, close enough to see the perplexed look on Francis's face at the question, followed by a look of hurt.

"Looking for Billy *Gilhousen*."

"In your dress-up clothes? With an umbrella?"

Soaked as he was, he still held the umbrella. "I got to go to work at eleven." Francis was night manager at the Truck Stop. Dave knew him from church, though he hadn't seen him there in three years; Dave hadn't been to church since Janey's funeral.

"Where's your light?" Dave said.

"Battery wore out. I guess. It stopped working. Had it in my back pocket, but I fell down and busted it."

"Jesus." Perhaps it was the utterance that made Dave notice anew the large, wooden crucifix Francis wore hanging from his neck. He'd always worn it, as long as he'd known him. A religious nut, Dave had concluded early on, though he'd always liked the man.

"Hurt my butt," said Francis.

"I don't wonder." Dave turned off his flashlight.

In the sudden blackness, Francis grabbed his arm. "What are you doing?"

"Saving the battery."

Rain slapping leaves in the moment of silence. "Oh." Francis released his arm.

Dave explained how it was done, walking in the dark from memory between bouts of illumination. He turned on the light. "Okay. We head down the slope here, between those two trees, remember where that stump's at, around, towards that laurel patch. Fairly clear, not too bad. We'll stop up there and look again. There's a ravine not too far down, if I'm where I think I'm at—little creek at the bottom. Got it?"

"I think so," Francis said.

"Stay close." Then he yelled, "BIIIL-LYYY!"

Francis caught on. "BIIIL-LYYY!" he yelled.

They listened for a moment to nothing but rain. Dave doused the light, they headed out. "Stay close," he repeated.

Francis said, "What do you suppose the odds are of you finding me?"

Dave thought about it. "About the same as me having venison in my freezer, I guess."

"But there's lots of deer out here. Only one of me."

"That's probably the same thing that buck in my freezer was thinking."

Francis was quiet. Dave wasn't interested in odds, which were nevertheless on his mind; he was interested only in getting through, finishing. In the racket of the rain he couldn't tell how close Francis was keeping but thought he heard clumsy footfalls not far behind. At the edge of the void, he flashed on the light; Francis was maybe halfway down the path, coming sluggishly through the fog, cross-first.

"Stay *close*," said Dave, waiting.

Francis caught up. Dave pointed the light down the slope, through the trees, scoping out their next route. "What do you suppose the odds are of us finding the kid?" Francis said.

Annoyed, Dave wanted to say *slim and none*. Instead, he called again, "BIIIL-LYYY!"

When Francis didn't repeat the shout this time, Dave yelled again. "GAAA-AWD!" It was spontaneous, surprising himself.

Francis caught on. "JEEE-SUS!" he yelled.

Seeing Francis's smile, Dave almost smiled himself. He put a hand to his ear, listening. "Nothing out there."

"They're out there," Francis said.

Dave flicked off the light. He stepped into the blackness, leaving Francis to follow. God could guide him. Before Janey's funeral, Francis and his wife, Mary Anne, had visited them at home, bringing comfort and a casserole, both overdone. Mary Anne had gushed and preached, Francis letting her do most of the talking. It had been apparent they'd steeled themselves for the mission, meaning to be pillars for Dave and Deb in their time of need. Sure enough, the tears had flowed, but it had been Francis who'd broken down, sobbing, followed by Mary Anne at the sight of her husband. Deb had been obliged to comfort them both. Dave had left the room, for the cellar and Janey's dollhouse.

Reaching out in the blackness, he felt the sapling's slimy bark, just about where he'd memorized it. He heard the rain thrumming on Francis's umbrella, heard him shuffling through the undergrowth. It wasn't that Dave didn't believe in God. Nor that he believed that if there were a God, it was necessarily one who didn't believe in him, a neglectful God, or a God who tested his faith. He remembered a sermon of Father Bill's comparing life to on-the-job training, God seeing what we could do with this tiny speck of dirt in the universe before He turned it all over to us. Good a theory as any, Dave supposed. But what did it have to do with him?

"Dave?" said Francis in the dark. Dave could barely hear him over the rain; he was lagging behind. "We miss you at church. How come you quit coming to church?"

Dave kept walking. He didn't respond. A few seconds later, he heard Francis again. "Dave?" He sounded more hurried, more anxious, more distant. "You're not going to find Janey out here, you know. You're looking in the wrong place."

Dave kept walking, the words swallowed by the rain and the dark. The dark, he supposed, was as good a place as any to be looking. The hill steepened. He hadn't noticed the sharper decline from above. His boots slipped in the soggy footing, he was sliding, through brambles, over fallen branches and rocks. Digging in his heels, he finally stopped. Turned on the light. Must have gone beyond his planned path, or strayed from it. He'd slid at the top of the ravine, stopping himself maybe halfway down, before it became even steeper. Near the little creek the fog was thicker, his sphere of illumination reduced to the inside of a milky globe. Francis was nowhere in sight.

"FRANCIS!" No answer. He climbed out of the ravine. Old trees here, stout black trunks in the fog, and he stood for a moment getting his bearings. Removing his hat, limp and drenched, he turned his face to the black sky, letting the rain wash over it. He pointed the light in every direction. "FRAAAN-CIS!" The irritating monotony of the pounding rain made him grit his teeth behind his beard.

"BIIIL-LYYY!" No luck with that one either.

"GAAAAWD!" Dave sat on a log and laughed.

He didn't know how long afterwards it was, he'd lost track of time, traveling farther along the edge of the ravine, using the same, on-again, off-again, light-and-dark method, trying to decide when to give it up, when enough would be enough. Weariness weighed on his body as well as his mind, his thighs growing heavy, his back tired. He stopped and yelled *Billy* again and again, and the last time he yelled it, a small, clear voice answered out of the rain and blackness: "I'm down here."

A cascade of chills crossed his skin and his breath caught high in his chest, a revelation, biblical in proportion, the purest, most singular sensation he would ever feel in his life.

He shone the light down into the ravine, at the little, white-headed boy looking up from the edge of the void.

"Who are you?" the boy said. "Where's my daddy at?"

The words tripped over his chattering teeth, he was shaking, wearing only a tee shirt and jeans. Two dogs slouched at his feet, shivering beneath matted coats. "Gotcha," said Dave, picking the boy up, wrapping his wet flannel shirt around him. Four steps took him across the swollen creek, and he climbed the other side, dogs close behind.

Afterwards, he would remember little of the trip out, fueled by adrenaline and ecstasy, eased by the luxury of the constant, dying light—no need now to conserve—the boy clutched to his chest, growing warm. The woods grew more familiar, he came to a field he knew, through more woods, out to an old logging trail he'd followed before. Fog thinning to wisps. Half a mile down, the trail came out on Shugars Road. He flagged down a pickup going by, an old farmer he didn't know. The dogs hopping in back, he climbed into the warm cab with the boy, out of the rain at last. Three minutes later they were at Gilhousen's.

He was exhausted. The old farmer carried Billy across the yard, to a flurry of cries and shouts, Dave trailing behind. Shadows converging, backlit by the lights from the garage and house. A small crowd, the two dogs trying wearily to celebrate with them. Badges, caps, helmets, teeth shining in the darkness, and the boy's mother was there, face twisted with joy, and a blanket appeared, engulfing the boy, and he was gone.

They were carrying him toward the house, the crowd moving as one. They were on the porch. The only creature not celebrating was the cat, who scampered away as though his tail were on fire, dismayed, no doubt, that the dogs had made it out. Dave thought of Mr. Whiskers, the pain in the ass, and gloom clamped down upon his mood. Then he saw his flannel shirt in the mud. He picked it up, as the last of the crowd disappeared into the house, leaving him alone. On the porch, the two dogs lay pointed toward the door.

Francis called in the morning, to assure him he'd made it out of the woods just fine, in case he was worried. After he'd lost Dave, he'd waited out the night under a sheltering evergreen, none the worse for the wear, though Truck Stops of America wasn't too happy with him for not calling in. But the good news was, they'd found the boy. The real reason he'd called. He wanted to let Dave know they'd found the boy, in case he hadn't heard.

That was all he said. "Did they say who found him?" Dave said.

"Not really," said Francis. "I guess some old guy brought him in, but he said somebody else found him. Nobody seems to know for sure." Dave felt slightly aggrieved, though he quickly let it pass. What had he expected? It had been his choice to leave, nobody else's. Francis said, "The important thing is he's all right. That's one lucky little boy."

One lucky little boy. Billy had been, certainly. Then what did that make Dave?

Deb was downstairs, vacuuming the living room, unconcerned about waking him. In her gray gym shorts, an old tee shirt, her bony arm pumping the vacuum in a monotonous rhythm, she didn't see him in the doorway watching her. When she turned to vacuum under the coffee table she noticed him, a near nod, near smile. She kept cleaning.

"Want some breakfast?" he said.

Looking up, Deb shrugged. "Sure."

He put on coffee, then sliced some scrapple, started it frying. Took a big yellow bowl, broke in six eggs, added a splash of milk, whipped them up with a fork. Breakfast was the only meal he cooked. He liked cooking breakfast. Deb came in in time to butter the toast, and they sat at the table by the tall window looking down the hill, toward the south side of Hartsgrove. Fog was still banked over the creeks at the bottom, but the rain had stopped.

"You make the best scrapple," she said, squeezing on a puddle of syrup.

"You didn't ask me what I did last night."

"You went out in the woods and found the kid."

"Yeah—did you . . ."

Seeing the shock on his face, Deb said, "You're *shitting* me."

Around mouthfuls, between gulps, he told her everything, the rain, the fog, the blackness, walking blind, falling—here he displayed his scratches and bruises—finding Francis Minick, losing him again, then, finally, finding the boy. He couldn't describe the feeling he'd had. So that was what he told her, that he couldn't describe the feeling he'd had. An abbreviated version to be sure, but more than they'd talked in months. If not years.

"That's what you do good," she said. "You're a hunter."

"Yeah." Sudden pride lifted the hairs on his neck. Of course. He wasn't a roofer, a drinker, certainly not a father or a husband. He was a hunter.

One lucky little boy meets hunter.

She asked him what happened next. How did they react to their little boy's rescue, what did they say, how did it feel to be a hero, was it going to be in the paper? He shrugged. An old farmer who'd given him a ride had carried the kid in, he said, and no one seemed to know it was Dave who'd found him. That's what Francis had told him.

Deb was dumbfounded. "Nobody said *any*thing to you?"

"No."

"Dave—didn't *you* say anything to anybody?"

"They all went in the house, left me outside, so I left. I was beat. It was raining."

"You should have *stayed*. You should have made sure they *knew*."

"What was I supposed to do? Jump up and down and start hollering, 'I found him, I found him!'?"

"You should have held *on* to him! What's the *matter* with you?"

He shrugged. "You mean like, have a tug-o-war with the kid?"

She slapped her fork to the table, turning to stare out the window. Dave, feeling suddenly empty, ate half a piece of toast in one bite. When she turned back, her eyes were damp, her lips narrow. "You *always* do that. You never get involved. I let Janey go with those kids. You should have *said* something!"

He watched bewildered as she left, heard her on the stairs. He stared at the empty doorway, at her unfinished scrapple. Then he went down to the cellar.

Mr. Whiskers was waiting on the worktable, guarding the dollhouse, fixing Dave in a baleful glare. He tried to sweep him off, but the cat escaped with a hiss, Dave kicking at him, "Little pain in the ass!" He pulled the dollhouse to the front of the table, studied it. It seemed as though he hadn't worked on it in days. Women. There was a hole in his heart too, equal to hers he was sure, but didn't you have to try to let it heal? After all, it had been three years. Three years, one month, and . . . four days. Wasn't enough enough? Wasn't there a statute of limitations?

After a week, it was apparent he was an unsung hero. He hadn't heard a thing from Gilhousens. The only people who knew he'd rescued Billy were the ones Deb had told, her father, Big Al, two or three at work, who'd only nodded politely. She'd given up. Dave never told anyone else, not his boss, not the other guys at work, no one. He'd never had much use for braggarts.

In the evenings he dabbled with the dollhouse, did battle with Mr. Whiskers, and convinced himself it didn't matter. What mattered was that Billy was rescued, not that Dave was recognized. But then his problem was that whenever he convinced himself of something, he could never be sure he really believed it. Believing in God, believing he'd been a good father to Janey, believing it didn't matter that his heroism would remain anonymous—did he really believe those things? Or had he just convinced himself it was what he ought to believe? This was why Dave couldn't be bothered thinking about it.

His heart wasn't in his work. He was totally dissatisfied with the way the dollhouse was turning out, yet totally stymied as to what it was lacking.

Then it came to him. In a dream, literally. He awoke at two in the morning, a vision of the perfect dollhouse in his mind, the dollhouse that Janey would love. A Tudor style, thick cardboard reinforced with basswood for the walls, a mixture of paste and paint for a stucco effect—and a garden! With a swing set, a picket fence around the whole thing.

The vision forced him from bed, down to the cellar. For the next three hours, he measured, sketched, sanded and primed a new plywood base, cut the picket fence, sanded, primed, cut, framed the new house out—his focus fierce and singular. He ignored Mr. Whiskers prowling restlessly in the cellar beyond the workshop, the occasional growl of discontent. He never thought about Billy. He never thought about Janey. At five he went back to bed, still high. Her shallow breathing told him Deb was awake, but they let it pass in silence.

At seven he went to work, tired and foggy-headed, but the vision of the dollhouse remained, and he was anxious to get back to it. The baseboards in the colonial he'd built last year would be perfect for the swing set frame. His daydreams overflowed with the textures and colors and angles of the dollhouse on his table and the one in his mind, watching the merging of the two in the light from the glow on Janey's face. As soon as he got home, he opened a can of beer, hurried down to the cellar.

On the floor in front of the worktable, the dollhouse lay shattered. On the table where the dollhouse had been, Mr. Whiskers sat grooming himself grandly, ignoring the intruder.

Two weeks to the day after he'd found Billy, Dave was again in the woods at night, behind the Gilhousens' place. He'd parked down Shugars Road where they wouldn't see him, toward the logging trail, and he didn't go into the woods as far, maybe only half a mile, and everything was different. It was dry, comfortable. Ambient moonlight from behind a thin cloud cover was enough—his flashlight never left his pocket.

It was almost mundane, just woods at night, same as daytime, only darker. He followed a deer path through undergrowth to a clearing in a stand of hardwoods, boots crunching through the rustlings, peepings, chirpings, squeakings of creatures hidden by the night. It was a different place. The blind, black-and-white, drowning, ghostly, frightening, exhilarating, magical forest of two weeks earlier couldn't have existed. It was almost disappointing.

He set the sack he was carrying—a pillowcase, actually—at his feet on the forest floor. The sack moved. It shifted once, paused, shifted again. It took Mr. Whiskers a minute to free his head from the cloth.

The cat looked up. Dave couldn't see his eyes, squatted for a better look. "How do you like your new home, Mr. Shithead? Tell you what." He pointed through the trees. "If it's not to your liking, there's a family lives right over there about a mile or so, probably welcome you with open arms. They got dogs, at least one cat, but I'm sure they got an opening for another one. I tell you, they're one lucky fucking family. You ought to like it there. You ought to fit right in, cause you're one lucky fucking cat."

He didn't think Deb would mind. Of course he didn't think it till the ride home. If she did mind, she'd get over it. She'd never spoken of Mr. Whiskers except in terms of annoyance, seldom thought to feed him. He thought of it even more seldom, probably what made the cat such an excellent mouser. Boosting his chances of survival. He was a good hunter.

A good hunter—a common bond. He nearly felt a pang of regret, but opted not to. He drove slowly past Gilhousens', pale beneath a hidden moon, yellow home lights gleaming from the living room windows.

Deb was in bed. She'd been out when he'd left, at her friend Lorrie's bachelorette party down at the Ice House. Lorrie was marrying the guy she'd been living with for eighteen years. Deb and Dave slept in the dark, as dark as they could make it, shades pulled tightly, yet there were always two pale, incomplete rectangles defining the walls of the bedroom at night, where the light crept in. He made his way through the darkened clutter to his side of the bed, undressed, got in. Deb was not asleep.

"Daveman. Out of the cellar." She'd been drinking. She wasn't much of a drinker.

"Yeah. Took a ride in the country."

"Oh? Sounds exciting." Just a hint of a slur.

Now was as good a time as any. "You didn't care that much for Mr. Whiskers, did you?"

"'Didn't'?"

"Mr. Whiskers went for a ride in the country too. Only Mr. Whiskers ain't coming back."

He listened to her breathing. "The caveman," she said.

"I had this great idea for the dollhouse, I was working like crazy on it, and I come home tonight and it's laying there shattered on the floor. I usually push it back in far enough he can't get at it, but I must have forgot."

Sighing, she rolled over roughly, her back to him. "Got some bad news for you, Daveman." He couldn't see her in the dark. She said, "Mr. Whiskers didn't wreck your fucking dollhouse."

An hour later he woke up, angry, disappointed. Angry and disappointed with himself, at his inability to be angry with Deb. He'd tried, but he'd succeeded for only a few minutes. He'd been unable to keep his eyes open. Deb's easy, innocent breathing beside him had been hypnotic, contagious. The anger, hurt, and resentment that he felt he should have been feeling had refused to stay with him, flying away even as he'd tried to grasp them tighter, flying away like all the helium balloons from Janey's small, clumsy fists over the years. In the end, he found himself nearly paralyzed by an odd tranquility, a peculiar lightness. As though along with Mr. Whiskers, he'd dumped a heavy burden.

Next morning he took the pieces of the dollhouse and stowed them away, far to the back of the worktable. He was not a craftsman. He was a hunter. And that would have to do.

Gilhousens were at the club a week later. Dave and Deb stopped for a beer on their way home from the Harmony Mills Mall where they'd taken in a movie—*Shrek*, which Dave had thoroughly enjoyed, while pretending not to. It was their first date in years. He'd never mentioned the destroyed dollhouse to her, nor she to him. Not a word. Their indifferent coexistence had become somehow more informed, somehow less indifferent.

Deb's father, Big Al, was at the bar. They joined him, Deb sitting between the two men. The Gilhousens were at a large, round table at the edge of the dance floor with two other couples, playing darts, drinking pitchers of beer, having a wonderful time. Billy was with them, and for the longest time Dave couldn't take his eyes off the boy, staring, mesmerized, as though watching a cherub in heaven. An unruly cherub, coked up on Coke and candy bars, trying to pitch darts from three feet in front of the board, missing miserably, heedless of the damage to the darts hitting the concrete wall. Dave watched the Gilhousens laughing, drinking, taking Billy for granted, as though his life was their right, was something that was owed them.

One lucky little boy. One lucky family. It had not been his fate to enjoy such luck, that much he understood. He'd been fated instead to bring that luck to someone else. Almost as if he were on a different plane. The peculiar tranquility returned, settling upon him at the bar, as he observed, as though from above, the mortals upon whom he had bestowed such good fortune, watching how wisely they spent it.

Deb was less understanding. She kept glaring at the Gilhousens, while Al slouched over the bar with his hollow cheeks, watching as well. Billy threw a dart that hit the board, and he threw his arms up and cheered, twirling, and when he did, he saw Dave. He cocked his head for an instant, then came running toward the bar.

Stopping short at the foot of Dave's barstool, he stared up without a word, mouth open. Dave stared back from on high. Who was the more mesmerized? Finally, Al said, "Hey kid—I'm gonna paint a pig on your belly," one of Al's long-ago games, and Billy quickly turned and ran away, back to his mother, jumping up on her lap. The Gilhousens glanced only briefly in Dave's direction, an idle moment of curiosity, a nod, then turned back to their friends and their beer and their boy.

Deb said, "I think he recognized you. I think he remembered."

"All he remembers is being scared shitless," Al said.

Dave agreed. "Saddest thing I ever did see."

"What?" said Deb.

"A woodpecker pecking on a plastic tree." One of Al's favorite nonsense verses.

For a long time they were quiet, soaking up the wisdom of the verse. The Gilhousens partied on. Finally Al leaned up, looking past Deb to Dave, bobbing his head in a nod that was as close to scowl-free as Al would ever come in this lifetime. "You done good," he said.

Dave nodded in return, saying nothing, goosebumps spreading across his back.

Going home, Deb reached across the front seat of the pickup, putting her hand on his thigh. She rubbed it in little circles. "I think I might have a fever."

It had been a long time. He took her hand, moved it up his leg. Stopped it from moving. "I better take your temperature."

"I know just where you can put your thermometer. I got a good place."

Holding hands they walked up the steps of the porch, Dave still on his higher plane, looking down. There, on the window sill nearest the door, on an even higher, more tranquil plane, sat Mr. Whiskers, watching his every move.